TEACH ME SOMETHING

AUBREY BONDURANT

Photograph and cover design by Sara Eirew

Text copyright © 2017 by Aubrey Bondurant

ISBN: 9781542709118

CHAPTER ONE

I once read that a woman has a better chance of being hit by a car than finding love as a thirty-something-year-old divorcée in Manhattan. I wasn't sure if it was true, but it was amazing how easily I believed it could be, now that I was card-carrying member of that group. For that reason, plus countless others, I was currently sitting in a chair and ready to part with a thousand dollars in cash in the very last place anyone would ever expect me to be: a sex club.

Closing my eyes as I waited for the hostess to greet me, I exhaled heavily and tried not to freak the hell out. I reminded myself this wasn't my first time here, and I shouldn't be so nervous. Relax Catherine, I told myself, but I ended up jumping when a familiar female voice greeted me.

The tiny woman greeted me using my alias, sporting pink and silver hair despite appearing to be in her fifties. She was outfitted to the nines in a knockout dress that looked to be Chanel, flattered by the signature red-bottomed Louboutin shoes. It was on the tip of my tongue to compliment her, but I couldn't take a chance on giving away my ties to the fashion world.

"I was pleasantly surprised to hear from you again, Kat."

1

Yeah, so creativity had eluded me when it came to making up my fake name, and I'd gone with a derivative of my real one.

When I'd first contacted the private club months ago, I'd given them a fictitious profile along with the bogus email address I'd set up to match it. The reason was simple: I didn't want to risk anyone here finding out my true identity. Paying in cash helped ensure there was no trace to me. Plus, I'd signed a contract that assured they would keep my profile confidential so long as I kept the club activities secret in turn. Since I wasn't partaking in most of those activities, this wasn't a problem for me.

And if that wasn't enough, I now sat with a mask covering the upper half of my face and a dark-haired wig disguising my ordinarily straight, blonde hair normally styled in a long bob. If all else failed and it was ever discovered that the editor of Cosmo Life magazine was here at a sex club, I'd use the excuse of going undercover to do a story.

"Hello, Mavis. Yes, well, I've been busy the last few months." It had been five, and it wasn't exactly true. After my initial session, I just hadn't gotten up the nerve to return. The first time I'd come here, I'd dragged my friend Sasha along to stay at the bar and wait for me, but for a variety of reasons I couldn't use that strategy again.

The older woman smiled at me with reassuring eyes. It was only the two of us in the small lounge area, which was posh and stylish in hues of soothing purple.

"It's okay, Kat. You don't owe anyone an explanation, whether it was you being busy or simply not feeling comfortable. Now then, you mentioned in your email last week that you'd rather see someone other than Derek this time. I believe I have just the guy. His name is Calvin. Although all of our staff are terrific, he has become one of our most requested. Unfortunately, he was away the last time you visited, but he has your file and is more than ready to get started."

Although Derek had been nice, I couldn't say there'd been a connection that had me anxious to see him again. His attitude had struck me as though he was working on commission and wanted me to upgrade to the, uh, more physical classes. That's why I'd hoped someone new might be a better fit for me.

"That sounds good."

Sure, there were less extreme options than visiting a sex club for working through my insecurities regarding the dating world and sex. But there was something about the anonymity and the ability to reinvent myself as an alternate character that had appealed to me immediately when my colleague, who'd also gone through a painful breakup, had confided in me about this place. She'd called it her 'secret' for getting beyond it.

So I did something very un-Catherine-like, going to an extreme—cue the sex club, in which, ironically, I didn't actually plan on having sex. My real hope was that it would enable me to climb out of my rut and breathe new life into my self-esteem.

Mavis's sincere smile helped to put me more at ease in my decision to give it a second chance. I imagined she probably had to employ this technique quite regularly to ensure no one felt judged.

"As we discussed the first time, Kat, you've signed up for a starter package, which is all about talking and has no physical aspects. That means no touching or taking off your clothes. The goal is to give you the confidence to get back out there in the dating world."

That's what I needed. Someone to build up the confidence that my ex-husband had shredded. I hadn't had sex in almost two years, and all attempts at self-pleasure had failed miserably. It was some shit when you couldn't get yourself off at thirty-four years old, but refusing to bash myself a moment longer, I plunked down the money, re-signed the confidentiality agreement, and squared my shoulders. Time to do this before I chickened out.

MAVIS LED me down the hall and opened a door. When I entered the room, I was once again taken aback with the simple elegance of the setting. It was decorated much like a comfortable living room, with two chairs at a center point of the space, tastefully done in burgundy and crème. The first time I'd come, I'd imagined I'd find the stereotype of leather and sex toys, but clearly Club Travesty's reputation of being classy was merited.

I hadn't expected the gentleman named Calvin, which I assumed wasn't his real name, would already be in the room, greeting me the moment I arrived. As Derek had, Calvin wore a black mask which hid the top half of his face. He was easily six foot tall, sexual self-assurance clinging to him with perfection, as did his tailored, white, button-down shirt with sleeves rolled up and the black trousers showing off his well-built physique. There was something about seeing a man in dress trousers and being able to make out muscular thighs that had me staring. Maybe it was because, in the professional world, I didn't see it often. Then again, if I did, I wasn't sure I'd be very productive.

His stunning smile, revealing perfectly white teeth, was only eclipsed by his gorgeous blue eyes as he moved closer to greet me. "Hello, Kat. It's nice to meet you."

Holy hell. What a voice. Husky and sincere in his welcome. His warm hand took my ice-cold one in greeting.

I nearly erupted into a nervous giggle when the tingle traveled all the way through my body down to my toes. A spark some people called it. I dubbed it the: *I haven't been laid in so long that a handshake is making me desperate* effect.

Probably a good thing Calvin was wearing a mask because if his face was half as attractive as his body or voice, I was certain I wouldn't have been able to get out an actual coherent word. You would have thought I was sixteen with the way I was acting. Pulling my hand away, I reminded myself I was in fact a grown woman who happened to be paying for his time and had an agenda in coming here that didn't include standing here ogling him.

His voice broke me away from my thoughts as he motioned toward a chair. "Please have a seat. Can I offer you a beverage?" I shook my head, realizing Mavis had quietly backed out of the room, leaving us alone. "No, thank you." Sitting down, I took a deep breath, trying to quiet my nerves and keep puking off the list of my accomplishments for this evening.

He poured some water and took a sip and then sat across from me. "So, it's been a few months since you've been here."

"Right, I was pretty busy and…" I sighed, thinking if I couldn't be candid regarding my actual reason for staying away, there'd be no hope I could be honest about anything else. "The truth is this place overwhelmed me the first time. Add to that, my friend who accompanied me that night as my safety net—by sitting in the bar to wait for me—ended up in a fight with her boyfriend over her coming here. Anyhow, I started to think it might not be worth it."

"And now?"

It wasn't as though I hadn't given the dating world some effort on my own, although I doubted speed dating in order to find Mr. Right really counted. "It turns out nothing has changed with regard to my dating life or lack thereof, so I came back. I guess you probably get that a lot here, people second-guessing themselves about coming to a, well, a—"

He smiled slightly. "A sex club."

I winced at his bluntness.

"It's more than that; otherwise, we wouldn't be doing what we're doing, which is talking, but I get it. And to answer your question, people come and go with or without notice. Some find love, others decide they don't want to come to a club like this again, or still others 'graduate' and feel they've received all they can from this experience. I know you saw Derek originally, so I won't take offense if you prefer to return to him next time. It's all about finding someone you're comfortable with."

"No offense to Derek, but I'm already more at ease with you. I think he wanted to upsell me to the other packages, which I believe he takes part in. But I'm told you don't, which, frankly, takes some of the pressure off."

Under no circumstances was I interested in paying for sex. Yeah, yeah, fine line when you go to a 'sex club,' and I wasn't being judgy. I mean, to each their own, but it wasn't something I could ever see myself doing. Although, talk to me after another year of celibacy and put someone like Calvin in front of me and see if I wasn't throwing more cash down in a hurry.

"Good, I'm glad to hear it. According to the notes and your original email, it appears there are two reasons you're here. One is to navigate the world of dating post-divorce and the other is to feel sexually confident. We'll work on both, but as far as your history is concerned, you have exactly three minutes to tell me about your ex-husband, and then all talk of him ceases. This is about your future, which means you're here to move on."

I appreciated his approach. Five months ago, I honestly hadn't been ready *not* to dwell on my ex and everything about my divorce. "Okay, I don't think it'll even take that long. We were together ten years, having met in grad school. We dated for two years, engaged for one, and were married for seven. Divorce was final—God, I can't believe it—almost two years ago."

And suddenly I was embarrassed that I'd been in a rut of eat, work, sleep for that many months while my life virtually passed me. Calvin's voice pulled me out of my depressing thoughts.

"What would you say is the single thing that contributed the most to the split?"

"His desire for a different life, which he's made clear he wants with a twenty-something-year-old replacement."

"Ah. Any signs up until then?"

How about the fact that he was always too tired for sex, that he seemed to resent me for making more money, and that he thought my career in fashion was frivolous compared to his in finance? Or the ultimate reason, which was far too personal to share. So I settled on the generic version of the truth, not willing to bare my soul to a stranger.

"Sure, hindsight is always handy that way, I suppose. But to answer your question, I'd simply say we grew apart, and he needed more attention than I could give him." He maintained he'd never cheated on me, but he'd moved on so quickly that I wasn't positive I believed him. Either way, it was a moot point now as he was happily out of our marriage and, the last I heard, planning his second wedding.

Calvin's eyes appeared sympathetic. "And what would he say if you were to ask him why it ended?"

Interesting way of voicing the question. "He'd probably say I loved my career more than I loved him."

"And did you?"

I shifted uncomfortably while he mitigated his question with an explanation.

"If your job is your number one priority, then it's important for me to know that when it comes to giving you dating advice. I'm not judging you for it, Kat. I'm only trying to understand what's important to you when it comes to this process."

I sighed, thinking about how to explain. "I don't believe that was the real reason, but it was a convenient poke at the way he saw my prioritization of our marriage. At the end, I didn't chase after him or beg him to stay, instead opting to throw myself into work. But if I'd given up my career, I have no doubt I'd have ended up in the same situation, and a fool to boot. My job is what tells me that, although my marriage failed, I am not, in fact, a failure." Shit, I didn't mean to get defensive, and yet there it was in my tone. I softened it immediately. "I'm sorry. Obviously, it's still a sore subject, but you should know I have no regrets about my choices."

7

"You were in a relationship for quite some time and returned to a dating world where things have changed in the last decade. Talk to me about how that's been going."

"Like I said, I've thrown myself into work since the divorce, which isn't hard given what I do. And, well, I've kind of put dating on the back burner. I go out for quite a few social functions and travel as part of my job, so it's not as though I'm a recluse, but I have a hard time meeting any dating prospects. I realize two years is a long time, but I think for the first year I was sort of reeling from it all, not yet ready to actively search for someone new. Then in this last year, I've kind of floundered." The thing about the fashion world was I was surrounded by women. There weren't a lot of straight men unless you counted the models, but I was about ten years too late for that ship.

He leaned forward. "Sometimes it's a good thing to spend time by yourself. People deal with breakups in all sorts of ways, but my opinion is that going through the motions of moving on when you're not ready, or rebounding, if you will, is only masking the grieving process of getting over a relationship. You were with him for ten years, and that's a long time."

I knew women who threw a divorce party or went into dating like it was the Olympics and they were trying to win a gold medal, but I'd needed time to lick my wounds. It was nice to hear someone appreciate that. "Thanks."

"Do you have anxiety about a first date and meeting someone new?"

I shook my head. People weren't intimidating to me in the least. For the most part, I enjoyed getting to know someone. "No, not at all. But something happens during my date which ensures there isn't a second one."

"Like what?"

I shrugged, reluctant to reveal my actual thoughts on the matter.

"Do you sense something off during the course of it?"

"Not really. Conversation, at least with my last two, flowed really well. One even texted me afterward to say he'd really enjoyed himself."

"Okay, that's good. How did you respond?"

"Uh, I can't recall, but I do confess flirting via text message isn't my forte. It's a convenient way to communicate with people to tell someone you're running late, but I find I much prefer having conversations in person or on the phone. I guess you could say I'm old-fashioned that way."

He made some notes before smiling. "As I said, and you've noticed, dating has changed over the last ten years. What used to be a flirty phone conversation is now being done over texting or via social media. What was once a blind date is now meeting someone for coffee based on an online profile and a few prior messages back and forth."

"Yeah, well, that's why I suck at it. My assistant thinks I should join an online dating service, but, uh, it's not really feasible." I'd been about to say I couldn't go and put myself out there because of my job and well-known status here in New York City. Hell, I didn't even have a Facebook or Twitter account for the same reason.

He seemed to clue in anyhow. "We get a number of individuals who prefer anonymity for obvious reasons. For those same reasons, I'm assuming you can't go and put a profile up online."

"Exactly."

"Have you considered a professional matchmaker? Matter of fact, I have a rather good one I could recommend. She's exclusive and very discreet."

"What would I have to do?"

"You'd fill out a list of the traits you're searching for in a man and answer some questions about your personality. From there she tries to make the best match. I have the profile sheet if you want to take it with you this evening to have a look. We can even go over it together."

He walked over to a small desk and returned with a piece of paper, handing it over.

"Thanks." I skimmed the contents, appreciating that they wanted a list of the attributes for which I was looking as the first item. Lists were something I could embrace. Lists were a source of comfort to me. They kept the world in order and allowed me to organize my thoughts. But, unfortunately, they likewise reminded me of the true reason I thought my dates weren't working.

"You're holding something back."

His read on me took me off guard. Maybe having the mask and wig had given me a false sense of privacy. I sighed, chewed on my lip, and ultimately reasoned that if I couldn't admit my problem out loud to a stranger who was being paid to help me, then I couldn't possibly fix it. "I believe the problem on the dates is me."

"How so?" His voice was soft and not at all condescending.

"I think that over the first few months of dating I talked a lot about my divorce. Then I realized that was about the biggest buzzkill for a first date ever, so I stopped doing it, but…"

"But what?"

My dramatic lead-up was making it sound like I had some sort of dysfunction whereby I started barking during the appetizer. "Sorry, it's just something my ex implied, and I shouldn't believe, but maybe it's true." I sighed. "I think I'm boring."

"Boring?" I was reasonably sure that if I could see his eyebrows, one would be raised in surprise.

"Yes. As in safe, dull, predictable."

"How so?"

Now that I was admitting it out loud, it came out like a fire hose. "I make lists for everything from groceries to reasons I should or shouldn't have come here tonight. I have a set night where I pay bills and attend to my taxes, and I enjoy doing both. And you know how New Yorkers will walk into the street and survey traffic before they'd look at the walk/don't walk signs? Well, not me. I'll sit there on the corner waiting for that little white man to appear on the sign for my designated time to walk. Basically, where there's a rule, I'm a follower. Where there's a risk, I avoid it."

His eyes showed some amusement before he tried to hide it. "Kat, you're currently sitting in a sex club, which I would argue is the opposite from safe, boring, and predictable. Matter of fact, it's pretty bold."

"And that's part of the reason why I'm here. I'm tired of being a golden retriever."

He'd been taking a sip of water and nearly spit it out. A low chuckle accompanied his handsome grin. "Did you just compare yourself to a dog?"

I nodded, having come up with the metaphor months ago, although I'd yet to share it with anyone. "Everyone knows you get a golden retriever when you want a reliable, safe-around-the-kids, not-too-much-trouble kind of dog. But there's nothing intriguing, unique, or overly exciting about one."

His mouth was twitching. "You're not a breed of dog."

"Fine, then I'm a Volvo. A Consumer Reports top safety pick which does well in a crash, but about which no one has a thrilling story. I mean, when's the last time you heard someone start an exciting story with, 'This one time when I was driving my Volvo…'? Nothing exhilarating happens with a car like that."

He didn't bother to hide his grin. "I'm sure all of that couldn't have been easy to share, but it gives me some insight. And as far as the term 'boring' goes, it's a matter of perspective. Say you pick a vacation, someone who craves adventure won't want to park their butt on a beach all week, and someone who loves nature isn't going to enjoy a busy city. Boredom depends on the viewpoint, as does every other attribute. At the end of the day, what somebody may find dull in a relationship, someone else may find adorable. What one person finds crazy, another person thinks as fun. And for the record, golden retrievers are the most popular dog breed for a reason."

"I suppose." I wasn't looking for him to convince me otherwise, but it did feel good to get it all out.

"How about you tell me three fun facts about you right now."

I froze.

"Don't overthink it; just blurt out three interesting things."

This wasn't a test, and yet I was anxious like it was. "Um, I've never been sunburned because I'm fanatical about sunscreen, I love a good horror film, and my birthday is on Halloween."

His encouraging smile made me feel as if I'd accomplished something even though none of those three things struck me as interesting enough to have said out loud.

"See, those are all things I now want to know more about. And a great icebreaker to ask someone on a date."

I let out a breath, thinking it wasn't a bad idea. But of course I'd have to come up with better things to share. I mean, sunscreen, really, Catherine?

"Did you enjoy trick-or-treating on your birthday while growing up?"

"No, in fact, I kind of hated it. I never understood the whole deal of getting candy from strangers in a costume that was uncomfortable at best when you could buy a bag of your favorite stuff and sit at home watching a good horror movie on television. All the best ones are shown on Halloween night."

"But what about your birthday—did you do a celebration?"

"We'd normally have a party on the weekend closest, which was fine. My mom once wanted to have a Halloween-themed birthday celebration for me, but I refused to combine the two. Maybe because I wasn't any fun when I was a child, either."

He chuckled. "Kat, there isn't anything you've told me that wasn't amusing. And it's kind of true about Halloween. There's somebody at the door giving you tootsie rolls when you could've bought a bag of Reese's peanut butter cups and enjoyed them yourself at home."

"See, I was always the kid that liked the tootsie rolls." Good grief, even my candy choice was dreadfully dull.

"So you're the one," he teased and then leaned forward, his eyes intent on mine. "Can I ask you something?"

"Of course."

"How committed to this are you?"

I thought about it for a moment before responding. "Very, but I'll be honest and say my free time is somewhat limited during the week, as I travel and have quite a few after-hour work commitments. This week is an exception."

"Can you come here for the next four nights?"

"Uh…" I hadn't been expecting that.

"Before you answer, let me explain. I'm not here full-time, and my schedule tends to fluctuate, but I have openings during the rest of this week. Rather than meet sporadically, it gives us at least four more sessions in which we could make progress. Since I assume you wouldn't want me listening in on your dates because then I'd know your identity, I want to use the time to act out exercises as if I'm your date."

"What would that entail?"

"We'd meet here and go over tips. Then I'd text you each day to gage your flirting skills. And before you ask, to keep the confidentiality, you'd need to obtain a separate phone with a new number. You can pick up those pre-paid devices almost anywhere now. "

I quite liked this idea. No pressure to actually date, but I could get tips and feedback from a man and figure out what I could improve upon. "Okay. I'll block out my evenings this week and pick up a phone for this exercise."

"Good. As for the other reason you're here."

Ah yes, the sexual confidence part. My face heated at the thought of discussing this particular topic. Derek, my previous instructor, had hinted that I might want to step up to the next class for physical lessons, so I held my breath as I waited to hear what Calvin would suggest.

"I have an assignment for you, and since you appreciate lists, this should be right up your alley. You're going to write down fifty things you've always wanted to do, and I challenge you to make at least half of them sexual. Perhaps your ex wasn't good at something in bed, or maybe it's something you've always wanted to do, but I want you to really challenge yourself. Be honest. Most of all, think of things out of your comfort zone. Those twenty-five sexual things should be your fantasy, whether it's being tied to a bed or joining the mile-high club."

I had no desire to have sex in an airplane lavatory. But considering my sex life with the ex had been generic-store-brand-with-the-ice-crystals-because-it-had-been-in-the-freezer-too-long kind of sex, well, I could definitely come up with some quality Haagen-Dazs type scenarios. "Okay, I think I can do that."

He leaned back and smiled. Then we worked out the logistics for timing the rest of the week before he checked his watch.

"We have a few minutes left. Do you want assistance with your fifty items?"

"Um, I think I'll be all right." After all, what else was Google for?

CHAPTER TWO

*T*he next day in my office, I didn't have a chance to focus on my assignment until I was scarfing down dinner at my desk that evening. I absolutely loved my job as the editor-in-chief of Cosmopolitan Life magazine. Although at the top of my career, I was hardly resting on my laurels. Instead, I was working harder than I ever had, ensuring the magazine kept up with the times and, most important, connected with readers. Of course, some of that hard work was due to my not having much of a life outside of my profession these days.

Shifting from my thoughts about my career to my task from Calvin, I sighed, unfortunately drawing a completely boring blank as to what to put on my list. Ask me fifty items of clothing expected to be hot this upcoming fall, and I could do it in my sleep. Ask me fifty of the top makeup tips, I'd have it down in no time. But ask me to make a list of sexual things without the assistance of the internet? Yeah, right.

You'd think the amazing corner office view from the forty-third floor of Times Square would lend itself to some sort of crazy inspiration, given the busy epicenter of the city below. But at the moment, it wasn't doing shit for my brainstorming ability to come up with twenty-five sexual scenarios.

Deciding to focus on the first half of the list, I found the going easier. Bungee jumping, sky diving, attending Carnival in Rio, and hiking Machu Picchu topped the first twenty-five of my exciting bucket-list type activities.

Next, I googled a list of sexual items, but after inadvertently accessing a couple hard-core sites, I had to shut it down for fear the IT department would call up to ask what in the hell I was doing. At least this is where being a magazine editor came in handy since we featured at least one sex article per issue. I could always use 'research' as a convenient excuse for having stumbled across porn. Meanwhile, my search had thankfully kick-started my thought process. Before I knew it, my list was filled, clearly a testament to the number of sexual things I actually did look forward to.

I felt better already about the first step in my effort to bring out a more adventurous side of myself. But before I headed to the club to show the list to Calvin, I had another mission.

This particular mission had me waiting on a phone call from my friend Haylee. She was on her way into town in order to do something special for someone we both adored: Sasha.

I'd met Haylee two years ago in London and learned she coincidentally worked for my friend Josh. We'd struck up a conversation about vintage fashion. Since she was a model and had a closet full of iconic treasures, I'd featured her along with those dresses in my magazine. That spread was still one of my favorite cover features. She and Josh had gone on to marry earlier this year and were now new parents of a beautiful baby girl.

Haylee had introduced me to Sasha, who didn't know it yet, but was to be proposed to this evening by her boyfriend, Brian. Haylee and I had been recruited by Brian to set up a romantic setting in his hotel suite for the big question. Yesterday, I'd had the pleasure of helping him pick out a ring.

I didn't take our task tonight lightly. For a man to go to the trouble to call in reinforcements to make the moment perfect for his love signified that romance was alive and well. It gave me hope to know there were men out there who wanted to make such an effort for the women they loved.

Once the call came in, I made my way over to the W Hotel where I met Haylee in the lobby.

She was beautiful and fresh faced as always with her natural, girl-next-door looks. She'd thrown her long brown hair up into a high ponytail and opted for a casual chic style in capris and a T-shirt. "Sorry. The train was running late, and I had to drop off the baby with Josh. Do you know if Brian got the ring?"

"He sure did. We met yesterday and he's all set, but where are the roses and champagne?" I surveyed the lobby, expecting a florist or delivery guy. Instead, I saw the familiar face of Will MacPherson as he walked in carrying a few dozen.

"Ah, right on cue. Thanks for the help, Will," Haylee said and then led us all up to the suite.

Will had not only modeled for my magazine a number of times, but also was building a name for himself in the fashion world. He was one of the nicest guys in the business, not to mention gorgeous, with his blue eyes, dark brown hair, and boyish grin. He was the quintessential clean-cut, every-woman's-fantasy type of guy.

"Hiya, Catherine. Nice to see you."

His charming Australian accent made me instantly wish he was ten years older. "You, too. I've heard you've been busy." He'd been signed by Calvin Klein and had also done several other high-profile modelling jobs lately.

His smile widened. "I'm lucky. Ever since you put Haylee and me on your magazine cover, I've had a steady stream of jobs."

It had been my pleasure to do it. One of the perks of being in my professional position was the opportunity to find new talent and give them a break in the industry.

Hearing the buzz of my phone, I took it out and frowned at the number. It was the second time my ex-husband, Michael, had called me today—and this after not hearing from him for months. Silencing the phone, I tossed it into my purse, knowing that whatever he wanted it would only ruin my good mood.

Fifteen minutes later, all three of us stood back and admired our work in the luxurious suite, having made it a romantic backdrop, just as Brian had asked. Then Haylee and I said goodbye to Will as we left the hotel.

"Let me text Brian that we're done. He's been stalling with Sasha," Haylee said, smiling. "Oh, and Josh and Brian already have plans together this weekend in Vegas. Assuming Sasha says yes tonight, they were going to make it into a bachelor thing. But since it's one of my last weekends off before school starts again, I thought us girls could maybe go to crash it and do an engagement party while we're there. Of course, I'll have to ask Sasha first, but if she's game, can you come?"

I laughed at Haylee's presumption, but decided it did, in fact, sound fun. "Uh, I think so." Wasn't like I had many plans these days over a weekend, and perhaps adventure awaited in Sin City.

BY THE TIME I arrived at Club Travesty an hour later, I realized the nervousness I'd initially felt last night over hiding my identity had been replaced by the anticipation of meeting Calvin and finding out what my next lesson would be.

The same mask greeted me, only this time Calvin was dressed in a charcoal gray dress shirt with black slacks. "Hello, Kat."

Hello, Mr. Sexy Voice. "Hi, Calvin."

"I take it by the paper in your hand you've completed your list?"

"Yes." But suddenly I didn't feel comfortable handing it over.

He must've sensed my hesitancy. "How about I take it and put it aside for now? Why don't we instead work on your match-maker's list of traits you want in a man? Give me an overview of the basics in what you're searching for in a partner."

Sighing in relief, I thought that sounded much less daunting than having him read my wish list of sexual experiences. "Okay. Well, I guess first off, he should be older. Established in his career and respects mine. He needs to be financially independent." Frankly, I didn't care for another partner I'd have to worry would be competitive and insecure about me making more money than he did or who'd resent my career. "And I need someone who desires marriage and a family, uh, soon, because of my age."

"I know being anonymous means I'm not privy to how old you are, but it does say you're in your thirties. That means you don't need to be in too much of a rush, doesn't it?"

I swallowed hard. "It feels like every year that goes by, I may be losing the opportunity, so you could say I need to ensure we're on the same page from the beginning."

"Okay, but why does he need to be older? Some younger guys adore kids. It doesn't have anything to do with their age; it's just the time in your life you want those types of things."

Jesus, I could practically hear my ovaries wake up and wonder if Calvin meant himself. *Down girls. He was only generalizing.*

"I suppose it's possible."

"What about characteristics? What's important to you?" He was writing down the things I'd said thus far.

"Integrity, loyalty, and I want him to respect what I do. He doesn't have to know every detail, but I need him to support me in what makes me happy and—" I paused, trying to think about how to vocalize something else. A trait I'd seen, but never experienced.

"And what, Kat?

Weird. For a moment his American accent sounded decidedly Australian. Must be a residual effect of having talked with Will earlier tonight.

"I want a man who puts forth the effort. It may sound silly, but in addition to the work which makes a relationship successful, I desire someone who thinks of me and loves to do those little romantic gestures."

"That's not silly; that's love."

My eyes met his for a moment, and I appreciated he was completely genuine with his words.

"And what about in the bedroom? What kind of man do you want there?"

Somehow I thought the response of 'one who is willing' might only highlight how long it had been. "Uh, I'm not sure how to answer that. Is it on the form?"

"No, but I think it's a significant question you should ask yourself. Sexual chemistry should be as important, at least in my opinion, as the mental connection you have with someone over dinner. Perhaps in the bedroom, you'd prefer to take the lead or—"

I shook my head. "Although I don't mind initiating…" which I'd often had to do in the final years of my marriage. "I kind of want a guy who'll take charge in the bedroom, almost as if he can't help himself. An alpha-male type perhaps?"

"Are you asking me or telling me?" His voice was laced with humor.

"I don't know because I've never really had a man be that way. But if the prospect is, uh, exciting to me, then I suppose it means I may like the change."

"It turns you on to think of being bossed around in the bedroom?"

I knew he was only asking professionally, but that question coupled with his voice was making me a little too hot and bothered. "I'm not sure the word bossy is the right one. More like I want a man who knows what he wants and isn't a gentleman every time when it comes to sex."

I sighed, thinking about way too many lights-out, under-the-covers lovemaking I'd experienced over the years.

"Sometimes a woman just wants to be fucked against a wall, hard." I slapped a hand over my mouth, not believing I'd let that thought slip out of my brain and into actual words.

To his credit, Calvin didn't laugh. But he did clear his throat and for a moment seemed at a loss for words.

Not waiting to hear his response to my word vomit, I quickly sought to change the subject. "So, I guess I'll finish filling out the form with my information and see if she might have a match."

Something told me *wall banging* might not make it onto the list.

Luckily, he picked up on my effort and went with it. "Great. And don't be discouraged if she doesn't have a date for you immediately. She'd rather find someone you'll have a connection with than hurry up and put you with someone you won't. You obviously don't want to settle. Right?"

"Uh, sure." I wanted to believe that.

"Now, then, I'm going to read a couple of things on your fifty bucket-list items. Are you comfortable with that?"

Nope, not at all. "Yes, I think so." My entire body heated with embarrassment over the things he was reading. But, true to his professional nature, he didn't linger over the paper, merely putting it to the side after a minute.

"Talk to me about the things you've used to try to masturbate."

Officially the most awkward question I'd ever been asked.

So much so it took me a moment to recover enough to answer. "Uh, well, nothing aside from my own, you know, hand."

He reached for a notepad and jotted down a couple of items. "These are the devices I recommend for maximum pleasure and to fulfill number one on your list."

Nothing like putting that out there in the course of conversation or having a man write down, from memory, the make and model to use for the ultimate female orgasm.

"Kat, there's nothing to be self-conscious about. You're coming out of a long-term relationship. Having to rely on yourself for your own orgasm is new."

"Actually, I should've bought one a while ago, considering my ex wasn't always interested in whether or not I achieved one."

"Did you ever fake it?"

"No, never. I made the mistake of faking it with a college boyfriend once. Not only did I do him a disservice, but I was stuck feigning them going forward. If I've learned anything after turning thirty, it's that life is too short to fake an orgasm."

He chuckled. "That would make a great T-shirt slogan. I like that you get the importance of that lesson. Your homework this evening is to order one of these devices. I jotted down a couple of websites which I recommend. They're discreet in the packaging and reasonable in their prices."

He leaned forward and my gaze traveled to his strong forearms. They weren't helping with the whole hot and bothered scenario, which had started with his husky voice when I'd first entered the room. I suddenly wondered if any of those websites had same-day shipping.

"My intention is to push you out of your comfort zone on some things. In this case, that includes buying a vibrator. I hope you'll take these tasks seriously. Did you get your phone?"

I swallowed hard and then nodded. "Yes." I rattled off the number and watched while he put it into his phone. I wondered if it was his real phone but reasoned it was most likely for 'work' only.

"After this week, do you think I'll be good?" I had to ask because I was the kind of girl who needed to see results to keep me motivated.

His smile grew from a small one to a knowing grin with which I was becoming familiar. "Kat, you've always been good. I have no doubt you'd eventually navigate this world of dating and also find your sexual confidence on your own. Think of this as a boot camp, if you will, in order to get you there faster. Are you ready to be a good student?"

I could do this. "If you're willing to be a good teacher, you bet."

AFTER ARRIVING HOME, ordering Calvin's suggested device for overnight delivery, and then crawling into bed, I let my mind replay the evening. One thing which struck me from tonight was Calvin mentioning I shouldn't settle for less. But I worried that if I was too picky I'd miss out on my window to become a mother.

That I may, in fact, already have missed out. It was that fear I hadn't revealed to him—or to anyone else, for that matter. I couldn't face sharing the harsh truth that I'd been in the middle of fertility treatments, one week away from an egg retrieval process for in vitro fertilization, when my husband had come home to announce he wanted a divorce. After a year of tests, unsuccessful previous treatments, and on the verge of our last and best hope, he hadn't been ready to start a family and had instead wanted out.

Nothing like being hyped up on hormones, hoping I was weeks away from two pink lines, only to have the rug pulled out from under me completely. In typical fashion, he'd tried to turn it on me, citing my career choices didn't show a true commitment to becoming a mother—that we'd been stuck in a rut, and he'd needed to breathe again. In short: I'd suffocated his potential.

I knew in my heart it wasn't true. I'd never been the type who needed to live in the spotlight, nor did I have any problem shifting my priorities for a child. But it had still cut deep. I'd been about to further a commitment to my husband by starting a family while he'd been checking out—without me having a clue. The whole thing had left me reeling. How could I have been so naïve?

Thinking of my ex, I finally got up the nerve to listen to the voicemail he'd left after he hadn't gotten an answer from me the first time.

"Hi, Catherine. It's Michael. We need to talk. Please call me."

I pressed delete, not wishing in the least to speak with him. After the initial shock of his divorce announcement had passed, I'd prayed for months that he'd call saying he'd changed his mind. But two years later, now he needed to talk? Hearing a ding coming from the kitchen, I got up and found my new phone, charging on the countertop, was lit up. I couldn't help but smile when I saw Calvin's text message. He was simulating that we'd just been out this evening for the first time.

"Enjoyed this evening and our date."

I chewed on my lip and wondered what I should answer, settling with, *"Me too."* That was good, right? In this scenario, I was making my date aware that I'd also enjoyed it without being too wordy. I was pleasantly surprised to see his quick response.

"When can I see you again?"

My pulse quickened, and I mentally slapped myself. This was not a real date, and he was not a man actually interested in me. This was an assignment with someone who was being paid to help me with my text-flirting skills.

"Tomorrow night OK?"
"Sure, see you then."

THE NEXT AFTERNOON I met my friend Sasha for what would be our last weekly lunch, now that she was moving from New York City down South. I gushed over her beautiful engagement ring, thrilled to have helped Brian with his proposal. I had never seen Sasha look so happy.

Sasha had been hard to read and fairly closed off when I'd first met her. But over the last year, we'd grown quite close, having a lot in common with our careers, love of fashion, and both being in our thirties.

"Although I'm ecstatic to move back to Charlotte and in with Brian, I'm going to miss our lunches and girl time together here in the city."

I would, too, and told her as much. "Hopefully, I'll still see you whenever you travel up here, and we have Vegas this weekend."

We spent some time catching up on our jobs and what was new and then delved more into the personal.

"So how's the dating world? Have you, um—" She paused, probably not knowing if she should ask if I'd returned to the sex club or not.

I decided I wasn't ready to share that I had. At least not yet. "I've signed up with a professional matchmaker and meet with her later this week."

"That sounds promising."

"Could be. And there's this guy I've sort of gone out with a couple of times." Yeah, so I wasn't being exactly truthful in bringing up Calvin in this context. But heck, if I was acting this thing out, it made sense I'd ask my girlfriends for some advice along the way as if it were the real thing.

"You're blushing, which I think means you must like him."

Oh, Lord, if only she knew that wasn't the reason I was turning pink. "Well, it's new, and I'm still not great at this whole new world of dating. It's intimidating as hell."

She sighed. "To be honest, I don't know what I would've done if Brian and I hadn't already been friends and coworkers before dating. I could talk a good game and get a guy's phone number in a bar, but I find the whole getting-to-know-them phase very overwhelming. And since my first impressions on anyone I meet are usually for shit, that sort of rules out a lot of people right off the bat, both as friends in general and as dates."

What was funny about Sasha was that she came across tough as nails and smart as hell, with an intimidating beauty in which a raised brow could send a man screaming for the hills, but I'd been privy to the softer side of her. The side she didn't let her guard down for very often. I was privileged to have gotten to know her as a friend. And I'd seen her practically melt whenever her fiancé looked at her. Plus, she was one of the most loyal people I knew.

My phone buzzed, and since it was my regular phone and could be work, I had to check it.

"Is that the guy you've been seeing?"

I shook my head as I read the text from my ex-husband.

"Catherine, are you okay?"

I nodded. "Yeah, my ex has been trying to call me the last couple of days. Since I haven't called him back, he just sent a text."

"About what?"

I showed her the message. "He's asking if he can come over tonight to talk."

Her eyes got big. "You don't think he wants to get back together, do you?"

I scoffed. "Not for a minute. It's been two years."

That ship had sailed. I typed back that I was busy and then

wracked my brain for what he might want, but came up with absolutely nothing. We'd had a prenup which had divided up our assets, so even if he wished to talk money, he didn't have a leg to stand on.

"We need to work on your texting," Calvin blurted out immediately as I sat down that evening for our third meeting.

"Okay." My first thought was the text sent from my ex, so it took me a moment to realize Calvin meant the ones I'd sent him last night. "What, um, what did I say that was wrong?" I'd politely responded I'd see him tonight and didn't get the problem.

"It wasn't wrong, but you missed an opportunity to flirt. To build interest and—"

"Not be boring," I finished on a sigh of defeat.

He shook his head. "I was going to say to set the stage for the next date. Did you contact the matchmaker?"

"I did. I'm meeting with her on Thursday night before I head out of town on Friday morning."

"That's right, you mentioned a trip. Any place fun?"

"Las Vegas, actually."

It was hard to read his reaction through the mask, but his silence was strange.

"Um, are you not a fan of Vegas?"

"No, I am. Maybe you can live it up a little, or is your trip there for work?"

I was a little vague in my answer, given that I didn't want to accidentally slip up and mention names or anything else specific. "Personal plans and sure, maybe I can live it up while there."

But he didn't seem ready to let it go. "Are you there with friends?"

"Yes, for a sort of girls' weekend." Friday would be a ladies' night involving not only Haylee and Sasha, but also Brian's younger sister, Kenzie. Then on Saturday the women would surprise their significant others and their guy friends and make it a group event. I looked forward to a weekend of non-work-related fun.

"Sorry, I didn't mean to make you feel like I was prying."

It could've just been me, but he appeared off. "It's okay. Are you all right?"

He recovered immediately. "Yes, of course. Did you receive your vibrator in the mail?"

Holy subject change.

"I did, but I haven't been home yet. I could hardly use it at work even if I'd had it shipped there."

Something told me he was raising a brow behind his mask. "Or you could do something very unconventional and bring it to work. I'm assuming you have an office, maybe a lock, and a lunch hour."

Wowsers, his voice had slipped an octave lower and I was a heartbeat away from asking if he'd call me on said lunch hour to talk me through it. Something told me his voice alone could make all the difference. "Uh, maybe."

"So let's go through some icebreaking questions you can ask on your first dates and some suggestions I have for flirting."

I GULPED down a glass of white wine and dubiously eyed the battery-operated device where it sat on my granite countertop. I'd already taken a hot shower, read the directions, and changed into a sexy nightgown. Why the last part, I didn't know. It wasn't like I needed to seduce my damn vibrator.

Rolling my eyes at the thought, I threw back the remainder of my glass. Knowing that Calvin would ask me about it tomorrow evening meant I needed to get on it. Literally. The buzzing phone startled me. For a moment I wondered if the vibrator had taken matters into its own hands by turning itself on. I blushed when I read Calvin's incoming text.

"How's your evening?"

Was he trying to hint at asking whether or not I'd played with my new toy yet?

"Good, yours?"

"Getting better. What are you up to?"

Good grief. No pressure, considering he probably had a good idea exactly what I was up to. Not knowing what to text back, I decided to pour another glass of wine and leave my response to wait. Maybe I'd have a clue how to respond after I was done.

Ten minutes later, and I could definitely endorse the makers of the rabbit. Oh, yeah, if I'd been a smoker, about now I'd definitely be lighting up. But with the two glasses of wine and the healthy afterglow of the first orgasm I'd experienced in almost two years, I was out like a light.

TO TEXT or not to text? That was the question I contemplated the next morning while I dressed for work. Calvin's subsequent text message had come in after I'd passed out and was still up on the screen, waiting to be answered.

"I'm looking forward to seeing you tonight."

Well, at least I had until this evening to figure out how to talk about masturbation openly. For now, I had a full day of work to get to.

By the time I walked into our usual meeting room at seven o'clock, I realized it would've been less awkward to have texted him back about last night rather than have to converse with him in person. And Calvin wasn't beating around the bush.

"Good evening, Kat. Although your flirting via text needs work, not responding is worse."

Call me old-fashioned, but I preferred my sex with a man in the room instead of via text message. "I understand, but here's the thing. I think there needs to be a comfort level or intimacy in order to sext message with someone. No offense."

"Uh, none taken, but I wasn't trying to sext you. Given the timing, however, I apologize for the misinterpretation, not to mention the interruption."

My entire body heated with the depth of my embarrassment. But I wasn't surprised at my miscue, given my propensity for entirely misreading a man's signals. "No need to apologize. It wouldn't be the first time I've grossly misconstrued something like this."

"You've thought someone was trying to sext you before?"

I shook my head, "Uh, no, not that. But I do tend to misread the signs as to whether or not somebody is into me, flirting or not. Come to think of it, maybe that's why I'm so terrible with flirting, because half the time I'm not sure if a guy is actually into me or just being friendly. Isn't it highlighted by the fact you simply asked how my evening was, and I went and thought it was a precursor toward phone sex?"

He smiled kindly, and I had a vision of him patting me on the head like the golden retriever to which I'd compared myself in our first meeting. Way to go, Catherine.

"It's not uncommon to wonder if someone is flirting or only being friendly. People have subtle and unsubtle cues. Reading them depends on if you already have a rapport with the individual, or if you're on a first date and have only just met."

"That makes sense, but my biggest blunder happened on the heels of my divorce with a friend with whom I'd sort of hoped for more. He was divorced, too, and we had a lot in common and went out a few times socially. Anyhow, I totally misread the situation, thinking perhaps he wanted more than friends and tried to kiss him after a few drinks. I thought—" I made the air quotes with my fingers. "—that he'd given me the cue, but he hadn't. It was embarrassing, and then I found out later he'd been in love with somebody else entirely. I'd been totally clueless."

"After your divorce, you had to be at your most vulnerable."

"That's a nicer description than the word *desperate*, but yes, I was. Luckily, he was gracious enough to pretend it never happened, and the friendship has endured. Matter of fact, his wife is a really great friend of mine now, and I'll see them in Vegas this weekend."

It had been almost two years ago that I'd been out with Josh Singer and tried to kiss him after a few glasses of wine. Given our mutual interests and our friendship over the years, I'd thought there might be the possibility of something between us, but he'd pulled away and given me the classic *I only think of you as a friend* speech.

I honestly wasn't sure whether he'd ever told Haylee, about the miscue, but at this point, it really seemed moot. Anyone who met the couple knew without a doubt they were destined to be together. Although I might be envious at times of their relationship and new family, it was only because I wanted to be that happy someday, not because I begrudged them their happiness together. Hell, if anything, their bond only raised the bar and proved there were such things as second chances. Josh had obviously found his.

"See, then, putting yourself out there even when it didn't work out the way you'd planned wasn't such an awful thing."

No, maybe not, but at the time, I'd been positive I'd die from humiliation. "Perhaps, although going forward, I have no intention of making assumptions or putting myself out there ever again."

MY INITIAL CONSULTATION with the matchmaker, Melanie Foster, was, for lack of a better word, efficient. She was a woman who appreciated lists, which automatically made me like her. She didn't mince words when she fired off her questions for me, making notes about what I was looking for. She also assured me she dealt in high-profile clientele and was discreet. By next week she hoped to be calling with possible matches.

After I walked out of her office, Sherman, my driver, took me to what I was now dubbing Club T for short. He'd been with me the last six years and was one of my most trusted employees. The man was in his late sixties and yet kept himself trim and in fighting shape. I had no doubt if ever I needed a bodyguard, Sherman could throw down. He was a man of few words whose voice sounded like that of Samuel L. Jackson, and he asked no questions, which is why he said nothing when he helped me, dressed in my mask and wig, out of the town car.

I was aware this was the last time I would meet Calvin before I left for Vegas tomorrow morning. This thought had me restless. There'd been something about the last few days and seeing him nightly that made me feel as though I'd gained a momentum that I was afraid to lose. However, the thought of scheduling an appointment next week and continuing to see him steadily worried me. What I absolutely didn't need was to develop some sort of dependency on meeting him regularly.

He greeted me with familiarity and immediately inquired about my appointment with the matchmaker. "Were you pleased with the way Melanie goes about her process?"

I had found her to be quite competent with her list of questions and in the way she'd written down my absolute no-go items. "Yes, she's quite confident she'll find me some possible candidates as soon as next week."

"Great. A couple of things I wanted to go over tonight. One, I'd like for you, if you're open to it, to initiate a text to me over the weekend. Pretend you've just met me, we've gone out a couple of times, and now you're traveling out of town. People appreciate knowing they're on someone's mind, and a text is a perfect, flirty way of doing that."

Okay, I could manage that, although why did he wish to text me over the weekend if this was our last appointment? Unless he didn't want it to be our final meeting?

"Secondly, while you're in Vegas, do something out of your comfort zone. I'm not necessarily talking about your list, but if you're there with friends, you should make an effort to get out and have some fun. And if any of them are in relationships, make them your wing women while you meet guys."

"All right, I'll try to put myself out there."

"I'm out of the office until Tuesday evening, but I hope you'll want to see me again next week. I know you're busy, but I can work around your schedule when I'm able to."

Again, I knew he was only being accommodating on a professional level, not because he couldn't wait to see me personally, but I still enjoyed it way too much to be healthy. "Okay. By then I should have my first date from the matchmaker scheduled."

He nodded. "And you're good with me texting you over the weekend? If you're not, then I understand. The last thing I want is to intrude on your personal time."

The thought of him keeping in touch over the next couple of days gave me something to look forward to. I reasoned it was only because I didn't have any other man texting me and could use the practice. But I think, deep down, it was a thrill to have any sort of attention, sadly enough, even from someone I was paying.

"No, no, it's fine." The thought occurred to me that I'd have my friends there, which might end up being really useful.

"Great. I'll put you down for Tuesday night. By then you'll hopefully be getting ready for your date. I have a good feeling about the matchmaker finding you someone, Kat. He's out there."

It was a subtle reminder that Calvin was in this to help me, which meant he was part of the process, not the solution. Meeting his eyes, I felt certain he had to make this clear with a lot of his clients, ensuring even someone as clueless as I wouldn't misread his intentions.

CHAPTER THREE

*O*n Friday morning I briefly went into the office to finish up a couple things so I could take a work-free, three-day weekend in Vegas. After that, Sherman drove me to the airport. Haylee had insisted that we take one of her husband's private planes since she was bringing her baby daughter, Abby, plus her nanny. I didn't object. This was quite the way to travel; plus, it allowed me to catch up with both her and Sasha while enjoying a glass of champagne in luxury.

As we were descending, I glanced at my phone and considered firing off a text to Calvin. He'd asked me to initiate one, but I wasn't sure what to say.

"Please tell me your ex isn't contacting you again?" Sasha questioned, looking over. She'd become fiercely protective since learning about his message that he wanted to meet me in person.

"He already did. I told him I was traveling out of town and would get back to him once I returned. I'm not exactly in a hurry to do so." I sighed and realized I craved a change of subject. My divorce had become a tired topic with friends and family. Not that they ever complained, but I no longer wished to rehash old news or talk about how he'd once again upset me.

"I was actually contemplating sending a message to this guy I've been seeing, but flirty texting isn't my forte. Wanna help?" I was suddenly excited about the possibility of enlisting reinforcements.

Sasha shook her head. "No way. I can barely manage the face-to-face stuff, so text flirting is definitely not my thing."

Haylee broke out in an excited smile. "Oooh. You met someone, Catherine? Is it serious?"

"No, we only met this last week." At least that wasn't a lie. "But he said to text him over the weekend. However, I'm not sure what to say except, 'Hey, in Vegas. Have a good weekend.'"

Both women laughed, and Sasha clinked her champagne glass with mine. "Sounds efficient and practical. I say go with it."

Haylee shook her head adamantly and rolled her eyes. "Don't you dare. When we land, you should say something like, 'Just landed and already missing you.' Then do one of those cute emoticons."

"An emoti-what?" Sasha asked, clearly as oblivious as I was.

Haylee smiled and then showed us her phone. I was instantly intrigued. They had icons ranging from a face blowing kisses to a piece of shit. Evidently, there were all sorts of ways to emote oneself.

"So I download them to my phone and then blow kisses or send hearts when I flirt."

"Or send him a horny devil and a cocktail and really get the message across," Sasha commented dryly, causing us all to crack up.

"Ha, don't knock it. I bet if you sent a symbol for horny devil, bed, and house, Brian would come home from the office in record time." As soon as Haylee said this, I immediately realized the potential behind some of the little symbols as a fun way to communicate.

Sasha chuckled. "I'm pretty sure if I simply texted him, 'bed, now,' it would have the same effect. However, I get what you're saying. There you go, Catherine. You have your ringer in this girl for showing you how to flirt all weekend long. And you'll have Brian's sister, too, who knows all of those little acronyms people text. I swear I had to look up PMSL the other day. I thought my future sister-in-law had lost her mind by responding to something funny with a comment she had PMS."

I grinned. "Even I know that one is 'pissing myself laughing.'" I couldn't stay current in my magazine without adopting some of the lingo of the twenty-something-year olds who were around me all the time. "But for the purpose of the guy I've been out with a couple times and haven't kissed, I'm going to skip the horny devil or saying I miss him just yet."

Haylee contemplated. "Actually, sending any kind of text implies you're thinking of him all on its own, which is what you want."

Calvin had said the same thing. "So what do I say?" I was ready to draft the message.

"Start off cool. Say something like, 'Landed in Vegas, how's your Friday night?'"

That sounded easy enough.

"Wait. Are you guys exclusive?" Sasha inquired.

Ha, the furthest from it as I was certain he had a long list of clients. "We've only talked, so it's kind of premature to ask about exclusivity."

"Then you should add after you say you landed that you're about to hit the town. Make him wonder and wish he would've had the talk before you left because now you're a hot, single woman, one who obviously has sexy friends to help set you up during a weekend in Sin City."

Why not? I typed out my message with the help of both of them and sent it a half hour later while we were climbing in the car that would take us to the hotel.

"Just landed in Vegas ready to hit the pool, then the town. Are you having a good Fri?"

Calvin's response came much quicker than I'd anticipated. *"I am now that I've heard from you."*

Apparently, he didn't need lessons on how to flirt via text. His response had my heart beating faster and both Sasha and Haylee oohing during the car ride to our hotel.

"Don't answer him yet. You're busy as far as he believes. But maybe before you go to bed, you can say something like 'sweet dreams,' so long as it's not nine o'clock, cuz that would be lame," Haylee offered.

Right, because I planned on being up at least until ten o'clock before I'd call it a night.

SATURDAY MORNING we all met poolside at Josh's hotel and surprised the guys. The group of men consisted of Josh, Brian, Colby, Mark, and Will. You'd think among these handsome men, three of whom were single, I'd be clamoring for a setup. Unfortunately, there wasn't a connection with any of them worth exploring.

Colby, Josh's younger brother, said hello first with a kiss on the cheek. In all the years I'd known him, he'd always been the charmer. Not only good looking, he also had charisma in spades. He was a huge ladies' man and I doubted he'd ever settle down if half the rumors about him were true.

As for Mark, he and I had been acquainted for quite a while, having attended many of the same events over the years. He was Josh's lawyer and a good friend to both Josh and Brian. He was attractive and surprisingly well built, but very quiet and apparently introverted. Unfortunately, according to Haylee, Mark didn't date at all. Not since losing his fiancée tragically a number of years ago.

And Will, as previously noted, was regrettably too young for me. But he sure was nice to look at, wearing only his board shorts and showing his chiseled abs and bronze skin.

We all hung out by the pool for a couple hours and then retired to our rooms before tonight's planned activities for celebrating the newly engaged couple. Thankful for the time, I booked a couple of spa treatments in the hotel, eager to have a relaxing afternoon to myself.

The knock on the door surprised me, but not as much as Will standing on the other side of it.

"Hiya. I just talked Kenzie into coming with me, Colby, and Mark. We're going to ride some go-karts, go shooting, and whatever else we may have time for this afternoon. You interested?"

I might've been tempted if I hadn't already made my appointments, especially since the activities he mentioned would've served as things outside of my normal comfort zone and I'd promised I'd do something like that this weekend. "I have a spa thing, but thanks for thinking of me. I'll see everyone tonight, though."

"Sounds good." He smiled.

As I watched him retreat down the hall, I felt a twinge of guilt over my promise to Cal that I'd put myself out there and try new things. Oh, good Lord, I'd inadvertently shortened Calvin's name as if it was his real one and we were familiar.

Stupid. Stupid. Stupid.

So dumb, in fact, that before I needed to be downstairs for my appointments, I fired up my laptop. Nothing like making a list of reasons not to fall for Calvin to keep me on the sane path of reality. Luckily, it really only took one item for me to start laughing at the absurdity of it all.

Because you're crazy. You shouldn't need a list to tell you reasons not to fall for a complete stranger with a sexy voice who you're paying to talk to you and give you dating advice. And his real name isn't even Calvin.

AFTER SPENDING a lovely afternoon getting pampered in the hotel spa, I was more than ready to hit the town. Haylee had scheduled a wonderful dinner followed by a dance club and then the quieter venue of a bar after that. I'd had a really great time throughout, but returning to the hotel and seeing happy couples pair off was a reminder of what it was like to be in a relationship. To have that person you couldn't wait to be alone with, someone with whom to chitchat about the night and fall into bed together. This is what I missed after being half of a couple for most of my adult life. So when Kenzie invited me to have a drink with her and Will in the hotel lobby lounge, I accepted, happy for the company.

"Where did Colby and Mark go?" I inquired.

Kenzie frowned. "Evidently to a strip club."

"Oh." It didn't shock me one bit regarding Colby, knowing his reputation, but that Mark would tag along did. He always seemed so shy. What also surprised me was that Will hadn't opted to join them, instead having a drink with the two of us ladies. But given the way he'd danced with Kenzie earlier, perhaps he was into her. Ah, young people, I mused, while feeling the buzz of one of my phones in my clutch.

I smiled when I pulled it out and realized it was a text from Calvin. *"Are you enjoying Sin City?"*

"That's quite the smile for someone," Kenzie commented with a smirk. We were sitting there alone while Will went to the bar to get us a round of drinks.

"Yeah. But how to respond is really my problem."

"Let me see. What's it say?"

I read her the message and realized I had the perfect teacher sitting beside me. She wouldn't hesitate to type out a flirty response. "Any suggestions?"

"Clearly he called it "Sin City" for a reason. So maybe you

respond with something like, 'Yes, but I'm still waiting for the sin part.'"

Oooh, I loved that, typed it right in, and awaited a response. Kenzie scooted her chair closer, and I realized this could be fun. His response made me laugh.

"Oh yeah? Any ideas?"

She grinned when I flashed his response. We both were startled out of our little fun when Will delivered our drinks.

He smiled and took a seat at our lounge table for three.

Kenzie noticed his beverage of choice. "What's with the agua, Will? You can't hang?"

"I have a stomachache or something. I think I must've eaten something bad earlier. Anyhow, what are you ladies up to?" He quirked a brow, evidently taking in the two of us poring over my phone.

Why not? I thought. The male perspective might be nice. "Kenzie is helping me flirt via text message with, uh, someone back home."

"Should Catherine tell him she's only sitting at her hotel bar or make it sound as though she's out partaking in the sin part of Sin City?"

Confusion flitted over his face for a second, but then he shrugged. "Uh, I'd always go with the truth. But maybe take a picture of your martini and send it to him. Let him think of the possibility of what could happen tonight after your drink."

We girls quite liked that idea. See, I never would've thought to take a picture. Truth be told, I needed Kenzie's help to figure out how to send the shot of my martini glass via text on this new phone. We waited a minute, but when we heard the chirp and I checked my phone, it wasn't from mine.

Kenzie pulled out her phone and sighed, draining her glass. "My phone is completely dead. Guess that means no text flirting for me tonight."

Must've been Will's, but unlike me, he wasn't in a hurry to

see who had contacted him. After shooting Kenzie a sympathetic look, he excused himself to go to the restroom.

As soon as he was gone, I had to ask, "So you and Will aren't…?" If I were her age, I'd have wanted to spend time with him as he appeared to be the perfect gentleman, on top of being attractive. Matter of fact, practically every woman in the place was watching him make his way to the men's room.

Kenzie laughed. "No, we're only friends. I'm actually in love with someone else, a man who at the moment I'd absolutely love to whack-a-mole."

I laughed at her form of punishment while taking in this news that she was in a relationship. "I'm sorry, honey. I'd say he's a fool if he lets a girl like you get away."

"Damn straight he is." She clinked her glass with mine in girl solidarity.

After a few more minutes, Kenzie checked her watch. "I wonder what's taking Will so long? I hope he's not getting sick. Did you get a response to your pic you sent?"

I didn't see Will, nor had I received a reply from Calvin. Maybe we were done for the night? Flirting was exhausting. "No response. Do I text him again?"

She shook her head adamantly. "No way. You want to appear like you're busy, not waiting on his response. Don't you think, Will?"

Will set down the new round of drinks he must've grabbed on his way back. While doing so, he gave me a strange look, and then turned toward Kenzie, who was now downing the whiskey he'd placed in front of her. "What's that?"

"We were saying that since Catherine had no response, she absolutely shouldn't text again. Gotta keep up the illusion of being busy doing better things, right?"

He nodded, appearing all sorts of distracted.

"Everything okay? Your stomach any better?" I questioned.

He sighed. "Sorry. No, I'm still feeling poorly, but I got some ginger ale, which should help settle it."

Kenzie patted him on the arm. "Poor thing. We shouldn't have danced earlier if I'd known you weren't feeling good. Well, you two, I'm off to bed and to charge my phone so I can give hell to a certain someone." Given the pointed look she sent Will, I assumed he must know who it was. "Catherine, it was so nice spending time with you this weekend. Thanks for helping me with the clothes shopping and good luck with the texting."

I hugged her and thanked her for the assistance.

Surprisingly, Will stayed with me at the table after she left, waiting for me to finish up my last glass of wine. "Has she been helping you all weekend with the texting?"

"Only tonight. But Haylee and Sasha assisted yesterday. Someday I'll get the hang of it on my own." I laughed but realized his eyes had narrowed. Had I said something to offend him?

"Don't you feel like he may be getting someone who isn't really you?"

"Uh, he's getting me, just a flirtier version who's more fun. Does it really matter?" I found it odd that he cared.

He sighed. "I guess not. I think I'm calling it a night. Are you on the eight o'clock flight tomorrow morning to New York?"

Haylee had offered me the opportunity to travel back with her family on the private jet in the late afternoon, but I'd wanted to get an early start on my return, so I'd opted for commercial. "I am. We could share a car to the airport if you'd like?" I downed the rest of my wine, thinking it was about time to get up to my own room, pack, and call it a night.

"Yeah, that sounds good." He stood up and walked with me to the elevator where he pressed the button for our floor—we were all staying on the same one.

Since Calvin wasn't actually someone I was seeing, I decided to ignore Kenzie's advice about sending another text and typed out one last message to him.

"Good night. See you on Tuesday night."

Will watched me curiously and then physically winced when his phone chirped in his pocket, indicating an incoming text.

"Weird timing," I muttered. My eyes traveled to Will's strong hands and forearms, a sight that I'd memorized during my meetings with Calvin. Snapping my eyes to the uncannily familiar blue ones, I observed the deep red he was turning and fought my panic.

It couldn't be.

One way to find out. I hit the call button and listened to the ringtone of Will's phone immediately come to life.

The elevator started to move up, and I recalled the time I'd thought Calvin's voice had inadvertently slipped into a slight Australian accent. His pause about me going to Vegas for the weekend, and lastly his reaction to having Kenzie help me text.

Will was Calvin.

Calvin was Will.

Oh, God. The air seemed to be evaporating from the small space in the elevator, and I suddenly couldn't breathe.

"How long?" I barely got out, feeling my face hot with humiliation.

He knew what I was asking and didn't bother to deny anything, instead looking me straight in the eyes. "Only since you texted me the picture of your martini glass earlier, but it's not a big deal, really."

"Not a big deal?" I could feel my voice rising. Since the elevator was dinging on our floor, I lowered it, afraid I'd be overheard. "I gave you a list, and we talked about—" I couldn't begin to go there in my head. The things I'd discussed with Calvin—I mean, Will.

"Catherine, it's okay. It was all in confidence and—"

I didn't let him finish, instead beelining for my room only a few doors down. "I can't. I can't possibly discuss this right now."

When faced with the fight or flight situation, my flight instincts were taking over, fueled by the humiliation that this man knew intimate details about my sex life, details I'd never shared with anyone. That we were in the same professional circle; he was a model with whom I'd worked. And that worst of all, he was within my inner group of friends.

"Let me come in a few minutes and we'll talk."

I turned and shook my head. "No, I'm sorry. I can't." And with those parting words, I bolted into my room and leaned up against the door once it clicked shut. I waited until I could hear his retreating footsteps before letting out the breath I'd been holding.

CHAPTER FOUR

I didn't sleep much after the revelation that Calvin was Will. Evidently discovering someone you were only acquainted with casually through friends now knew that you wanted to be tied up in bed, the make and model of your vibrator, and all of your insecurities meant a restless night.

I'd taken a long, hot bath, hoping to relax last night, but it hadn't helped. So of course I'd stayed up to make a list of the reasons I shouldn't worry, which only made me more anxious. Thinking about it in retrospect the next morning, I realized I should've taken the time to talk it out last night instead of fleeing into my room. As I packed up the last of my things to get ready for my flight, I noticed the message on my second phone from Calvin, aka Will. Apparently sent last night, it simply said,

"I would never tell anyone and I'd hope you would offer the same courtesy in return. If you don't wish to share a car in the morning to the airport, I understand. I don't want things to be uncomfortable between us."

How could I possibly be angry with him for this situation? It wasn't like he'd caused it any more than I had. I regretted the way I'd left things last night, and now in the morning light, I wanted nothing more than to smooth it over as quickly as possible. It might be extraordinarily awkward, but I responded that I'd meet him in ten minutes down in the lobby to share a ride to the airport. Then I figuratively put on my big girl panties to face him.

He wasn't there. Since his last text had come in after he'd left my door last night and he hadn't heard back until I'd responded just now, the chances were he'd gone on without me. Realizing I couldn't wait any longer if I was to make my flight, I got in the car and texted him again on the way.

"I'm on my way to the airport. Hopefully you're already there?" Then deciding to offer an apology for last night, I typed, *"I'm sorry about my reaction last night. I guess I needed time to process."*

No response by the time I'd made it past security and sat waiting in the boarding area. I'd opted to skip the first class lounge in the hopes of seeing him, but it wasn't until I was about to board that I heard his sexy voice come up behind me. I couldn't believe I didn't realize he was Calvin sooner. There should have been no mistaking his husky tone even if he had been covering up his Australian accent with an American one at Club Travesty.

"Hiya, Catherine. Sorry I missed your text this morning. I was running late."

I turned to face him and immediately noticed how pale he appeared. "Are you still not feeling well?"

He shook his head. "Nope, not so much. I think I must have food poisoning. Anyhow, you didn't have to apologize."

I cut him off. "No, I did. I overreacted."

He started to chuckle but then gripped his stomach. "Ow, laughing hurts. You definitely didn't overreact; you just reacted to quite the shock. Anyhow, I think they're calling for first class, which is probably you, right?"

It was, but for a moment I was reluctant to leave him or this conversation. "Right. So we're okay, then?"

He nodded, giving me a wan smile. "Of course we are."

"Are you certain you'll be all right for the flight?"

He took a sip of his bottle of water and nodded. "Yeah. I plan on sleeping most of the way, anyhow."

After I took my seat in the second row, I found myself scanning the faces of each person who boarded, waiting for his. When my pulse raced upon seeing him walk in, I convinced myself it was only because I was anxious about his knowledge of so many personal things about me. That had to be it.

He tipped his head and smiled before proceeding back into the coach section to take his seat.

We landed after the four-hour flight, and I was one of the first to deplane. But I waited for Will, who must've been sitting in the rear since he was one of the last ones off. He didn't look well at all, which was saying a lot since normally he was exceptional to look at.

"You're not well, are you?" I asked.

He looked shocked at seeing me standing there. "No, not great. Were you waiting on me?"

His eyes were glassy. Before I could register the appropriateness of my action, I put the back of my hand to his forehead. He was on fire. "Jesus, Will, you're burning up. Do you think you may have the flu?"

He shook his head. "I don't think so, more like shooting pain on my right side. And you didn't answer my question."

"I only waited to assure you that I wouldn't say anything, either. You know, what you said in your text from last night."

He nodded briefly before grimacing in pain and clutching his side.

"Do you think it could be your appendix?"

His expression flashed panic before we both walked slowly

towards the exit. Apparently, he hadn't checked a bag, either. "I sure hope not. Maybe it was something I ate yesterday."

"I think you should go to the hospital to make sure. My driver should be outside, so I can take you."

He shook his head. "I don't really do doctors." Again with the agony etched on his handsome features.

"I don't think that's the best motto at the moment considering you look like you're about to pass out with pain." Growing up the daughter of a physician, I definitely didn't share his viewpoint.

His pallor had gone almost green now, and sweat beaded on his brow. "It's just that I don't have medical insurance, so I don't want to go to the emergency room if I can help it." The way he swallowed hard with the words told me this admission didn't come easy for him.

"Look, my father is a doctor. A heart surgeon, actually, but I'm sure he has a clue as to what appendicitis is. Come on, let's get in the back of the car, and I'll call him."

He hesitated, and I took his arm. "Will, I'm not leaving you here or in a taxi when you're feeling this way. We'll have a five-minute conversation to see if he thinks you should go to the ER."

He finally nodded, and we headed out to the waiting sedan. I said hello to Sherman, handed over our things, and popped inside with Will, who cringed as he scooted into the backseat.

Calling my dad on a Sunday was always a crapshoot as he could be on the golf course, but luck was on my side. He picked up the phone.

"Hi, honey. How are you?" he greeted.

I smiled whenever I heard his kind voice, full of endless energy though he was in his sixties.

"Good, Dad. Um, I have a friend, though, who's having some severe pain on the right side of his stomach and seems to be running a fever."

"Is he with you now?"

I glanced over at Will. "Yes, we're in my car, and I'm wondering whether to take him to the emergency room or not."

"Call me back on FaceTime." And just like that, my father hung up.

Taking a deep breath, I realized Will and I were about to cross over a personal line by involving my family. I hoped my smile was reassuring. "My father wants to FaceTime you if that's okay."

He seemed mildly surprised, but nodded his consent.

I dialed. My dad's concerned face came into view after two rings and I had to smile because he was already in doctor mode with a medical book in front of him.

"Hello, young man, my name is Dr. Davenport. But if you're a friend of Cathy's, you can call me Tom."

Will took the phone, giving him a half smile. "Hiya, Tom. I'm Will. Thank you for taking the time."

My dad, long used to getting calls from neighbors, family, and pretty much anyone who had his number, waved him off. "Not a worry. Tell me about your symptoms, son."

Will rattled off that he'd first felt nauseous yesterday morning, but the fever and terrible pains in his back and stomach hadn't started until overnight, progressively getting worse. The whole time he spoke, I thought about my selfishness in retreating to my room while he'd been feeling this way. But he hadn't let on. My ex-husband would've been whining to anyone who would listen about a simple hangnail.

"Do me a favor, Will. Have Cathy take the phone and point it so I can see your stomach. I need to view both sides as I'm checking for swelling, particularly on the right one."

Holding the phone, I positioned it above Will's impressive six-pack after he lifted his shirt. But instead of the sound of my father's voice, my mom's unfortunately came through.

"My God, would you look at those abs? Cathy, please tell me

the word 'friend' is only a cover so your parents won't know you're in reality sleeping with this man."

My mother never failed to embarrass me with her lack of filter. I could practically feel my ears turning pink. Although I was horrified, Will, despite his pain, was cracking a smile.

"Mom, would you please let Dad examine him?" I put the phone toward my face, giving her a pointed look which said, 'contain your crazy please.'

Her shrug let me know she was only giving in for the moment.

After she returned the phone to my father, he apologized. "Sorry, kids, had to grab my glasses. But I see your mother doesn't need any. Aim the phone toward his left side, then his right."

I did as he requested.

"It's hard to tell if the right side is distended or swollen on the screen. Cathy, can you be a dear and feel both sides to see if the right one feels more swollen than the left?"

My face started to heat at the prospect of touching him, and he didn't help my predicament when he bit his lip. Whether in pain or not, his action was sexy as hell.

Taking a deep breath, I put each of my hands on either side of his abs, simultaneously noting how soft his skin was. Probably because he was so young. And that's what I needed to remind myself. I wasn't a cradle-robber. His baby-smooth skin was because he was closer to a child than to my age. Okay, maybe that was an exaggeration, but still, he was way too young for me to be this turned on by touching his taut, tanned, completely lickable…. *No, no, no. Get off that train of thought, pronto.*

My Dad's voice snapped me out of practically drooling over poor Will sitting there in an immense amount of pain.

"Press down slightly on both sides, letting go of the left one first. It should be most painful, Will, once she releases the pressure on the right side."

Following directions, I felt the breath leave him with only the slight pressure I put on his left side. But he almost looked like he was going to pass out when I lifted my fingers, as my father had instructed, on the right one.

"It definitely feels a little swollen and, judging by his face, I'd say when I released the right side, it's much worse."

"Get him to the ER stat, Cathy. I'm nine-five percent sure you have appendicitis, young man, and need to get it out, especially if you've been suffering with the symptoms for some time now."

Will grimaced while I thought back to the fact that he didn't have any medical insurance. But this had the potential to be serious, so I directed Sherman to drive us to New York Presbyterian Hospital. Hopefully, on a Sunday afternoon there wouldn't be a lot of traffic into the city.

"Thanks, Dad," I said, waving goodbye as my mother's face came into view again. I should've guessed she wasn't done yet.

"You bring that good-looking hunk of a man up for dinner any time. Oh, and the shirt is completely optional."

I rolled my eyes. "Mom, he can hear you." Stealing a glance toward Will, I noticed the amused smile tugging at his lips.

"Doesn't bother me. And I make a mean Irish stew, although if you're English—I have a hard time telling those foreign type accents apart—you might not want that. What do the English eat, Tom?" she yelled toward my dad.

"How the hell would I know? I'm American. Fix him ribs or burgers. I'm sure it'll be fine."

Okay, I needed to end this conversation before it careened even more out of control. This comedy routine, although typical for them, was embarrassing as hell for me. Will didn't help when he answered her.

"I'm Australian, for the record, and ribs or burgers sounds fantastic. Thanks again for your help, Dr. Davenport, and nice to meet you, Mrs. Davenport."

I knew my mother was probably beside herself with his lovely manners. She got out a "We're only a short train ride away near Boston—" before I hung up on her. I loved my mother dearly, but she had a tendency to drive me batty.

"Ow. Laughing hurts. Your mother is a top chick," he commented with a smirk.

"She's certainly something," I mumbled, figuring the translation of that had to be something with the word crazy in it. I then amended. "In her mild defense, she's sort of turned into a matchmaker momzilla after the divorce. She tries to set me up with every eligible bachelor she sees. Having your shirt pulled up clearly put you as a frontrunner in a hurry."

A smile crossed his face. "No worries. Mine's not so different about trying to set me up."

"But you're practically a baby." One who had an amazing body with golden skin that made my body tingle with desire. *Bad, bad Catherine.*

"I'll be twenty-eight in April. Not so old that my mum should be worried I'll never settle down, but hardly a babe."

While smiling at the adorable way he said mum, I felt surprised he wasn't closer to Haylee's age at twenty-four. Not that it made a difference. I was over six years his senior. "Right. Um, how does it feel now?"

He sighed. "Still in pain, but I keep hoping by the time we arrive, I'll miraculously feel better. By the way, if you want to just drop me off, you can. I appreciate the ride."

"Oh, do you have someone else who'll meet you there?" It occurred to me that, for all I knew, Will had a girlfriend.

"No. My Dad lives in California, my mum in Australia. But with any luck, I'll be in and out after an exam."

My father was a renowned heart surgeon who'd practiced medicine for nearly forty years. If he was betting ninety-five percent that Will had appendicitis, then I could guarantee he was right. However, I kept my thoughts to myself. Will would find out for sure soon enough. "Yes, here's hoping."

Twenty minutes later, we pulled up to the emergency room doors, and I thanked Sherman, asking him to wait curbside until I texted him. Luckily, the ER wasn't too busy. After Will filled out some paperwork, he was taken back quickly to be seen.

"I understand if you don't want to wait," he murmured.

I shook my head. "No, no. I'll be here. Matter of fact, my dad already texted me asking how you're doing, so at the very least I need to give him an update."

Will gave me a small smile of thanks and walked with the nurse through the double doors when his name was called. Thirty minutes later, a woman in scrubs came out and called my name. When I stood, she motioned me to follow her into the elevator.

"I'm Nurse Tina. They're prepping your friend for surgery right now. He asked me to come see if you were still here."

I sighed, aware that surgery was the very last thing Will had wanted but grateful my father had convinced him to come to the hospital. The nurse showed me to a small curtain which cornered off his pre-surgical space. When I walked in, I was unprepared for the sight of Will looking so vulnerable in his blue hospital gown and lying on a gurney.

"Looks like your dad was correct, unfortunately. In ten minutes, I'm being wheeled back for surgery."

"I'd really hoped he wasn't. Um, do you have a phone to call anyone? Your family maybe?"

"If I rang them, they'd only worry, and there's not much they can do, being so far away. But I do have a favor to ask?" He appeared nervous as he held out a note for me.

"Sure, anything." I meant it. This unforeseen medical emergency had ended up propelling us past any residual awkwardness from last night's discovery.

"I don't expect you to stick around for the operation, but I was hoping you could put your number down so the hospital can let you know once I'm out. And if for some reason there are complications, these are my mum and dad's phone numbers."

My eyes met his, and I saw him valiantly trying to hide the worry. No doubt he'd already had the anesthesia spiel where they explained the risks of going under. I took the folded piece of paper and sought to ease his mind. "Are you having laparoscopic surgery?"

"Yeah, how'd you know?"

"My dad. He said it would mean less recovery time."

He nodded. "I'm hoping to be discharged tonight."

"Really?" My brow arched. "I'm surprised they're letting you go so quickly." Especially since it was already late in the afternoon.

"I'm not staying overnight. The bill will be high enough as it is." His lips flattened to a firm line. He clearly didn't want to discuss it any further, but then he sighed. "Sorry, this whole thing is so unexpected. Um, do you mind writing your real cell phone number down?" He indicated the form on the clipboard on the side of the bed.

"Of course I don't, but I feel terrible leaving you here."

He waved me off. "No need to feel bad. I'll be fine."

But the note in my hand told me there was a small part of him that was nervous. I might not know him very well, but I'd spent enough time with him to know he was a good guy who didn't deserve having to go through this all by himself. "Do you want me to call Haylee?" I knew they were good friends, and he was even close to Josh.

He shook his head adamantly. "No way. I'll be okay."

"All right." I watched the doctor come in.

"Ready, William?" The older man was dressed for surgery in scrubs.

Will grasped my hand and let out a breath. "Thanks for taking me here and calling your dad."

I had to swallow past the lump forming. My emotions would

have been mystifying except that I hated he was here on his own. No one should be alone before, during, or after surgery. "I'll be here when you wake up."

His eyes widened. "You don't need—"

I cut him off, squeezing his hand. "I want to. So I'll see you in a couple of hours. And who knows? Maybe you'll be one of those crazy people saying weird stuff as you come out of anesthesia, and I'll film you and send it to all our friends."

He laughed before clutching his side and then clasped my hand in return. "Sounds like a plan."

I watched as they wheeled him away, feeling nervous for him. What a crazy twenty-four hours this had been.

I HAD Sherman take me to my condo to drop off my suitcase and change my clothes before driving me back to the hospital. After an hour of waiting in a small sitting room outside of the surgical wing, I was finally told that Will was out of surgery. Soon I'd be able to see him in recovery. It was such a strange thing to walk back to recovery in order to see a man whom I barely knew. Yet I felt a connection to him, albeit an unconventional one.

For the moment, however, he was a guy who was alone. If there was anything I could relate to, it was that. My solitary state had felt especially driven home when I'd removed my husband's name from my emergency contact form. I had put my parents down even though I knew they were too far away to come quickly and be by my side if anything ever happened. Nothing says lonely like having to think about who to write down for your emergency contact and realize there's no one within a car ride who could be there for you.

When the nurse opened the curtain to his post-surgery recovery spot, I could see him asleep on the gurney. He looked a bit paler than normal, but otherwise still remarkably hot, despite the ugly, blue hospital gown.

"He's been in and out. We could wheel him up to a room, but he's insistent that he's leaving tonight," the nurse told me.

"And what does the doctor say?"

"He said he'd consider a release if your friend could prove he has someone to take care of him over the next twenty-four to forty-eight hours."

"I have my roommates," Will mumbled, flicking open his eyes. He'd obviously caught the tail end of the conversation.

"Well, unless one is coming here to sign the form and ensure they'll be there for you, I doubt the doctor will buy it," the nurse returned.

Without thinking, I blurted, "I'll sign him out. He can stay at my place overnight."

Will shook his head while I lifted a brow as if to say 'what's your alternative?'

"Okay, I'll get the paperwork ready." The nurse had disapproval in her tone as she left the room.

"Although I appreciate you—"

I held up a hand. "I'll drop you off at your apartment if you do, in fact, have people who'll take care of you. But this gets you out of here quicker than having to wait on anyone else to arrive."

He breathed a sigh of relief. "Thank you. That would be great, and my roommates will definitely do that for me."

Two hours later, after Will had promised the doctor to follow the discharge instructions to the letter and we'd filled his prescriptions, we were in the back of my sedan heading toward Queens.

When we pulled up in front of his multi-story brick building, I noticed it was older, but the place still appeared to be in decent shape. Will was climbing out the door before Sherman could open it or I could help him out.

"Thanks yet again for everything." He appeared haggard and struggling with pain.

"You're welcome, but at least let me walk you up."

He shook his head. "I'm fine. Really."

I blew out a breath, not believing him in the slightest. "Yes, so you've said multiple times, and I'm sure you are. But no offense, it's my name on that sheet saying I'd ensure you were taken care of. And, as previously discussed, I'm an annoying rule follower who would end up stressing out if I don't make certain, at the very least, that you don't collapse in the elevator. Plus, there's no way you're lifting your bag yourself, Mr. I'm Fine. Fair enough?"

Thankfully, he didn't argue, instead giving me a smile. "Fair enough."

We were quiet on the way to the fifth floor. After getting off first, I watched him sway with his first step. By holding his arm, I helped him balance by taking some of his weight. "Almost there. Then you can slip into oblivion with your painkillers. Also, my dad said it's critical you take all of your antibiotics." Great. Now I sounded like a worried mother.

He nodded, taking out his keys from the bag I held and opening his apartment door. "I owe you big time."

I shook my head. "No, you don't. So good night, then."

His crystal blue eyes met mine. "Good night, Catherine."

The door shut, and I couldn't shake the sensation that something was off. But he was home, and I should be relieved as I could now return to my own place and get a good night's sleep. I had work tomorrow with a busy week ahead.

When I climbed into the back seat of my sedan, I spotted the white prescription bag containing Will's pain medication and antibiotics. Maybe that's why I'd been feeling unsettled. I'd subconsciously known he'd forgotten the bag. After telling Sherman I'd be another few minutes, I returned to Will's apartment and knocked.

Opening the door was a very attractive man with olive skin and black hair. He appeared to be Will's age but had a heavy Italian accent. "Hello. How may I help you?"

I held up the bag. "I have Will's medication."

"Ah, okay. Yeah, he don't look so good. He's in the first room to the left." He pointed down the one hallway leading off the main room.

"Uh, thanks." I sure hoped this wasn't one of the roommates who was supposed to be taking care of Will because he seemed clueless as to why his friend wasn't 'looking so good.'

When I stepped further inside the apartment, I noticed a couple on the couch engrossed in the television and two more guys in the kitchen. No one paid me any mind, most likely because there were five people, not including Will, within the first two hundred square feet of the space.

The door to the bedroom was slightly ajar, so I tapped on it lightly while opening it further. The sight inside shocked me. There were four mattresses on the floor of the small room with Will lying on one of them. His arm was over his face, and he hadn't bothered to take off his clothes. *Roommates that would take care of him, my ass.* He was basically staying in a boarding house where he rented a mattress on the floor.

Crouching down, I said his name. "Will."

He moved his arm, and his eyes focused on me. "Catherine, what are you doing here?" He tried to sit up but winced in discomfort with the effort.

I held out the bag. "You left these in the car."

He reached out and took it, murmuring his thanks. "That would've been bad in a couple of hours. Thank you."

I surveyed the room and sighed.

"Don't say it," he said tightly.

"Will, you need a proper place to recover. You can't honestly tell me any of those people out in the living room are aware that you had surgery a few hours ago, let alone that they are going to take care of you."

"Just because my room doesn't meet your standards doesn't give you the right to judge it."

He was defensive and I knew the last thing he needed from me was an ounce of pity. "Don't treat me like a snob simply because you're annoyed that I'm right. The way I see it, you have two choices. You can either come with me and recover in a real bed where someone can keep an eye on you, or I can make a phone call. You have five minutes to make up your mind."

He smirked. "A phone call to who? The hospital paper-work-enforcement police? Are they going to take me in because I'm not following my discharge instructions?"

I had to fight the smile that threatened and shook my head. "Nope, worse. I'll call Haylee and tell on you."

His eyes got big. "The last thing she needs is to get bothered with this. She's a new mother and doesn't have time to fret over a friend merely because he had his appendix removed."

"And yet you know she would. So that leaves option A, then. Glad we settled it." I stood with my hands on my hips, turning when the couple who'd been on the sofa came into the room giggling and already trying to undress one another. They looked at us like we were the ones who were intruding. I crouched down and whispered, "That only proves my point. Your roommates are oblivious."

"You shouldn't be here. Someone could recognize you," he said on a whisper. "And for the same reason, I can't come back to your place."

It could be tough to explain if someone saw him. At the moment, though, I wasn't sure I cared. "I have another idea. Come on. Let me help you up."

CHAPTER FIVE

*B*y the time we returned to my waiting car, Will had a fine line of sweat on his brow and was looking in rough shape. "So what's the plan?"

"I'm putting you up in a hotel." I handed the bag which he'd hastily repacked to Sherman and pulled out my phone.

"Fine, but I'm paying you back, so please don't make it the Four Seasons or the Ritz." He closed his eyes and leaned his head on the seat, exhaustion obvious in his features.

I thought for a moment before calling information and then asked my driver to head into Manhattan. I knew just the place. Once I was connected with the one-eight-hundred number, I made my request for New York City. "Three nights starting tonight, and please use my points which are about to expire," I said to the woman who'd answered the phone. I next rattled off my loyalty card number.

Will opened his eyes and quirked a brow.

I shrugged as if to say, 'what?' I did, in fact, have a few hundred thousand points. This way he didn't have to worry about paying me back.

For a man in his twenties, his pride was decades older. "I don't need three nights. One would be plenty."

Turning my attention back to the woman on the phone, I confirmed the three nights, making the reservation in the W Hotel one block over from my office. That way I could go by tomorrow and check on him. Hanging up, I didn't let him fight me on it.

"Look if you want to leave the hotel room empty for the last two nights, wasting it, then so be it. But either way, it's booked, using points for which I pay nothing. Matter of fact, it'll be nice, for a change, not to have them expire."

He seemed as if he would argue but instead sighed. "Why don't you use them to take a vacation or something?"

"Because vacations for one are no fun. Jesus, now I'm rhyming like I'm advertising for a dating site run by Dr. Seuss. Anyhow, the hotel is close to my office and condo, so I can check in on you, unless you object to that, too."

He held my gaze for a while before shutting his eyes. "If I wasn't in this much pain or drugged and laughing didn't hurt like hell, I'd find your Dr. Seuss comment funnier. And I'll be fine."

"Oh, yeah? Did the last time you had your appendix removed show you how well you recover from that type of surgery?"

He chuckled and then grabbed his side. "Ow. Now you're just being cruel by being funny."

I pursed my lips. "Mm, I'll keep it in mind in case you disagree with me again."

"I'm sorry. I don't mean to appear ungrateful."

"Then take the help where it's offered and pay it forward to someone else." I understood pride, but human kindness was something about which I wasn't willing to compromise. "Do you have any modelling gigs coming up or, um, other work?"

We both knew I meant his double life as Calvin. He shook his head. "I already called my job from the hospital and told them I wouldn't be in until later this week. And I don't have another shoot scheduled for two more weeks, so I should have time to fully recover. I only hope whatever I'm wearing for it will cover the scars."

"If not, they'll use body makeup. I've seen it done for appendix, c-section scars, and they even managed to cover the entire back tattoo of one model." I noticed we'd pulled up in front of the hotel. "Oh, good. We're here."

By the time I managed to get Will settled in his room and then arrived home, the fatigue from the last twenty-four hours started taking hold.

I took a minute to admire the view out my picture window of the beautiful city I called home and poured myself a glass of wine. Loneliness washed over me in that moment as it often did during the nighttime hours. I missed having a partner. Someone who cared when I came home and missed me if I didn't. Maybe that's why I felt a kinship with Will tonight and wanted to ensure he wasn't on his own.

Not for the first time, I wondered why Will was working at Club Travesty. I'd had to bite my tongue a couple times to keep from asking; knowing it wasn't any of my business. For all I knew he loved what he did or made great money. Although if it was the money then why was he living where he was?

As I climbed into bed, a smile tugged at my lips at the text he'd sent me on my real phone, using his real name this time.

"Thanks again."

I typed back. *"You're welcome. See you tomorrow."*

I fell asleep telling myself it was only concern that had me anxious to check in on him the next day.

I WAS in solid meetings at the office until noon. I had texted Will first thing in the morning to make sure he was feeling okay and told him I'd drop by to bring him lunch. At the hotel, I knocked on his door, waited, and then sent a text letting him know I was here. After no answer and five additional minutes, I started to get worried. That's when I slid my in-case-of-complications-and-him-dying-emergency-key into the slot.

"Will," I called out. The bed sheets were rumpled, but there was no sight of him. But then there he was in all his glory, wrapped only in a not-quite-small-enough towel around the waist. He was obviously fresh from the shower.

Evidently, hot Australian men without their shirts made me lose the power of stringing together coherent sentences. "Knocked and, um, lunch. Was worried."

He grinned. "Sorry, I lost track of time and was in the shower."

I finally came to my senses. It wasn't as if I'd never before seen an attractive, half-naked man. Being in fashion, I'd viewed plenty of shirtless models. "Right, sorry. I brought you lunch, but I'll set it on the table and leave you to change."

"Let me grab my clothes and go into the bathroom to get dressed. If you have a few minutes, do you want to eat with me?"

I nodded. "Sure. Okay."

Blowing out a breath when he shut the bathroom door, I thought, *Catherine, get it together.* The poor guy had just had surgery. Yet here I was lusting after him like some teenager. Although I certainly hadn't had this sort of dirty thoughts running through my head when I was in my teens.

By deciding to busy myself with setting out lunch on the small table over by the window, I was able to recover by the time he came out in shorts and a T-shirt. "How are you feeling?"

"Much better after a good night's sleep."

"Good, but hopefully you'll stay here the next two nights to ensure you get more rest. It's what you need to heal."

He regarded me thoughtfully while eating his soup and then spoke quietly. "I've been thinking and want you to know I meant what I said in Vegas. I have no intention of telling anyone your secret."

My face heated with the unfortunate reminder of Club Travesty. Then it dawned on me why he was bringing this up. "You think that's why I'm helping you?"

He ran a hand through his hair. "To be honest, I'm not sure. But if it is, I wanted to tell you it's unnecessary."

"I know enough about you through Haylee and Josh to have trusted you when you gave me your word the first time. And I don't feel an obligation if that's what you're worried about. I just didn't feel good about leaving you post-surgery on the floor in your apartment where no one even knew or seemed to care about what had happened."

He sighed. "About that. I'm hoping since I can trust you're not telling anyone about my second job, that you'll also not mention the apartment to Haylee and our other friends."

"I would have no reason to, but can I ask you something?"

He shook his head. "It's not a subject I want to discuss if it's about money or why I live there." His jaw was set.

"Okay, then."

"Look, it's personal, okay?"

I lifted a brow. "And would it be terrible to share something personal with me after I confided some pretty private things about myself with you?" Frustrated that I'd go there, I cursed internally. "Forget I said that." Why was I hurt he didn't want to share something with me? It wasn't as if we had the type of relationship where the unbalanced information should bother me.

He met my eyes, clearly not willing to let it drop. "You mean the list of your most intimate fantasies?"

Flushing at his bluntness, I muttered, "Yeah, so maybe you could see that document is shredded."

"I could, but only if you have a copy for yourself. The fact I now know who you are doesn't change what the list is about. It's about expressing and opening yourself up to new experiences.

Nothing we talked about in that room was fake, Cath. If you want, I'm happy to still see you at the club."

So not happening. "No offense, but I don't see myself returning to Club T. And how did we even get on the subject?"

"Nice nickname for the club and I'm sorry for bringing it up, I just feel bad that we didn't finish."

"You shouldn't, and it's fine."

There was an awkward silence while we both ate our food until he suddenly broke it. "I send the money that I earn home to my family to help them out."

"Oh." He'd caught me off guard with his admission. My tone softened. "I didn't mean to guilt you into telling me, but I appreciate that you shared it."

"It's okay. I didn't want you thinking I had a gambling problem or something. Which by the way, the trip to Vegas—I had a sponsor thing that paid for the flight out on Friday, and then Josh invited me for the weekend."

There was a touch of defensiveness in his tone, as though he needed me to believe he wasn't taking frivolous vacation weekends. And because I couldn't contain my curiosity, I flipped back to the previous subject. "Would you adjust anything about the advice you gave me as Calvin now that you know my identity?"

"Mm, it's not like you followed my instructions in Vegas, Ms. Opting-For-The-Spa instead of going out and trying new things. Not to mention, you enlisted your friends to help you with the flirting via text assignment." A smile curved his lips with the memory.

"I did feel a pinch of guilt over the spa, but I'd already made the appointments when you knocked. And in my defense of group texting, I learned a lot from the girls. I even downloaded emoticons."

He laughed heartily before leaning back to study me. "You mentioned your dates go to shit and you don't know why. Now that I'm aware of who you are, I could put a microphone on you and listen in. It would allow me to offer my feedback afterwards. I've done it with a couple of clients who were okay with me knowing their identity."

Something about being called a client turned me off from the idea completely. "I'd have to think about it."

He smirked. "Translation: not a chance in hell."

His eyes held amusement and made me smile at his candor. "Pretty much, but I appreciate the offer. Um, I should return to the office, but I can bring you dinner."

He hesitated before answering. "If you're sure I'm not taking you away from other plans."

Aside from drinking wine alone while shoveling something into my face over my kitchen sink or at my desk in the office, not so much. "No plans this evening."

"Any luck with Melanie?"

And just like that, we were back into weird territory with this reminder of Calvin's suggestion for a matchmaker. "I have my first date on Friday, actually. Anyhow, I'll come by after work tonight, about seven o'clock. Any requests for food?"

He stood up gingerly, walked over to the nightstand, and grabbed his wallet. "Nope, I'm not very picky. Here's a twenty. Since you got lunch, let me buy dinner."

I was about to argue but realized it was important to him. So I took the money without a protest, promising to meet him later.

I WASN'T sure what to get for dinner with Will, and after spending fifteen minutes perusing menus, I realized I was spending way too much time stressing over it. This wasn't a date, and I wasn't out to impress him. This was a guy recovering from surgery who needed sustenance and company. And maybe breakfast for the morning while I was at it. I had my assistant, Erin, place the order before she left for the day.

When I showed up at Will's room with food in hand, I was amazed to see him looking so good—I mean recovered—when he answered the door. His blue eyes appeared brighter, and his skin color had returned to normal.

"You look much better."

"I'm feeling better after sleeping most of the day. I can't remember the last time I've channel surfed and napped like this."

We took seats at the small table, and I took out the contents of the bag I'd brought, which included pasta, chicken, and garlic bread. Nothing said comfort quite like carbs. "Your body needs it. My dad wanted me to ask you if—" I took out my phone to read the text. "If you have any sign of fever, redness, or warmth around the incision site?"

"I don't feel feverish, and the incisions seem good, I think." He pulled up his shirt to reveal the bandages, peeling them back slowly. His eyes met mine, and he apologized. "Sorry. You're not squeamish about this stuff, are you?"

I shook my head. Nope, but I was in the process of becoming completely stupid at the sight of his impressive body. "No, I'm a doctor's daughter. It looks like it's healing."

We ate in silence until he inquired about my date coming up on Friday. "What do you know about him?"

Deciding it was easier to show him, I brought up Melanie's email with my date's profile information and handed it over. Will took a few minutes to read it, and I found myself wondering what he thought. Paul was an investment banker, divorced, with no kids. He was forty, loved to play golf, and appeared to take care of himself if his profile picture was any indication.

"It appears he checks all of your criteria," Will commented, handing my phone back to me.

His voice sounded flat, but I decided I must be imagining it. "Yes, he sure seems to."

"Tell me about your family. You said your dad is a heart surgeon?"

"He is. My younger brother is a doctor, as well."

He raised a brow. "Impressive. Is he in Boston, too?"

"No, he actually does Doctors Without Borders and has been in Africa the last few months. Although he's brilliant and amazing for doing that, I think secretly he does it to get away from my meddling mother."

Will laughed. "She tries to set him up with all available females?"

I smirked. "No, it's worse. My brother is shy and because of his medical studies and travel doesn't date much which of course led my mother at one point to think he may be gay. And in order to show her unwavering support of either preference she'd test him by whispering very loudly, 'What about her? Are you attracted to her? Or how about him, dear? Do you prefer the penis?' Obviously, it's beyond embarrassing and sent him all the way across the world."

Will nearly spit out his soup. "You're kidding?"

I shook my head and recalled another story, enjoying the conversation shift to our families.

TONIGHT WAS Will's last night in the hotel, and I found myself making up an excuse to go see him with dinner even though we hadn't discussed it. My plan was to bring up a modelling opportunity with a photographer with whom he'd previously worked. I didn't dare examine why I was practically giddy about seeing him again, but I did acknowledge I'd grown accustomed to his company.

We'd taken some time getting to know one another last night. I'd learned he had an older brother and a younger half-sister from his mum—still adorable when he called her that. His father and mother had divorced when he'd been ten. He'd moved to the States with his father, who was American, before returning to

Australia where he'd attended college. Then he'd moved to New York when a modelling scout had taken notice of him. He took classes part time and hoped to be a counselor some day and work with people. I could see it. Will was very easy to talk to.

After knocking on his door, I smoothed down my hair and waited. I rapped one more time and sent a text telling him I'd brought dinner by. Not that it was a bad thing to walk in on him fresh from the shower, as experience dictated, but I didn't want to make it a habit. So I waited five more minutes before sliding my key in. But instead of turning green and letting me in, it only clicked red. His incoming text message explained why.

"Sorry, I had a modelling gig that I received a call for down in Miami. I checked out this morning so they would credit your account with the unused points. I can't thank you enough, not only for taking care of me, but for your company over the last couple of days. I'd like to think of us as friends now."

I swallowed hard with disappointment even though I knew it was stupid to go there. I hoped being on a plane this soon after his surgery wouldn't cause him any pain. But obviously, he wasn't going to turn down a job when he needed the money, especially with his unplanned medical expenses. And that reminded me; I had a phone call to make that would hopefully help ease his burden.

CHAPTER SIX

$\mathscr{I}$t was Thursday. It had been three days since I'd last seen or spoken with Will, but I was slammed with work, which proved to be a welcome distraction. With New York Fashion Week coming up next month, including many events I'd be attending, my fall was shaping up to be quite packed, per usual.

I'd put the latest issue of my magazine to bed and finally could start thinking about my date tomorrow night. I'd already made a list of things I could talk about and another of the items off limits. Funny how the *not to talk about* list was longer, topped with the subject of my divorce or anything having to do with my ex-husband. I'd learned my lesson. The topic was an instant turnoff, and I would steer clear of it. Knowing my date had been married previously took some of the pressure off, though, since we'd have that in common.

As I was about to pack up and call it a day, Erin buzzed me. "Ms. Davenport, a Will MacPherson is here to see you. He says he doesn't have an appointment but, uh—" She lowered her voice to a whisper. "He's freaking hot as hell, and it could be my pregnancy hormones talking, but if I were you, I'd make it a point to see him."

I smiled at my assistant's assessment. "Okay, then. Send him in."

Standing up when the door opened, I then had to grip the edge of my desk to keep from having a physical reaction to how good he looked in his slacks and button-down shirt. Unfortunately, the distraction of his appearance left me unprepared for his anger after he shut my door.

"Did you pay my hospital bill?" He didn't raise his voice, but the tone and the pulsing of his jaw left no doubt regarding how pissed he was.

"No," I replied without hesitation. But I was clinging to a technicality, and he had my number.

"Fine, let me ask the question another way. Did you make an anonymous donation to New York Presbyterian Hospital which covered my expenses?"

Shit. I tried a new tactic. "Will, I make a lot of charitable donations, and they took very good care of you there. I expressed my gratitude and wanted to—"

"Cut the bullshit, Catherine. It's a yes or no question."

I sighed heavily and took a seat. I had no idea who at the hospital had told him his bill had been paid, but clearly my anonymity hadn't been as guaranteed as I'd hoped. "Yes."

He paced my office, irritation evident on his face. "How much was it?"

"I only have an estimate." And that was the truth. I'd donated thirty thousand, knowing it would cover the surgery. Even on the high side, that would only rise to twenty five thousand, but I knew they'd put the extra to good use. I hadn't asked for an actual invoice.

He swallowed hard and took a seat across from my desk, eyes fixed on mine. "Why?"

I wasn't sure I had a good answer for him, aside from the fact it made me feel good to do something nice for people when I had the means to do so and that I'd hoped he'd never find out. "I give money every year to hospitals. With my dad being a surgeon, and my brother also a doctor, we've always made such donations a priority in my family. So for once, why shouldn't I have that gift go toward someone I know who can use it rather than to a faceless stranger?"

"I don't need you feeling sorry for me." He scrubbed a hand over his face in agitation. "I pay my own way, always have."

"I don't doubt it, but that's what makes people want to do something for you. You didn't ask to get appendicitis without medical insurance. And given that you send the money you do make home to your family, I have nothing but respect."

He appeared to calm some, but it was short-lived. "I'm paying you back once I find out how much it was. What was the estimate?"

"Twenty-five thousand on the high side or seventeen on the low."

He sucked in a breath at the staggering amount. Even I'd been taken aback initially, I could only imagine how much a more complicated procedure involving many days in the hospital could cost without insurance.

"Holy shit. Imagine if I'd spent the night."

"I know."

He suddenly looked as though he had an idea. "Your date is tomorrow night, right?"

Of all the things for him to ask, this particular question I hadn't expected. "Yes, why?" There was a good amount of trepidation in my voice.

"Since I can't pay you that amount of money right now, I'm going to work it off."

"Excuse me?"

"You need assistance with your dates, and I need to pay you back."

"This isn't—I mean, I don't need help."

"Yes, you do. Otherwise you wouldn't have come to Club T in the first place."

My face heated with the reminder, and I shook my head. "Can't you just take the donation for what it was?"

"No," he said simply. He was being stubborn and clearly felt it important not to take charity from anyone.

And the truth was, maybe I could use his help. But the reason I didn't want it at this point had more to do with my attraction to him and less to do with any lingering awkwardness.

Sensing my hesitation, he used a tactic I wasn't expecting: Vulnerability. "It would mean a lot if you'd let me do this. You wanted to help me, and now I'd like to return the favor."

How in the hell could I say no? But I needed terms to ensure this didn't drag out. "If I let you do this, then you agree that for every hour a thousand comes off the total. And we go with the low estimate of seventeen."

"One thousand is too much…"

"It's what I paid at Club T." I realized he had no clue how much clients paid by the expression on his face. It made me wonder what he ended up earning out of that thousand.

"I'll agree to the thousand per hour, but only if we go with the higher estimate."

"We'll split the difference between the numbers at twenty-one." The illogical part of my mind was already coming up with a lot of different scenarios regarding the way to spend those hours, none of which had to do with him assisting me in dating.

"Deal. Do you want to do the earpiece tomorrow night with only the microphone, or I can give you real-time feedback by talking you through it?"

I shifted, not liking the idea of my date unaware he was being recorded. Nor did I want the distraction of Will listening in. "Neither. At least not yet. It just feels weird to have you in my ear or my date oblivious to the fact we're not really alone.

What if you sit nearby in the bar or something, and I can excuse myself to go to the ladies' room and touch base with you if I need pointers or assistance? Then we can do a recap after or something."

"Whatever you're most comfortable with. Shoot me the logistics and plan to meet me there thirty minutes ahead of time."

"Okay."

He stood and crossed toward the door, but before leaving, he turned. "And, Cath?"

I swallowed hard at the familiarity implied by his shortening my name. "Yes?"

"Thank you."

I WAS NERVOUS, but it had nothing to do with meeting my date Paul for the first time and everything to do with knowing Will was there in the bar only ten feet away. He'd given me a pep talk earlier, and I could still remember his breath close to my skin when he'd leaned in and given me a hug while telling me I'd do fine. Clearly I needed to get laid so I'd stop lusting after any man who breathed on me.

Standing up when Paul came in, I appreciated that he actually resembled his photograph, with dark hair, chiseled jaw, and brown eyes framed with dark lashes. He stood six foot tall, as his profile had indicated. I'd heard stories that this wasn't always the case, but then again, if Melanie was as good as her reputation, not to mention her asking price, she wouldn't overlook such details.

"Hi, Catherine. I'm Paul, but I guess you already knew that."

I smiled, taking his outstretched hand in greeting, and we took our seats. "Yes, nice to meet you, Paul."

"Likewise. Nice restaurant choice, by the way. I've been here a couple of times."

The restaurant was a quiet venue with tables spaced far enough apart to have a private conversation. With space being a premium in Manhattan, it wasn't always so. I was also a big fan of the laid-back atmosphere and muted classical music in the background.

We made small talk for the first few minutes. I appreciated his manners and the way he was wearing a sport jacket and slacks, showing he'd taken time to dress nicely for our date. The casual conversation was what I was good at; at least I thought so. Talking about New York was second nature to me since I'd lived in this city since college. We ordered wine and then an appetizer and settled into more personal dialogue.

"So, I have to put it out there that I've worked with your ex-husband a time or two on some business deals."

The wine stuck in my throat on the way down, but I managed a forced smile and an "Oh yeah?" So much for worrying I'd be the one to inadvertently bring up my ex.

Paul must've thought my noncommittal comment was a green light to continue. "Yep. Matter of fact, we've played golf together. I texted him on my way here to tell him that, of all people, I'd been set up on a date with you."

This time I choked on my drink. "You did what?"

"It's okay. He was cool with it."

That was the last thing I worried about. What I actually hated more than the fact that Paul thought it was 'cool' to contact my ex and tell him he'd been set up with me was that my ex-husband was now aware I'd had to seek out a matchmaker.

In this moment, it was obvious to me that Paul wasn't getting a second date, but did I continue to suffer through this one? If I was Sasha, I would simply get up and leave with an epic tell-off, but I was way too nice and polite for that, so I set my mind toward getting through the meal.

But wait, maybe I didn't have to. After all, wasn't that the beauty of being in my thirties and knowing what I did and didn't want? To not have to put up with the crap and waste time. I excused myself to go to the ladies' room before the waitress returned to take our dinner orders. But instead of going there, I made a beeline for the bar where I found Will sitting in a stool.

He quirked a brow.

I slid in next to him, not really caring at this point if Paul got up to look for me. "Would it be rude to slip out a bathroom window?"

He laughed. "That bad already?"

I gave him the lowdown of Paul texting my ex-husband.

"Who the hell does that?"

"Exactly. I'd feel bad ditching him without an explanation, though, so I guess I'll tell him I received a phone call or something."

"Or you could finish the date to gain the experience."

Was he being serious? "Experience doing what: trying not to tell someone to 'fuck off' after he tells me my ex-husband is 'cool' with him going out to dinner with me?"

This he found hilarious. "Sometimes you surprise me, Cath. Anyhow, how about you think of it like you have nothing to lose? So, it won't end up in a second date or a forever match. Hell, knowing that may in fact take the pressure off flirting."

I blew out a breath. There was some sense to what he was saying even though I wasn't thrilled about wasting the next hour. Grabbing his drink, I tossed back the contents of what was unfortunately only seltzer water. Just my luck.

He shrugged, giving me a grin. "Sorry, no liquid courage. Go and try to have fun."

"Fine, but keep your phone on because if I need a rescue, I fully expect you to come over and save me."

He winked. "Fair enough. Maybe I'll come up with an outrageous story just in case I need to. Now, off you go."

To Paul's credit, once I returned to the table, he grew better as the meal progressed. He ticked all the boxes that I'd given to

Melanie about being successful, confident, and ready to settle down and have kids—if his hints were any indication about his priorities shifting toward family now that he'd hit the milestone of forty.

So why was it all falling flat?

It could've been the first impression he'd made with the deal about my ex, but it was something less tangible. After dinner, he paid the bill and saw me out to my waiting car in front.

"So, how do you feel about doing something tomorrow night?"

"I have a charity event, but thank you for dinner. It was nice meeting you, Paul."

His smile didn't reach his eyes. "In other words, you'll tell Melanie what the problem was but not me."

This matchmaking thing was new to me, but I'd thought that was the whole point. Go back and give Melanie the scoop without the necessity of an awkward conversations. But in doing that, I was avoiding direct dialogue with the person involved. Since that seemed impersonal, not to mention chickenshit, I decided to be direct, but kind.

"Look, Paul, the whole texting my ex-husband to see if he was okay with you going out with me was—well, not cool. How would you like your ex-wife knowing you'd gone to a match-maker or any of your personal business, for that matter?"

He had the decency to turn slightly red. "I didn't think of it that way."

I noticed there was no apology, which sealed the deal for no second chance. "Yes, well, take care." I squeezed his hand and got into my sedan quickly, while attempting to appear like I wasn't running away. It wasn't until Sherman pulled out into traffic that I let out a resigned breath.

"Dating sucks," I muttered and then wondered where Will was. Pulling out my phone, I thought about texting him, but instead found myself wanting to hear his voice. So I dialed.

"Hiya. Nicely done with giving it to him straight."

"You heard me?" I leaned back in the seat, smiling and kicking off my shoes.

"I was standing to the left by the valet station, so I caught most of it. I didn't think about New York being a small world for you sometimes."

"Yes, it is. Way too small in the case of tonight."

"Did I hear you say you have a charity tomorrow night?"

"That part was the truth."

"If it's for the New York Women and Children's Center, I'll probably see you there."

My heart beat faster at the thought of seeing him again so soon. "It is, so I guess I will. Uh, when did you want to do the recap?"

"Sunday okay? Maybe we could meet for lunch. Would that be *cool*?"

I could hear the amusement in his voice. "At least you asked me instead of my ex. Oh, good grief. Speaking of which, he's calling me on the other line."

"Why? Because he heard about your date?"

"Maybe. He's wanted to get together since last week to talk about something."

"Sounds cryptic. And you don't know what it is?"

"No clue, since he won't tell me in a voicemail or via text. I'm really not in a hurry to see him." It was more than annoying for him to call when he had to be aware I was out on my date, so I let it go to voicemail. I hoped he'd think I was having a great time with Paul.

"Good. Have a nice evening, Cath."

Ah, that sexy voice did something to a girl. "You, too."

———

I LOVED WEARING A BEAUTIFUL DRESS, accessorized just right,

and feeling red-carpet worthy. It was that love which had pushed me to pursue a career in fashion in the first place. I was a communications major in college, wanting to go into some sort of print media. But my adoration of fashion design had led me to a career at Cosmo Life.

I took one final look at my blond hair back in a low chignon and the simple, yet sparkling, chandelier earrings complementing the diamond rope necklace which dipped low into my cleavage. Both the neckline and the slit up the left side were a little more provocative than what I normally would wear, but I hadn't been able to resist the champagne color of this Versace gown with the Jimmy Choo nude heels to match. The shoes elevated my five-foot-seven frame another three inches and made my calves look good, if I did say so myself. I might be almost mid-thirties, but I wasn't dead yet and could still feel sexy.

I gave up telling myself the extra attention to detail wasn't because of the possibility of seeing Will this evening.

When I got in the back of my car, I checked my watch, grateful I was right on time. This particular charity was near and dear to my heart as it funded women's shelters around New York City. I'd been involved since my very first year with my magazine when we'd done an exposé on domestic abuse which included the resources available for women when they chose to leave, many of them with their children. I made a point to clear my schedule every year for this gala and volunteered at some of the shelters around the city at least once per quarter. After all, it wasn't just about writing a check. At least not to me.

As much as I wished I had a date for tonight, I was very accustomed to attending this type of thing alone. My ex-husband had a very busy work schedule in investment banking which meant he'd traveled quite a bit during our marriage. It was rare that we'd actually attended an event together.

After getting out of the car, I walked the small red carpet and smiled for the photographers while rattling off the designer names of the clothes I was wearing. Once I entered the beautiful hotel ballroom, I accepted a flute of champagne.

I'd done this scene a thousand times the world over, for fashion shows, charities, and parties. For the most part, I enjoyed mingling and meeting new people, but tonight I felt a foreboding as if something wasn't quite right.

I should've trusted my gut instinct and run for the door, I realized, when my eyes landed on my ex-husband. He was dressed in a tux, looking twenty pounds lighter and better than he had in years. His sandy blond hair and brown eyes made him the quintessential all-American executive, and he was making a beeline for me.

"Catherine." He leaned in and kissed me on the cheek.

"Michael." I returned the same cordial greeting, but then couldn't help asking, "What are you doing here?"

He smiled, making it appear to anyone who might be watching that we remained on good terms and were simply having a friendly conversation. "You won't return my calls or see me."

"I have a busy life, one which no longer includes you. I asked you what it is you wanted, and you chose not to respond."

He had the decency to wince. "I know, but what I needed to talk to you about was better done in person."

"So you thought confronting me at a charity gala would be the appropriate place?"

He sighed. "You didn't leave me a lot of choice. And how the hell did you come to date Paul Morris?"

"You're not going to question me on who I'm dating. What is so important that you've decided to stalk me here tonight?"

"I needed to talk to you about getting a church annulment. Brittany and I want to get married, and she wants a Catholic ceremony."

"I see," was all I could manage. It wasn't enough for me to

feel like I'd failed at making the marriage work; he wanted me to pretend it had never happened in the first place. Ouch.

"So you'll agree?"

I hated that he'd put me on the spot here, of all places, and needed a minute to process. "You could've asked me this via text or email. Your decision to come here tonight is pretty shitty, Michael."

He blushed slightly. "Look, I know, but time is of the essence and—"

Thankfully, one of the main sponsors came up and inadvertently rescued me by leading me away to meet with the board members. "I'll call you tomorrow and we'll discuss," I offered Michael as I walked off. I hoped he'd leave me alone for the rest of the evening.

Unfortunately, after I spent the next hour mingling with the foundation's leaders and staff, I spotted Michael again. He was hanging out near the entrance, apparently trying to make sure I didn't leave without speaking with him again. I'd looked around for Will but saw no sign of him. Since I wanted to avoid another encounter with the ex, with the potential I might get emotional in public if he casually asked me—again—to annul our marriage, I nicely inquired about getting some fresh air. Someone mercifully pointed me toward a rear entrance.

I sent a text to Sherman to meet me at the back of the building, but before I could make my escape, one of the volunteer coordinators cornered me. It was only a three-minute conversation, but it was enough time to worry that Michael might figure out where I'd gone.

When I heard his voice calling out, I practically ran into the nearby bathroom, but the unfamiliar sight of urinals greeted me. Too late, I realized I'd picked the wrong one. Just my freaking luck.

The sight of a man in a tux at the sink washing his hands

capped off my humiliation. But fate was a weird thing. When he turned around, I saw the man was Will, of all people.

"Fancy meeting you in the men's room, Cath. I understand you wanted to be a little more adventurous, but, uh, I can think of some better options." He smirked.

"I didn't—I mean I was hiding from—You know what? Let me get out of here." I turned tail and out the door.

Will was right behind me. "Wait up. I was only teasing. Who are you hiding from?" He pulled gently on my arm and peeked over my shoulder. "That bloke there?"

My eyes tracked where his had landed. "Yeah. My ex-husband and an awkward conversation."

He glanced at my face and then over my shoulder again. "Is this my cue to kiss you silly and make him uncomfortable enough to want to leave?"

Yes, please. But that thought had nothing to do with my ex and everything to do with how unbelievably gorgeous Will looked in his tux and the feel of his warm hand on my arm.

He must've interpreted my shocked expression for panic. "Relax. I was joking. Not only would it be cliché, it would come off as desperate and look like you were trying to make him jealous."

"Uh huh." Wouldn't want that.

"Catherine, can I please speak to you one more moment?" Michael's voice interrupted. "In private," he added, basically dismissing Will.

"You want me to stay with you?" Will asked in a low voice.

Although I was tempted, I shook my head. "I'll only be a few minutes."

He squeezed my hand, flashed Michael a pleasant smile, and walked about twenty feet away, where he leaned up against the wall to wait.

"Who the hell is he?" Michael questioned.

"None of your business." He had some nerve to ask.

"Fine. I made an appointment for us with Father Daniels at eleven o'clock tomorrow."

My seldom-seen temper flipped. "And, what? I'm supposed to drop everything to be there?"

His face showed irritation. "I knew you would fight me on this. That you wouldn't wish for me to be happy."

"Get over yourself, Michael," I yell-whispered. "You want the annulment, fine. I'm not going to fight you on it. But that you'd spring this on me in a public place or make an appointment without checking my schedule is over-the-top rude. And I don't get your hurry. You've been engaged for over a year. I hope you're aware it can take up to two years for them to grant an annulment."

Considering he hadn't once stepped foot in church the entire time we'd been married, I wasn't surprised when his eyes bugged out at this news.

"Two years? Are you fucking kidding me?" His voice rose with the question, and I saw Will pop off the wall. He looked uncertain whether or not to come closer.

I held out a hand, waving him off for now. "I'm not kidding," I told Michael. A friend of mine had been through it, and it had taken a very long time.

He raked his hands through his hair. "Brittany's family is devout, and we can't marry in a Catholic church without it."

"The best I can offer is to set up my own appointment with Father Daniels later this week and give them whatever they need." I wasn't sure what grounds Michael would cite for the annulment, but at this point, I didn't care. I just needed to be done with this evening and with him, for that matter. I felt like my offer was more than fair.

"You should've told me when we got divorced that an annulment could take this long."

My eyes narrowed. "How the hell is it my responsibility to educate you on the workings of the Catholic Church? You're the one engaged, so you should've researched it yourself once you knew you wanted a religious ceremony."

"I don't have two years. Brittany's pregnant."

Blood roared into my ears, and I had to remember to breathe. A punch in the stomach would've felt better than hearing those words. The annulment request had stung, but this—This was so much worse. When I thought about how much I'd wanted to have children and how close we'd almost been—Tears instantly pricked my eyes.

For a moment I thought he'd say something for the almost-mother-to-his-children that was sympathetic, but instead he barged on with his agenda. "Do you think if we contributed a large donation it might make a difference in how fast they can process it?"

"You really don't give a damn about anyone but yourself, do you?" My voice was louder than intended, and Will didn't hesitate this time. He walked right toward us.

Deciding I didn't want either man to see my threatening tears, I quickly turned on my heel and fled out the rear doors.

Thank goodness for Sherman who, upon seeing me, popped out to open my door.

"Home, please," I managed.

His kind, sympathetic expression was almost my undoing as he simply nodded without a question.

Will's voice called out my name. When I turned, I saw him running down the steps after me. I didn't protest when he slid into the back seat with me.

Sherman started driving, and I sat there stunned.

"Are you okay?" Will asked softly.

I shook my head, letting a tear slide down despite my best efforts.

"How about I walk you up, and we talk about it?"

We were nearing my place already and all I could think was

that I wanted to be alone. "No, thank you. But, um, Sherman can drive you home if you like."

He stepped out with me anyhow onto the curb. "The way I see it is you have two choices. A, you can let me come up and ensure you're all right, or B, I can call Haylee."

My eyes went wide. He was using my own ultimatum back on me, the one I'd given him when he'd had appendicitis. With a sigh, I realized I had no energy left to fight. "I guess I'll go with option A, then."

CHAPTER SEVEN

*W*ill smiled with the mild victory of turning the tables on me and followed me into the building. Inside, I gave a nod to the doorman and led Will into the elevator. The cab didn't stop until the thirty-sixth floor. My two-bedroom, two-thousand-square-foot home wasn't fancy by any means, but I'd wanted it for the view—not to mention the impressive closet space.

His eyes went straight toward the large window taking up most of the living room and overlooking the city. "I can see why you bought the place." He moved closer to the glass.

Murmuring a "yes," I slipped off my heels and plunked down my clutch on the granite island that separated the living room from the kitchen. Hating that this would most likely sound bitchier than intended, I blurted out, "I'm fine. I was merely taken off guard tonight with him showing up."

Will turned toward me, lifting a brow. "In other words, you're dismissing me?"

"Look, I'd feel terrible if you left your date behind or I cut your evening short."

I found myself swallowing when he shed his jacket and loosened the bow tie of his tux exposing the slightest hint of skin.

"My roommate is dating a woman who helps run a shelter in Queens. Since she knew she'd be busy tonight talking to all of the sponsors, she invited me to keep him company. So I didn't bring a date, and I don't have anything else going on. It's a worthy cause, by the way."

"It definitely is." The small talk was helping ease the awkwardness. I watched as he took in the room, which boasted an open floor plan from living room to kitchen.

"You going to tell me what happened?"

I sighed. "I'd rather not. Matter of fact, I'd love nothing more than to change into yoga pants, pour an extra-large glass of wine, and not talk or think about it at all."

"How about I wait for you to do the first part while I facilitate the second, and then I promise not to bring up the third part unless you wish to?"

A smile tugged at my lips. I definitely couldn't turn down someone who was trying to be a good friend to me. But then a doubt creeped in that maybe friendship wasn't why he was here. The thought he might intend to 'work off his debt' left me cold. "I appreciate the offer and know you feel obligated to work off your hospital bill, but I'll need to decline tonight."

His instant anger surprised me. "You think that's why I'm here?"

"I don't know, honestly," I whispered. I could hear my own vulnerability lacing the words.

He stepped closer to me, searching my eyes. "The lines may be blurry when it comes to our history, so let me be crystal clear: I'm here right now because we're friends. I want to be that for you without a thought toward our deal."

I took a deep breath and let it out slowly, forcing myself to relax. It was clear there wasn't one ounce of him that wasn't sincere. "Okay."

He walked over to the kitchen and perused the wine rack on the kitchen counter. "Any of these bottles okay to open?"

"Either those, or there are whites in the refrigerator. Opener is in the drawer next to the stove. I'll only be a moment."

Once I'd changed into comfy clothes and come back out into the living room, he greeted me with a large glass of red. I sipped and approved of the dry Malbec. It suited my mood tonight much better than a fruity white wine would have.

We took seats on my plush sofa overlooking the city. Although I had a television mounted on the wall, it rarely was turned on since the view was all I needed in here. The expanse of lights and buildings visible for miles was awe inspiring.

Will leaned back, sipping on his wine. "Did you live here with your ex?"

"No. I bought it after the divorce. I needed a new space without the memories."

He raised his glass. "Good choice."

We drank in a silence which, surprisingly, wasn't awkward. His husky voice after a few minutes took me off guard, but not as much as his words.

"I was a baby when my older brother was diagnosed with cerebral palsy. He was about two years old at the time, and I guess wasn't developing like he should've been. We lived hours away from the nearest major city, and I remember having to travel there constantly while I was growing up. My mum quit her job to take care of him and my dad—Well, by the time I'd turned ten, he'd had enough of that life, I suppose. I remember overhearing a fight on my tenth birthday where my dad said it wasn't fair to me to live a life in and out of hospitals. He claimed she'd forgotten my birthday because my brother Thomas had been very sick the entire week."

I could see him swallow in the shadows of the room. I turned toward him and moved closer, mindful this wasn't easy for him to share. "It must've been difficult on her though."

His smile was sad. "I didn't appreciate that fact until I was older. Once they divorced, my dad moved me with him to California. My mother remarried when I was a teenager and then had my sister. By the time I went back to spend a summer with them, Thomas's care had become more efficient with technology, and his medications were better. But I finally saw through mature eyes what it was like to be my mother every day. How hard it was and how much it took from her."

He paused, taking another drink of wine. "But worse, I realized how much my brother, who was almost an adult by then, hated being a burden on her. I vowed then and there that I'd have the type of job someday where I could put my brother into an assisted living community where he could live his life and finally give my mum the break she deserved. I was able to achieve that goal three years ago when I began working at Club Travesty. It was steady money while modelling was more hit or miss. So I live where I do in order to keep my expenses minimal because Thomas's care is costly."

I was blown away that he'd made both his brother and mom such a priority and by the type of load he shouldered for the sake of his family. "I can only imagine."

He glanced at me, shaking his head. "And I swear to God, Cath, if you so much as think about paying one cent of—"

I held up my hand. "I would never. Even I wouldn't cross that line."

His features relaxed. "My mum took a vacation last year for the first time ever."

"You're an incredible son and brother. How old is your younger sister?"

"Janet is fourteen and in high school. She's a good kid. Next week I'm traveling to Australia to see them all. It's been over a year, so I'm looking forward to it."

"That sounds really nice. Thank you for sharing your story

with me about your family." He'd clearly made a difficult effort to do so, but I didn't feel ready to reciprocate with my baggage.

"I didn't do it because I have an expectation you'd do the same. I simply want you to trust we're friends now. In fact, there isn't one other person who knows about the things I've just confided to you."

I took a gulp of my wine, downing the contents, and got up to pour another. When I returned with a full glass, I blurted it out. "Michael wants an annulment in the church because his fiancée is Catholic. In order to have a second Catholic wedding, you need one granted from the first marriage."

"Ah. I take it you're not exactly feeling like doing him any favors?"

I sighed heavily. "That's not what really upset me the most. Although his timing was sucky at the gala, I'm not going to deny him the annulment." I pulled the pins from my hair, letting it down. "It's all so personal."

"I won't pretend to know how you're feeling as I've never been married or in love, for that matter, but I am a good listener."

Maybe it was time I had one of those. "I was three days away from an IVF egg retrieval procedure in order to try to have a baby when Michael came home out of the blue and told me he wanted a divorce."

"Jesus. That's shitty."

I fought the tears as I recalled the day he'd announced he wasn't ready, after all, and then left. No wavering, no discussion, just moved his things out that very night. I remembered sobbing in my shower, a hormonal, bloated, and shocked mess. I'd convinced myself he'd come back, that he'd only panicked temporarily and would come to his senses in time.

"Tonight he told me he needed the annulment stat because his fiancée is pregnant and she comes from a Catholic family. He went on to vent his frustration about me not telling him sooner how long an annulment can take—as if it's my responsibility to inform him that annulments can take years."

Will set down his glass on the coffee table to give me his full attention. "Wait, he ambushed you this evening to tell you he's having a baby with his fiancée and wants you to help get him the annulment—after your history together? Then he blamed you when he found out it would take a while?"

I drained the last swallow of my new glass of wine, thinking it had gone down rather fast. "It would appear so." Suddenly I needed more alcohol and some levity in the heavy conversation. "You know, they say there are four glasses to a bottle, but clearly they aren't aware what an actual full portion should be."

Getting up off the couch, I headed for the kitchen in order to uncork a new bottle, but Will came up behind me.

His strong hands took the bottle out of mine and set it on the counter. Turning me, he rested his hands on my shoulders, letting his blue eyes, full of sincerity, meet mine.

"Cath, I'm really sorry. You didn't deserve to be hijacked tonight or at any other time. He should've been more sensitive than to treat you that way."

That did it; the dam broke. I guess I should've been grateful they were silent tears and not ugly sobs, but still, not exactly my finest moment. Before I could register what was happening, he'd steered me back onto the couch and enveloped completely in his arms, allowing me to cry it out on his chest. His hands stroked my hair and my back, and he was quiet in his unwavering support.

Finally, when there were no more tears to shed, I hiccupped and spoke softly.

"The thing is, I don't love him any longer, but I once thought he was my forever. I'd believed we were starting a family together. So to now hear he wants to erase me like a mistake so he can have that future with someone else really hurts. I convinced myself when he left that it had to have been a midlife crisis or something. He'd needed someone younger in order to have a life with less responsibility. That an impending baby and added commitment had made him freak out. But now I know that wasn't it, which means it was me. And to add to it all, they couldn't ever diagnose why we couldn't get pregnant naturally after years of trying, so now it's obvious that was me, too." The verbalized, deeply personal thought set off a fresh round of tears.

Will didn't hesitate pulling me closer in his strong arms. "You might not believe this yet, but he never deserved you."

I let out a humorless laugh. "God, you're sweet, but I'm far from perfect, Will. I didn't even notice my marriage was falling apart. Looking back, maybe I should've done more to ensure it didn't. Hell, I didn't even make any effort to go after him once he left, so what's that say?"

"I have no doubt you took your commitment very seriously to make it work, but were you truly happy? Would putting more effort into it have made you happier—or just him?"

"I wasn't happy or unhappy. Rather, I was simply going through the motions, at least in the final years. At some point, I felt empty, and I believed a baby would fill that void. But now the thought of having a child in which I'd be sharing custody with him right now is sobering. So I know the timing of the divorce was for the best even if it was devastating to go through at the time."

"And now you have the power to never settle for anything again."

I reluctantly left his embrace, missing his heat almost immediately as I moved toward the kitchen to put space between us and the subject at hand. "Speaking about settling, we should recap about Paul."

He watched me pour more wine. "I think we can save that conversation for another time."

It occurred to me he was most likely trying to keep the lines clear between paying me back and being a good friend. The sound of his stomach growling broke the silence. I lifted my eyes to his. "You're hungry."

He grinned sheepishly. "A little. The appetizers at the gala were on the small side."

Thankful for something to do, I realized I was starving, too. "I only have a few things I'm decent at cooking and of those, only two can be made from the ingredients on hand or under the influence of the amount of wine I've just consumed. So it's buttered noodles with parmesan or cheese quesadillas. Or we can order in."

"Noodles sound great." A smile played at his lips, and he took a stool at the island to watch. "So what happened with the egg retrieval? Did you end up going through with it?"

I swallowed hard, having never shared this with anyone but my doctor. "I did. At the time, I thought Michael would change his mind. And after all those drugs, not to mention the money…"

"You don't have to justify it, especially not to me."

"You're the first person I've ever told. I'm guessing talking about frozen eggs might not make a good first-date impression, so I should probably add that to the list of what not to bring up."

He chuckled. "Probably best to wait on it."

We ate in silence there at my kitchen island, side by side, enjoying the simple meal.

You would've thought I'd made something gourmet from his compliments. "That was really good. Thank you."

I scoffed. "You're obviously easy to please."

He winked and then did the hottest thing ever: he washed the dishes.

I DON'T REMEMBER what time I'd finally closed my eyes, but when I woke up on the couch, I found Will was still asleep on the other side of it. I took a moment to observe him in his slumber. He was sexy even in his sleep. Not only was his body incredible and his face cover worthy, but also his charm and caring nature were absolutely incredible. We'd sat there talking about life until the early hours of the morning as we watched the city come alive. I don't think I'd ever laughed or enjoyed someone's company as much as I had his. And instead of feeling embarrassed about everything I'd shared with him, I realized it had been cathartic.

After tiptoeing down the hall to the bathroom to brush my teeth, I then ran a comb through my hair and made sure my makeup—what was left of it—wasn't completely smudged. I walked out tentatively, wondering if I should wake him up or let him continue to sleep. The unexpected knock on my front door took the decision out of my hands.

Will popped up suddenly. "Sorry, I meant to catch the subway first thing this morning, but I must've fallen asleep." He stood up to straighten the pillows and throw blanket.

"No, no, it's fine. I should've offered you the guest room." Or my bed with me in it, the naughty thought crept in.

Another knock sounded, reminding us that someone was at the door.

"Uh, should I go hide?" He looked adorable, rumpled from sleep and eying the door with apprehension.

"No, it's probably a delivery. The doorman would call up with anyone not on the list, and the only people on there are—" I gave an obligatory peek through the peephole. "—my parents," I finished on a groan. I couldn't believe they were here.

"We know you're there, Cathy, and don't you go hiding that man we hear in there with you until I get a good look," my mother's voice called out.

"Shit." I threw an apologetic smile toward Will. "I had no clue they were coming." I kept my voice at a whisper.

Luckily, he was grinning and not freaking out at the situation like some guys would have been. "The least I can do is go rinse my mouth out with water," Will murmured.

Meanwhile, I tried to decide if waiting out my parents and pretending I didn't hear them would convince them to leave.

"There are new toothbrushes under the sink, if you want, and toothpaste in the drawer," I offered in the same quiet tone. It was absurd that I'd have to whisper as an adult in my own home. But I couldn't deny that I felt as though I'd just been caught by my parents.

He smiled in thanks before retreating down the hall.

Taking a deep breath before opening the door, I was unprepared for the immediate engulfing hugs from my parents. I let them in and asked the question I felt inevitable considering it was nine o'clock on a Sunday morning and they'd arrived without notice. "What are you guys doing here?"

"Surprising you, that's what." My dad wheeled in his suitcase.

My mother patted me on the cheek, sympathy etched in her features. "We received a text from Michael last night."

What the hell? My ex was texting my parents now?

"What did he say?" My voice was calm, but in my mind I was plotting a very grisly death for the man. If he thought he'd manipulate me or my decisions by going to my parents like I was twelve, he had another thing coming.

"He said he'd upset you last night and that we might want to give you a call to make certain you were doing okay. He didn't think you wished to hear from him. So we decided, why not take a quick flight down to see you instead?" my father offered.

"Oh." Well, that deflated my anger somewhat. Although it might be more convenient to hate my ex-husband, he wasn't the sort of guy who really inspired that emotion. Was he selfish at times? Absolutely. Did he have awful timing in confronting me last night? Yes, definitely. But he didn't try to be an asshole on purpose. Most of the time. Ironically, it might've been easier if he had.

"I'd say you're doing a lot better than Michael knew, for sure." My mom was all smiles, looking beyond me to where Will had appeared with a sheepish expression on his face.

She made a beeline for him once he stepped into the living room. "Are you the young man from last week in the video with the impressive abs?"

"It would be awkward right about now if he wasn't," I muttered.

Will was the only one who seemed to be paying attention to my words. He fought a grin. "I am, and it's nice to meet you in person, Mrs. Davenport. And Dr. Davenport, it's a pleasure to thank you in person for taking the time last week. As you probably heard, you were right about the appendicitis." He shook hands with my father after squeezing my mother's hand warmly.

My mother didn't skip a beat. "Please call me Liz. And don't you need to check on his incisions, Tom? Lift up your shirt, Will, and let him have a look."

It was official: my mother was a pervert. I rolled my eyes while my father managed to unintentionally embarrass me further.

"I'm sure if he's healthy enough to partake in, um—" He suddenly stopped as he must've realized whatever he assumed Will was *healthy enough* for was with his daughter.

"It's good. The surgeon did a nice job," Will assured them. "Uh, I was about to say goodbye, but I hope you enjoy your visit."

If I were him, I'd run far, far away. At the same time, the thought of him leaving had me instantly wondering when I'd see him again.

My mother, however, was on it before I could process anything to say. "How about lunch later today? Would you care to join us, Will?"

It was on the tip of my tongue to tell him he didn't have to, but I found myself curious to hear his answer. I was also happy for an excuse to see him again.

"That sounds great. Just text me the address and time, Cath, and I'll meet you all there."

I nodded and walked him to the door, well aware that neither of my parents were moving or bothering to pretend they weren't trying to listen to our conversation. For that reason, I shut the door on them, putting Will and me out in the hallway.

We both were quick with our words and back to whispering. "If you have plans or don't wish to come, I understand."

"I don't have anything going on, but if you don't want me there…"

"Are you kidding me? I think my mother wants you there more than she wants her own flesh and blood."

He chuckled and then hugged me close to whisper in my ear. "I'll try to stretch up and let her catch a glimpse of my abs if she's good."

I burst out laughing. "You'll probably have to shake her from your leg if you do that."

He winked, and I watched him walk toward the elevator.

It occurred to me that with an ass like his, my mother might not be the only one making a spectacle of herself during the meal.

WILL SHOWED up at the restaurant fresh from the shower and looking casual, yet sexy, in jeans and a soft gray Henley, a shirt which showed off his impressive chest and arms.

And if I hadn't noticed, my mother certainly did. Out loud, of course. "Catherine, this young man is gorgeous. Please keep him."

"Subtle, Mom, real subtle, and he's not a puppy." If he were, though, I'd totally keep him. And pet him and love him and squeeze him.

I'd already explained earlier that we weren't romantically involved, but considering they'd found him this morning in last night's wrinkled tuxedo, they hadn't believed it. It hardly seemed fair to be labeled his sex partner when I hadn't actually had the opportunity. But I pushed the thought aside. We were friends.

Will only smirked, giving me a wink. This had all of my girly parts rebuking the friend-zone thoughts and my mother sighing at the gesture.

"I'd like a Bloody Mary, double vodka, please," I requested when the waitress came up to take our drink order.

Will chuckled, ordering only water.

My mother clucked. "You know, she won't tell us what Michael said last night to her at the party, but I've never seen her order a double."

I thought it interesting she believed my drinking had more to do with my ex than with her and her nonstop inquisition all morning. The truth was not even my parents knew I'd been going through in vitro when Michael had announced he was leaving. We'd decided to keep it quiet in case it didn't work. So to delve into all of that personal history at this late juncture would've been exhausting, not to mention moot. So I'd simply chosen to explain to my parents we'd argued and leave it at that.

Will was diplomatic in coming to my defense. "Some things are better left private, don't you think?"

"I like this young man, too." My dad announced his approval as if the very subject wasn't sitting right there next to us.

As the waitress set down our drinks, I noticed my mother had her phone out typing away. "Who are you texting, Mom?"

"Your idiot ex-husband to let him know you've obviously moved on to better things and didn't need consoling from us."

I gasped. There was no word for the horror that instantly flooded my brain. "You are not. Put the phone down." I was not only embarrassed she would step over the line, but also that Will, trying not to crack a smile, was here to witness it.

"Too late. It's sent."

I could only stare her down, wanting to say so much. But of course I couldn't in front of Will and a whole host of other witnesses.

My mother shrugged, not appearing apologetic in the least. "Don't go giving me that look, honey. The way I see it is I restrained myself from asking your friend—" She punctuated 'your friend' with air quotes. "—from lifting up his shirt and sending a visual along with the note. It annoys me no end to think of Michael picturing for one moment you crying over him. So I just made sure he's aware that's definitely not the case." Then she leaned over and said in a conspiring whisper to Will, "I do hope you can help shave off those corners of her square and show her a bit of fun."

"Just remember who your power of attorney is for making future medical decisions, Mother," I mumbled, knowing the threat was as empty as my Bloody Mary glass. I signaled the waitress for another round, anticipating I'd need it.

She cackled. "Please, you adore me. I mean, what's not to love?"

My father glanced over toward me in sympathy and shushed my mother. "Take it down a notch, Liz, before you scare the young man off and make our daughter an alcoholic."

I shot a smile of thanks toward my dad who luckily, my mother did listen to upon occasion.

"Fine, fine. Sorry, Cathy. Guess you could say I have issues with not saying exactly what's on my mind. But love it or hate it, at least I'm never boring."

I instantly tensed up. My mother had never heard me refer to myself as boring, so she absolutely wasn't targeting me now, but it hit home nonetheless. Ironically, perhaps it had been my mother's unconventional outspokenness and affinity for marching to her own drum that made me so conservative in contrast.

"No, you're never boring, Mom," I said on a sigh and felt Will take my hand under the table and squeeze it.

When the waitress came over to take our orders, sidetracking my parents, Will leaned in and whispered, "Boring people don't order double vodkas in their drinks."

I smirked. "Maybe the ones who want to be more fun do."

While the meal progressed, I sipped on my second double vodka Bloody Mary and Will handled my mother like a seasoned pro. Unfortunately, the thought reminded me of his job at Club T, where he'd probably mastered the technique.

We all made small talk during lunch. I thought it might get awkward when my dad asked Will where he worked, but he handled it beautifully by telling my father he not only modelled, but he also moonlighted as a bartender in a club while taking classes.

"In fact, I need to get to work," he stated, pulling out his wallet.

My father waved him off. "No, son. I have a rule that absolutely no one younger pays while I'm at the table. We sure hope to see you again soon, maybe if you come up to Boston for those ribs and burgers."

Great, now my dad had hopped on the not-so-subtle freight train with my mom. I wondered if that's what caused a look of irritation to pass over Will's features when he flicked his gaze toward me.

"Sure. It was nice meeting you both, and thank you for lunch." Will stood up and glanced over at me. "Do you mind walking me out, Cath?"

Once we were on the sidewalk, I spoke first. "Thanks for coming and sorry about the countless innuendos. I promise I told them we were only friends, but given how they found us this morning, it doesn't look like they believe it." I blamed the vodka for my nervous chatter.

He chewed on his lip and appeared distracted before answering. "I didn't mind. Did you, uh, tell your dad about my financial situation by chance?"

Ah, so that was the annoyance I'd witnessed. "Absolutely not. I've tried my whole life to pay a check for my father, even for his own birthday, and never won. He's old-fashioned that way."

His smile was apologetic. "Sorry, I jumped to conclusions—" He ran a hand through his hair. "Anyhow, enjoy the visit with your folks, and I'll talk to you later."

Right. Later could mean tomorrow or three weeks from now. He leaned in and kissed me on the cheek. I returned to the table already wondering when I might hear from him again.

CHAPTER EIGHT

$\mathcal{B}$y Wednesday of that week, I'd put my meddling, yet supportive, parents back on a plane north to Boston; met with the priest who had married me for my 'interview' regarding the annulment, where I'd experienced enough Catholic guilt to last me a lifetime over a failed marriage; and had coffee with my ex-husband, who'd whined about the process taking so long but had at least apologized for his behavior the night of the gala. In all, it had been the type of week that left me feeling meh. I told myself none of it had to do with not hearing from Will.

My parents had encouraged me to come home next week and take a breather before things got really crazy at work as it typically did in the fall. Considering I hadn't taken a real vacation in years, I was sorely tempted. However, my idea of relaxation needed to involve more sand and less of my mother. I loved her and my father dearly, especially that they would drop everything to come down and check on me, but small doses normally ensured I appreciated them more.

I was feeling restless, almost anxious for something new, but not knowing quite what it would be.

Will's text came as a nice surprise.

"Do you have time for me to come by your office? I can bring lunch if you haven't eaten."

I typed out my response immediately. *"Lunch sounds great, thanks. I'm free from 1-2."*

Then I buzzed my assistant, informing her he'd be on his way up soon.

Glancing down at the blood-red Armani dress which hugged all my curves, I smiled at my choice for today. I was a mood dresser. Today's ensemble had been inspired by refusing to dwell on anything depressing this week. It was my armor, so to speak, but the fact that it looked downright sexy and I was about to see Will didn't hurt, either.

If I was being completely honest with myself, I knew I was rapidly developing feelings for him outside of the friend zone despite knowing it wasn't smart. Not because he wasn't a terrific guy and not even because he didn't meet all of the criteria on my 'perfect' mate list, but because I was going to get hurt. He saw me as a friend. If I'd learned anything the hard way, it was that I needed to heed those boundaries. Even if I thought he was giving mixed signals, there was no way in hell I'd ever put myself out there again. I was well aware of my tendency to misread things after the debacle I'd had a couple years ago with my friend Josh.

Too bad the decision was easier thought than followed when I took one look at him walking into my office.

"Hiya," he said, grinning. He was dressed in a suit, which most likely meant he was heading to Club T afterwards.

"Hi, yourself." I wasn't quite sure how to greet him any longer. A hug, a handshake—

Thankfully, he took the uncertainty out of my question when he leaned in to give me a kiss on the cheek.

We moved toward the small, round conference table where he set the food down. I watched him survey my office and wondered what he was thinking as he scanned the framed magazine covers on the walls and the accolades on the shelves behind my desk.

"I hope I'm not disrupting your day?" His eyes fixed on me.

"No, not at all. Matter of fact, the next couple of weeks are the calm before the storm, so to speak. We're really busy here in the fall. Um, we can eat here at the table or over in the sitting area." I pointed toward the couch and loveseat near the window.

"On your white sofas? No, the table is good." He started taking out containers. "I think this year's Fashion Week will be a busy one. I'm already booked for three shows."

I smiled, impressed, as this wasn't a small feat. "Good for you."

"You look great, by the way. Red is certainly your color."

And now I could feel myself turning that particular shade from the simple compliment. Jesus, Catherine. He was being nice, not anything more.

He set out the food, and I was pleasantly surprised to see the chef salad from one of my favorite restaurants. When I looked at him in question, it was his turn to blush.

"I swear I'm not a stalker, but I noticed the menu on the front of your fridge with this item circled. I hope it wasn't too presumptuous."

If I'd held a gun to my ex-husband's head and asked him the type of salad I preferred and from where it came—even with the menu in plain sight—he wouldn't have been able to say. Not at any point during our entire marriage. But Will had been over once and was now apologetic over appearing presumptuous that he'd noticed. "No, not at all. Actually, it's very thoughtful. Thank you."

We started eating and settled into small talk. "You're leaving for Australia soon, right?"

"Yeah. Actually, that's why I came by. With our Sunday plans for recapping your date getting waylaid by your parents showing up and me leaving this Friday, I wanted a chance to give you my feedback on your date with Paul."

Ah, and just like that I was painfully reminded of the real reason he was here: to work off his so-called debt. I tried not to let my disappointment lace my tone. "Sure. What are your thoughts?"

"I think we need to get you out of New York City for your dating."

I paused mid-bite, and then swallowed it down with the help of some water. "Although it might be nice to have some anonymity, meeting someone who doesn't live local would make it difficult when it comes to beginning a relationship, don't you think?"

A smile played at his lips. "Agreed, but I've been thinking and believe you may be putting too much pressure on yourself to get out there and meet *the* one, when you should be out having fun." He laughed out loud. "See, now I'm rhyming like Dr. Seuss. Anyhow, you need to learn how to feel comfortable flirting and dating without the pressure of trying to find forever."

That didn't sound so bad, after all. "What do you have in mind?"

"It's easy. I think you should come to Australia with me."

I was sure the shock was evident on my face. "Um, that's a long way to go." Not to mention, the fact we'd be together wouldn't exactly help my respect of our friendship boundaries or my mixed signals radar.

"The further away from here, the better. The way I see it, Manhattan is pressuring you to follow certain protocols based on your high-profile job. But you travel to the other side of the world, and no one will know who you are. Plus, compared to the States, Australia is much less politically correct and so much more down to earth."

"That's probably true, but—"

"Hear me out. There, you could not only meet guys, flirt,

dance, and escape the pressures of finding the perfect someone, but also you wouldn't have to stress about somebody knowing your ex-husband or worrying you'll end up on page six for gossip. Gain that confidence, then return home and put it to good use."

"Meet some Aussies, huh? Is there someone you have in mind?" Like him.

"No one specifically, but I'll be there as your wingman and have plenty of friends."

Okaaaay, that wasn't the answer I'd been hoping for, but I had in fact expected it. Then I thought about what it would be like to have an anonymity similar to that I'd enjoyed when I'd gone to the sex club as Kat. No one would know who I was or have an expectation about how I should act. Did I have it in me to shed the boring, proper Catherine persona? Or would I make a fool of myself by trying too hard?

"What's going on in that pretty head of yours?"

"I'm thinking about the possibilities of anonymity a world away. How long will you be there?"

"I have a shoot in Sydney, so a couple days there. Then I'm traveling to visit my family, which is north of the city, for another week. You could come with me there, too, and stay any amount of time. You'd have Internet, so you could work if you needed to."

"Wouldn't it be weird for me to meet your family?"

He shook his head. "No, not at all. But I'll warn you they'll probably make the same assumptions yours did about our 'friendship.'"

"Where would we stay?"

"My mum and stepdad manage a resort. Not the kind you might be thinking of—it's made up of cottages laid out over a number of acres. It's off-season, so they'll have cabins available for us to stay in."

It was sounding more appealing by the moment.

"Do you need to make a list of pros and cons?" He was teasing about my list-making propensity, but in a gentle way.

"Probably," I admitted. Then something dawned on me. "Oh, I'd miss Haylee and Josh's little girl's baptism. It's this weekend."

He sighed, looking at me dead in the eye. "And they'd understand. They already know I'm out of town, and it's not like there won't be other opportunities for you to get together with them. I'm not trying to sound harsh here, but when's the last time you've said no to anyone?"

I smirked. "You realize you've just challenged me to say it to you."

He chuckled. "Maybe, but you know you don't want to."

No, no, I didn't. But it did remind me of the problem at hand, and why it might be a bad idea to spend a vacation with someone to whom I was so attracted.

But he wasn't giving up so easily. "My point is you can be a good friend with a big heart and still say no. And you said yourself that vacations by yourself are no fun and that you work too much. Plus, when's the last time you picked up and went on an adventure? You wanted to break out of your shell and do something spontaneous, so here's your chance."

I swallowed hard, aware he wasn't wrong. "You're leaving Friday morning?"

"Yep. And just so we have full disclosure: if you come with me, then you're at my complete mercy."

A guy as hot as Will shouldn't ever be allowed to tell a woman she'd be at his mercy, especially in his delicious Australian accent, unless he had something to tie her up with immediately following that statement.

"Uh, what would that mean, exactly?"

"It means a boot camp on meeting, flirting, and dating guys will be in full swing."

Although in the back of my mind, I still wondered if this trip might further my attachment to Will, it only took a moment to contemplate the alternative. That was to sit home and not change a damn thing about my predictable life. No, thank you. I'd been there, done that plenty. "Okay, I'm in."

His smile was contagious. "Really?"

"It would seem so. Text or email me your flight details so I can try to get on the same one?"

"You bet." He winked and was out the door minutes later, leaving the panic to set in about rearranging everything.

Of course it was nothing a few lists wouldn't cure.

As I went through security at JFK airport on Friday morning, I felt someone watching me. Turning, I saw Will in a different line a few people behind, tracking me with his eyes. I also noticed the female TSA agents taking notice of him. Could I help it if his smile that focused on me gave me a thrill? He was striking, but beyond that he had a way of making me feel like I was the only woman he had eyes for despite the fact we were only friends.

"Hi," I breathed, sounding like I'd run a race, when he met me on the other side.

He smirked as if guessing the reason. "Hiya. Any idea why when I checked in I was bumped up to first class?" We proceeded toward the gate together.

I'd already rehearsed my response, knowing he probably wouldn't be happy about it, given his pride about such things. "Because we're traveling together for the next thirty-some hours, and I wanted company. You did say you were putting me through a boot camp. Since I'm about to embark on a whole new adventure of being casual, flirty, and fun, well, where better to prepare me than on the plane?"

He arched a brow in amusement. "You practiced that little speech, didn't you?"

I laughed. "It annoys me how quickly you have a read on me, but yes, of course I did. As previously established, spontaneity is not my strong point." We reached the first-class lounge and sat down.

"Hmm, speaking of which, I have something for you."

He pulled out a small, wrapped box which instantly aroused my curiosity. I mean, what woman didn't enjoy getting a surprise gift? But his smirk had me proceeding carefully. Especially with his lips now twitching.

"What?" I asked.

"You're pulling it apart perfectly as if you're planning to save the paper. Don't you want to rip into it?"

"Maybe I like to savor the anticipation."

The smirk got bigger. "Good to know."

Had I inadvertently flirted and made a sexual innuendo without trying? Maybe there was hope for me yet. When I finally fished out the contents, I held a round black ball with a white eight on it. I fixed my eyes on Will. "Is it an eight ball?"

"Uh-huh, a magical one, or some people call it an answer ball."

"For what?" I turned it to where the circular window was visible, and a blue triangle floated up, but before I could read it, he snatched the ball from my hand.

"One of the things you most need to work on, if I'm being blunt, is being a little more relaxed and a little less analytical about your decisions."

I arched a brow. "I won't bother to argue that point, but how does this ball come in?"

"Simple, really. When it comes to your decisions on this trip, you'll ask a question, and the eight ball answers."

"And I follow the advice of this ball?"

"Yes. It'll force you to go with the flow. At least while in Australia. Deal?"

My first inclination was to think about it, which was ironic considering the reason he'd given me the gift in the first place. So I took a deep breath and shook it up. "Dear Magic Eight Ball: I need to loosen up and learn to be more fun. Should I allow you to make all of my decisions on this trip?"

I flipped it over to see the blue triangle that eerily said, *"As I see it, yes."*

Hm. "I have one caveat, though," I blurted out.

"I'd be disappointed if you didn't," he said, chuckling.

"You should be impressed I only have one. See, I may have to work on this trip. So if I have anything come up work related, then no ball."

"Deal." He pulled out of his pocket a smaller version on a key chain.

I raised a brow.

"This is in case you need a backup."

It was so silly that I couldn't help smiling, but then shit got real once we were on the plane, and the flight attendant passed out the menu for dinner service. Will plopped my eight ball in front of me.

"Seriously?"

"Come on. Be adventurous."

I sighed. "Fine. Should I have the beef or the chicken?"

I turned the ball over and it said: *'No'.* "Explain to me how that's helpful."

He laughed. "You're supposed to ask it yes or no questions only. Now ask if you should have the beef."

"Fine, should I order the beef?"

He turned it over, and it said, *'Decidedly yes.'*

"And should you have the red wine?" he asked.

"Of course I should. Red goes with the beef."

He smirked, turning my ball over to reveal a *'NO.'* "The eight ball disagrees. Time to walk the walk."

"Oh, yeah, drinking white wine with beef is really living it up?"

He shrugged. "Think of it as breaking the mold with something outside of the norm."

"Maybe I want a second opinion."

Pulling the smaller version from his pocket, he handed it over. And wouldn't you know it? It said the exact same thing, much to Will's amusement.

When the friendly flight attendant came to take our orders and poured the wine, she automatically reached for the red, but I stopped her. "Actually, I'll have the white."

She gave me a condescending brow raise. "But red goes with the beef."

I tossed an 'I told you so look' toward Will and then focused back on her. "Yes, but I'm living on the edge and defying all social conventions because his balls told me to."

She poured the white and couldn't move on quick enough while Will burst out laughing.

"You know something, Cath? I believe there's a wild and sarcastic side to you that's anxious to get out."

I held up my white wine for a cheers clink to his. "Here's hoping."

After a short layover in San Francisco, we arrived in Sydney thirty-two hours later, having lost a full day with the time difference. After we checked into our separate hotel rooms, I was surprised when Will announced he had to go straight to his model shoot. Good thing we'd each slept a decent amount on the plane.

He'd made me promise to get out and not stay in my room doing nothing, so after consulting the magic ball about some tourist options, I ended up taking a ferry over to the Taronga zoo.

After a few hours exploring the amazing zoo, I was happy I'd gone ahead and seen the koalas alone. Maybe there was something to allowing the ball to make decisions for me. By the time I arrived back at the hotel, Will had left me a message on my room phone that he'd returned and I should get ready for a night out.

I'd just finished applying my eye makeup a bit darker than usual when the knock came on the door. Looking down and noticing I was still in nothing but the hotel robe, I smiled. 'Do I get dressed before answering?' I asked the ball.

'My reply is no'

So there I had it. I puttered to the door, peered out the peephole in case it was a stranger, and then opened it to a slightly shocked Will.

"Uh, I can come back," he stammered, taken off guard at seeing me so underdressed.

"Nope, come on in. I would've put on my clothes, but the ball told me not to bother."

He chuckled, stepping inside. "You're really embracing this aren't you?"

"You know, it's kind of liberating. By the way, the ball had me raiding the minibar as well, so I'm two vodkas in if you wish to help yourself while I change."

"Ah, you now have someone to pin the blame on."

"Exactly," I called over my shoulder as I walked into the bathroom. There I slipped on the black Herve Leger dress which hugged my curves and showed enough leg to make me hopefully appear sexy.

Coming back out, I enjoyed the appreciation reflected in Will's expression.

"Um, that's some dress, but we're only going out to a bar."

"And this isn't okay?" I smoothed my hands down over my hips and walked over to check my reflection in the closet mirror. I'd be fine in any of the bars in Manhattan dressed like this.

He laughed. "Not here it's not. Do you have a pair of jeans?"

"Yes. Of course." I guess I could do more casual, and the upside was I'd be more comfortable.

I rummaged through the closet, grabbing my skinny jeans and a gorgeous black-and-white silk top. After changing and walking out, Will's frown gave me pause. "What?"

"It's not that you don't look good," he hedged.

I lifted a brow and watched him crack a smile.

"It's just that you're intimidating as hell looking like that or in anything, really, I've ever seen you wear. Well, the yoga pants are an exception, I suppose, but even those appear to be designer."

They were, but I kept quiet and wondered how the heck I was intimidating. "What should I be wearing?"

"Something less, I don't know…"

"Fashionable?"

"Expensive."

I motioned toward my closet, as if to say, be my guest.

He perused the contents a moment before turning to meet my eyes. "Did you have more hangers brought up and have these clothes dry cleaned?"

I folded my arms across my chest, feeling a bit like a petulant child as I defended myself. "I bring my own steamer, and yes, I did call down and ask for more hangers."

Instead of being put off by my tone, Will smiled and stepped in closer to lay his hand on my shoulder. "I'm not making fun of you. Honestly, it's kind of adorable."

I shook my head, not believing him for a second. "My OCD is adorable?"

"You don't have OCD. You simply prefer things neat and tidy. But you're not high maintenance about it, considering you steamed your own stuff. I get fashion, and I especially understand why you, in your position, would have designer clothes. But tonight when we go out, I want you to be Catherine the woman, not Catherine in charge of a major fashion magazine in New York City."

"Okay," I whispered, well aware of his hand still touching me. "But in that case, I probably need to go shopping."

He glanced over toward my suitcase. "Maybe not. What's in here?"

While he walked over and looked through the contents, I tried not to let my lacy thongs and bras turn me bright red with embarrassment. I hoped he didn't find the condoms I'd tucked in the pocket in case my adventurous side included that type of fun on the trip. Not that I expected it. But when I'd seen my ex on Wednesday, the first thought that had popped into my mind had been regret he'd been the last man I'd been with. I hoped to be able to channel my inner Kat, a woman who would be confident enough to maybe have a fling, and so I'd packed them just in case.

"Earth to Cath."

I blushed at the train of my thoughts. "Yes, sorry. Um, those are my workout clothes and pajamas."

He pulled out a long-sleeved, black cotton V-neck. "This is good. Put this with the jeans, wear the black heels, and your hair down."

I'd twisted my hair up, thinking it went better with the dress. "It's a yoga top," I protested.

"It's casual, which is perfect for the bar." Then he smirked and pulled out his little eight-ball key chain. "Should Catherine wear this black top to the bar?" Flashing it at me, he showed me the '*YES*' and then pointed to the bathroom.

Something told me that ball was just getting started for the evening.

CHAPTER NINE

*A*fter walking a couple of blocks from the hotel in downtown Sydney, Will led me into a bar which looked half sport themed. On the wall were framed jerseys and mounted televisions showing rugby and soccer playing. The other half of the bar consisted of a soon-to-be dance floor, if the DJ setting up lights and speakers was any indication. Glancing around, I saw several pool tables and dartboards off to the left in a separate room. There seemed to be something for everyone here. In surveying the laid-back crowd, I was glad he'd insisted on me dressing casual.

I resisted the urge to tug at the form-fitting yoga top and was completely taken off guard when Will suddenly stopped and turned toward me.

"Before you meet this crew, you should know that Jack and Adam are harmless, so feel free to flirt away with them. Rich, however, is married, although he won't tell you, and Paul is definitely not your type."

"Okay." I felt as if I'd been fire hosed. Shouldn't I make some of these judgements on my own? I thought that was the whole point of this exercise.

After leading me over to a table in the corner, he greeted the men there and turned to introduce me. "Cath, I'd like you to meet my mates from my time here at university. This is Adam and Jack. Over there is Paul, and I guess Rich hasn't arrived yet. Everyone, this is Catherine."

"Hi, guys," I said, smiling as I watched Will give bro-hugs all the way around.

Adam scratched his head and turned toward Will with an awkward expression. "Um, Bridget is here, mate. Sorry about that, but she found out you were in town."

I was clueless who Bridget was, but Will sighed and scanned the room apprehensively. It wasn't long before a sexy brunette, dressed in leather pants with a silk camisole top—definitely not used for yoga—and four-inch heels came running over. She engulfed him in a hug that was more than familiar.

She was beautiful. Petite, curvy in the right places, fashion-able, and young. Young like Will. Matter of fact, in seeing them together, I realized they fit. It was as if the universe was reminding me that I, on the other hand, did not. Judging by the irritated look on her face, she wasn't keen on the fact that he'd brought me here with him.

"Who's she?" Bridget gave me what I interpreted as the universal 'stink eye.'

Never one to allow someone to talk about me as if I wasn't sitting there, I held out my hand. "Hi, I'm Catherine. Nice to meet you."

She didn't take my hand but instead turned her pout toward Will. She then dragged him away from the group, toward the bar and out of earshot.

I had to remind myself that she was twenty-something and merely lifted a brow at her behavior. I focused my attention on ordering a drink once the waitress came over.

I smiled at Adam, who offered the seat next to him.

"She's not normally so bitchy, but, uh, she's had a thing for

Will for years. They dated at university and modelled together over the years."

I told myself I didn't care. "It's okay. We're only friends."

Adam and Jack exchanged looks, and then Jack slid into the seat on the other side of me. "In that case, I'm Jack, and I'm quite single."

"Hold up. You're not the only one. Did Will mention I'm the most handsome of the lot?" Paul teased.

I thought, nope, but he had mentioned that Paul wasn't my type. Now I was curious as to why. After laughing off the attention, I learned that all of the guys had met while playing rugby while attending university together and had kept in touch over the years. Since Will had told me he was still taking online classes, I'd assumed he hadn't graduated yet, but now I wondered if that was true.

When the guys ordered a round of shots, I didn't bother to consult the ball in my clutch because I knew what I wanted it to say. Why not? Time to let loose and have some fun.

Looking annoyed, Will returned with Bridget beside him.

A straight-up sour expression marred her beautiful face. "I, um, I'm sorry for earlier. It's nice to meet you."

Yep, it was official. Will was the woman whisperer if he'd been able to convince her to apologize.

"It's okay. Happy to start over. Nice to meet you, too, Bridget."

She glanced at Will as if to say 'are we done now?' and gave me a fake smile before returning to her friends sitting at the bar. Oh, well. Catty women in my industry were a dime a dozen and I'd stopped letting them bother me a decade ago.

"Everything okay?" I asked Will.

He blew out a breath. "It's better now. Thanks for being gracious."

He took a beer from Paul and sat across from me while he caught up with his friends. I heard them make plans to go surfing tomorrow morning. The image of him in a wetsuit had me momentarily distracted until a couple of tall, handsome guys walked over, one with sandy and the other with dark hair. Their arrival caused another round of exuberant greetings from the group.

Turned out the dark-haired man was Rich, the conveniently-without-his-wedding-ring friend. And the blond-haired guy was introduced to everyone as Liam. He was Rich's friend and was in town visiting. After another round of beer and more chairs pulled up, I found myself sitting with Liam to my left and Will on the right. Unfortunately, Bridget and her two friends sat on the other side of him, having now joined the group at the tables.

"So, how you going, Catherine?" Liam inquired, flashing his dimples.

"How am I what?" I'd had a couple of drinks and a shot, so it was possible I didn't understand what he was asking.

"How you going is like how are you doing, but the Aussie way?" he thankfully explained.

Ah. "So do I answer with: I go fine?"

I realized when the entire table started to laugh that everyone was listening and amused by the American girl's take on Aussie greetings.

"Nah. You say. I'm good. You? Try it as you'll hear it everywhere."

"Okay. How *you* going?" I fell into my own fit of giggles because I sounded more like Joey from *Friends* with 'How YOU doing?' and far from natural. "I think I'll stick with 'how's *it* going.'"

Liam smiled and then perked up. "Sounds like the DJ started in the other room. Do you care for a dance, Catherine?"

Because I was feeling playful, I pulled out my magic eight ball.

"What's this?" He flipped it over to reveal a *'YES'*. "Did you lose a bet or something?"

Standing up, a smile stretched across my face. "More like I decided it might be fun for the evening to let the ball decide. Luckily, it worked in your favor. Shall we?"

I took his extended arm and glanced toward Will, who now had Bridget whispering in his ear with her hand on his leg. I tried not to care. I was here tonight to flirt and meet someone new and that involved channeling my inner Kat. Besides, Liam was very handsome.

Turned out he had some serious dance moves. If nothing else, I could say definitively that I was good at dancing. And it wasn't dull. Matter of fact, given the way he was looking at me move, I was feeling uncharacteristically sexy.

We returned to the table after a couple songs, and he motioned for the waitress, ordering a gin and tonic.

I tried to ignore Will's frown as I sat back down and continued to chat with Liam. Wasn't this the whole reason I was out tonight? So why did Will seem unhappy with me?

"Where are you from, Liam?" I questioned, sipping my cocktail and wanting to get to know him a bit more.

"From Brisbane, but in Sydney for business and visiting Rich, who I used to work with."

"Oh, what is it you do?"

He shrugged, appearing put out that I was engaging him in conversation. Maybe this was the downside of meeting a guy in a bar. That he didn't want to get to know me better unless it included taking off my clothes later. Yep, this part about my college years was flashing back to me now.

"I do a little of this, little of that. I fancy myself a bit of an entrepreneur."

I wasn't a snob by any means. He could've told me he worked a farm, did landscaping, or was a painter, but his vague answer grated on my nerves. Yes, I was aware I'd put down *having a man who was financially independent* on my matchmaker's criteria, but I was quickly realizing I wanted a man who was passionate about what he did, no matter what it was. I had to remind myself this wasn't a date, however, and I wasn't looking for a relationship. So I made myself figuratively shrug it off and continued my mission of flirting.

After a few more minutes of small talk, Liam excused himself to take a phone call. "Sorry about this; it's work." He walked down the hall toward the restrooms, where it was probably a lot quieter than the bar, which was getting louder as the hour got later.

As soon as he was out of earshot, Will turned to me. "He's a class-A douche, Cath," he whispered.

"He's not that bad. And…" I pulled out my trusty 'get out of jail free card' eight ball. "Do I keep talking to Liam?"

'It is decidedly so' flashed up, and I shrugged, trying not to get annoyed that Bridget, on his other side, was now rubbing his arm possessively.

Turning my full attention back onto, uh, uh, Liam, yeah, Liam, when he returned, I had to request him to repeat the question he'd just asked.

"I'd asked you what it is you do?" Liam's voice was low and throaty, but instead of being turned on, I was distracted by the thought of Will possibly returning to the hotel with Bridget tonight.

"I work in fashion."

"Yeah, like in retail?"

I gave him a small smile, not bothering to tell him anything about my career. For one, he wasn't my type, and for two, I was trying to leave the fashion magazine editor persona behind in New York. "Sure. Something like that."

"Well, you dress nice."

"Thanks. I like clothes." I don't think I'd ever said anything lamer in my life. I was officially a hair twirl away from having to excuse myself to beat my head against a wall. "So, um, tell me more about yourself."

"Should be his favorite subject," Will mumbled in my ear, and I tried not to giggle.

Liam didn't help things when he flipped his hair, Justin Bieber circa 2010 style. Good Lord. Although I could definitely say he was handsome, I was growing less attracted to him by the second. After a couple more minutes of prattling on, he startled me by trailing his fingers down my arm seductively. "Tell me: are all your decisions dictated by the ball tonight?"

Taking it out of my pocket, I shrugged. "I should probably ask it that question."

He took it out of my hand and showed me the *'YES'* which floated to the top.

"Guess I am." I hoped it came out braver than I was actually feeling.

He leaned in, whispering. "Then maybe you should ask the ball if you're going back to my hotel room with me tonight."

I was a deer in headlights, but forced myself to lighten up. Shaking the ball, I wondered if I should entertain the idea of a one-night stand with Liam. After all, he was the sort of guy where you knew up front what you were getting, and it had been two very long years. I took a deep breath, flipping the ball over with a shaking hand.

Up came the non-definitive answer of *"Reply hazy, try again."*

Nervous laughter erupted from my throat, and I took the temporary reprieve for what it was. "And that's my cue to use the ladies' room."

He looked disappointed but hopeful. "All right, but I expect a second try once you return."

"Sure."

Do not overthink this, Catherine. Get out of your own head. I tried to talk myself into it while I walked down the short hallway, but it was no use. If I felt this relieved when the ball hadn't come up with a definitive yes, then clearly this wasn't something with which I was comfortable. Unfortunately, there were some things I wasn't able to leave up to the ball, after all. Even fun, flirty Kat had her limitations. This meant no one-night stands with a handsome Aussie man I'd just met in a bar. Damn.

Taking one last glance in the mirror and freshening my breath with a mint, I figured I'd return to the table and play it cool, maybe lose the ball. But when I walked out the door into the hallway, I ran straight into a brick wall of Will MacPherson.

"Oomph." The breath came out as I steadied myself against his hard chest. I blushed when I saw his gaze fixed on me and saw my hands remained on his pecs. Dropping my hands quickly, I took a deep breath. "Sorry. I didn't see you there."

"Are you seriously thinking about sleeping with that wanker?"

Grasping that he'd followed me in order to ask that question, I didn't appreciate his judgy tone, so I automatically got defensive. "You're not exactly one to talk, with Ms. Insincere Apology hanging all over you. I'm assuming you're taking her back to your room, so what does it matter what I do?"

I realized too late that I'd revealed my true thoughts with my jealous tone and watched his eyes narrow.

"Is that what you want? Me to be with her and you to sleep with Liam?"

What was he asking? We stood there, our gazes locked on one another until Bridget's voice broke through, along with the sound of her heels as she walked down the corridor.

She looked between us. "There you two are. If you don't mind, I'm going to take my man out onto the dance floor."

"We need another minute," Will said, not even sparing her a glance.

She was instantly put out, murdering me with her eyes before moving to the end of the hall on the edge of the bar where her location meant there would be no way to walk by her without her knowing.

Will ran a hand through his hair in frustration. "I'm trying to look out for you," he whispered. The intense moment from which we'd been interrupted was now long gone, if ever there'd been such a thing.

Frustrated with myself for reading into things and possibly taking his concern at more than face value, my irritation spilled over. I seemed to have forgotten I'd already talked myself out of a one-night stand. "I'm a big girl, Will. And you're the one who said I needed to lighten up and have some fun. Maybe this is a way to do that." I was only thinking out loud, but I could tell by the sour expression on his face he wasn't happy with my answer.

He threw up his hands, exasperation lacing his words. "You're right. You are a big girl. Do what you want, then, but just so you know, your prospect is now flirting with those two at the bar." He pointed at Liam, who was within sight and acting touchy-feely with two young girls who appeared to be all over him.

What the hell? Nice Catherine would've let it go. Polite Catherine would've walked by without another thought. Kat was neither of those people. Kat was not okay with being dissed like this. I intended to give him a piece of my mind or maybe simply glare at him while I walked by—because, let's be honest, I wasn't exactly in a position to go banshee on a guy I'd just met and wasn't actually going to sleep with. Before I could, I was surprised by Will grabbing my hand.

"No, don't."

I raised a brow. "You accuse me of being too nice, too accommodating but now want to stop me from walking by and at the very least give him a dirty look?"

He sighed. "I told him you weren't coming home with him and to find some other conquest for the evening."

"Wait. What? Why?"

He shifted uncomfortably. "Because it's not you. Listening to you flirt with him wasn't even close."

Oh, my fucking God. Frustration wasn't a strong enough term for what I was feeling. "Of course it wasn't me. The whole point in traveling across the globe was to stop being the same old boring me."

Did he have any idea what it took to get my head wrapped around acting casual and thus shed my *Catherine New York* persona? But I was more disgusted with myself than with him. Why had I imagined for one moment that coming here to the other side of the world would change things? I grabbed my reprieve when an employee opened up a door at the far end of the hallway, revealing the back of the restaurant. I bolted out the rear door and didn't stop.

Thankful the hotel was within walking distance, I set out on foot. Unfortunately, I didn't remember what direction to head. Regardless, I began to walk, hoping for once I'd get lucky with my fifty-fifty choice.

I could hear Will's voice calling after me a few minutes later. "Cath, hold up. Would you wait?"

Once I realized he was catching up, I slipped off my heels and took off in a run, tears streaming down my face. The very last thing I wanted was for anyone to see me this way, especially when I didn't even have the words to describe what I was feeling. When the lights of the hotel came into view, I threw up a little note of thanks to the universe and decided to take a shortcut across an empty grassy lot next to the hotel hoping it might keep Will from catching up with me. Regrettably, my appreciation of fate had been given too soon. My bare feet sank into six inches of mud.

"Shit."

Will stopped short, evidently recognizing the lawn I'd thought to run across was nothing but a mucky mess. "At least you had your shoes off." He stood with his hands on his hips at the edge, hardly out of breath despite having run after me.

"Can you please take them?" I held my shoes high, hoping at least I could avoid ruining my designer heels.

He sighed and stepped forward. "Are you really that much of a princess? A little dirt never hurt anything."

I fumed at the name, feeling like he was adding insult to injury tonight. "I'm not a princess, but when my shoes are worth over three thousand dollars and my clutch another two, the last thing I want to do is take a chance on ruining them."

He cursed under his breath and grabbed the shoes, along with my purse. "That's more than my first car was worth and only re-emphasizes the princess comment. Your phone is ringing, by the way."

He helped himself, taking the device out of my clutch and then flashed me the screen with a smile. "Who is *Why the hell is he calling me now?*"

"I'll give you one guess." It was my ex-husband, and his newly dubbed contact name said it all. "Are you going to help me out of this or what?"

He put my phone away, chuckling, and then reached his hands out to grip mine. "Sure thing, princess."

His newfound nickname snapped something inside of me. I made the mistake of letting go, which flung me back on my ass into the mud where I didn't bother to get up. That was it. I was about to lose my shit in the muck of a vacant lot on a starry night in Sydney, Australia.

"I'm not a fucking princess. I appreciate nice things, and I run one of the best fashion magazines in the world. Half these things were given to me by the designers; I didn't buy them. And I would think that being in the same industry, you'd have an appreciation for the fact the editor of Cosmo Life cannot go around in clothes from Target, although I think that might be nice for a change. Furthermore, I work hard for a living; I always have. I didn't grow up poor, but I certainly didn't enjoy some lavish childhood which afforded me a silver spoon. I always worked: in my father's office, volunteering at the hospital, babysitting. So don't you dare call me a princess as if I've led some sort of pampered lifestyle that I don't deserve. I've earned every penny and every stitch of clothing, whether it be expensive or not."

He regarded me a moment before smiling. "Exactly. So don't ever diminish yourself again in front of anyone, especially that wanker in there. You work hard, and you're damn good at your job. Be proud of that fact."

I huffed out a breath, getting whiplash from his unexpected response. "Was this some sort of test?"

The smug bastard shrugged. "Listening to you tell that asshole you work in retail like you fold clothes at the Gap was not the Catherine I know. You have a career which means something to you, that you worked hard for, and that you should be proud of."

Exasperation flowed through me. "You convinced me to come here and leave my New York image behind. You told me I was intimidating in my regular clothes and had me change tonight. You encouraged me to be fun and flirty, which obviously isn't me. And then you proceeded to sabotage it once I'm finally doing a decent job of it. Was I really supposed to invest time in telling Liam what I do for a living when we both know he didn't care? He only wanted to get laid."

His jaw flexed. "Yeah, well, I changed my mind. You should be yourself from now on."

I stood up slowly, flexing my hands in the wet earth, and then did what any thirty-something-year-old woman at her wit's end would've done. I threw mud at him. The look of shock when my pitch hit him square in his pretty-boy face was definitely worth the momentary loss of maturity.

"Did you really just do that?" He grinned like he couldn't believe it, either, wiping it off with his hand.

"With precise aim, which I'm about to do again unless you

give me one reason why I wasted my time and took this trip, gearing up for something you're now saying is a bad idea."

He offered me his free hand, pulling me out of the mud, onto the sidewalk, and then flush against his body. My eyes widened at the contact and I thought for a moment it must've been an accident until he banded his arm around my waist, pinning me to his body intimately.

"Is this reason enough?" he murmured huskily before dropping his lips to mine.

Fire. It's what my body felt at the contact. I was absolutely ignited with heat the moment he kissed me. There was nothing tentative about it; instead, it was pure passion as he plundered my lips, his tongue delving inside.

"I'm so confused," I whispered the moment he pulled back.

"You're not the only one, but I think this may finally clear things up. Now, either kiss me back, or tell me to stop."

"My hands are all muddy," I pointed out because, you know, the whole OCD thing was tough to turn off. I didn't want to get his shirt dirty.

"I don't fucking care. Kiss me, Cath."

I wrapped my muddy hands around him, one at his waist and the other reaching up behind his neck, pressing myself further into him and meeting his lips again. When his tongue met with mine, a shiver ran down the length of my body and heat pooled at my center, which practically ached for his touch. He consumed me with his kiss to the point that I forgot where we were.

It wasn't until somebody walking by shouted "get a room" that we broke apart.

He brushed my hair from my face. "We're just rolling with this and not overthinking it. I mean it, Cath. You're going to turn your brain off and listen to your body, which I plan on being inside of in about five minutes."

I was pretty sure if my body had anything to say about it, I'd make it three.

CHAPTER TEN

*W*ill's hand took mine before I could utter a word, not that I had any coherent ones, and he led me the short distance to the hotel. Once there, much to my astonishment, he hoisted me up over his shoulder, carrying me as he walked toward the elevator.

"What are you doing?" I urgently whispered, noticing a few people in the lobby staring.

"Ensuring you don't leave muddy tracks through the hotel."

"Oh." How quickly I'd forgotten I was completely covered in the stuff.

Upon arriving on our floor, he wasted no time striding the hall and whipping out my key from my purse in order to let us both into my room. As soon as the door shut, my shoes and purse dropped from his hands and he slid me down the length of his body. Every hard inch. His blue eyes simmered with lust, devouring me with the power of his stare.

"You're so beautiful, mud and all," he whispered, dipping his head and taking my lips again.

I moaned when his kiss turned carnal, eager for more, and yet while my body was on board, my brain wasn't following suit.

So while he trailed kisses down my neck and his hands nimbly unfastened my jeans, I had to ask. "Aren't you worried this might—I don't know—might change things between us?"

He nuzzled my ear, his hands working my jeans down. Once they were off, he backed me past the bed and toward the bathroom on the far side of the room. "How so?"

Oh, Jesus, his fingers were sliding beneath the material of my lacy thong straight into my heat, and I was losing my grasp of why, in fact, I was asking anything that could conceivably stop what was about to happen.

"Possibly jeopardizing our newfound friendship," I murmured, sucking in a breath when his finger entered me and curled up, finding the perfect spot for pleasure.

"Are you saying we can't be friendly with my fingers inside of you?"

"I—God—I can't think."

"Good. Everything else we'll work out after."

His mouth took mine again and left no doubt that I was far past the point of being able to overanalyze or question anything. In this moment, I didn't care what the consequences might be so long as he didn't stop. I hardly noticed when he maneuvered me into the large glass shower. Nor did I care about the warm water from the glass enclosure that was now beating down on us, drenching us both, still half dressed with mud pouring off onto the shower floor.

Will made short work out of shedding his clothes. Before I could do the same, I saw him completely naked and I froze.

Holy Perfection.

He was absolutely beautiful. Although a man might not appreciate that particular adjective, there really was no other word for it. As if his pretty-boy face with arresting blue eyes wasn't enough, it only got better from there. His chest and arms were sculpted to perfection. A trim waist, previously mentioned lickable abs and, good Lord, his hardened uncut length jutting out proudly literally had my mouth watering. He was unabashed in his nudity as he stalked toward me.

"You're staring and clearly still wearing too many clothes."

"I can't help it. You're gorgeous." I couldn't muster up the grace to be embarrassed by the blurted-out compliment because it was the unbiased truth. He was an absolute feast for my eyes. The moment I realized I had free license to touch him, I couldn't move fast enough.

He grunted when my hands skimmed down his chest, feeling the planes of his muscles.

"Fair is fair, let's get this off."

Pulling my black top over my head, he flung it somewhere to land with a sopping splat. It occurred to me that the old Catherine would've been concerned about the fabric care of my expensive clothing strewn about and covered in mud, but at this moment I didn't care if anything was permanently ruined. All that mattered was that his hands kept touching me, where they made quick work of stripping me of my bra and panties.

Once I was standing completely naked before him, he took a step back to leisurely view my body from head to toe. "You're absolutely stunning."

I flushed at the compliment. It was doubtful he hadn't seen a better-looking woman considering he'd been in the modelling world for the last few years. But not one to be self-conscious about my body since I made it a point to keep in shape—hello, what else were the thirties for?—I didn't give the thought any energy. "Now you're staring."

His grin was both sexy and playful. "Damn right I am." He locked his eyes on mine while palming both my breasts, letting the weight of my B cups fall into his hands and brushing the nipples with his thumbs to hardened peaks. "Your skin is like pure silk. So perfect," he murmured, taking my lips.

My hands weren't to be denied the opportunity to touch him as much as possible, so I reached down, taking his length in my hand. I enjoyed his sound of pleasure at the contact and the velvety softness of his skin. As I slid my hand up and down his hardened length, his breath came faster as my pace increased. Then it was my turn to gasp when his finger entered me again. I let my eyes float closed, thinking of nothing but the awakened desire he was evoking. I'd never climaxed this quickly before, and yet my body was starting to tingle, letting me know I was close.

"Come for me, Cath," he murmured. He then bit down on my ear lobe, which cued my body for release. My legs shook, and my pussy clamped down on his fingers like a vice grip with the power of my orgasm. He added two more fingers, working my wetness deep inside of me, stretching me exquisitely.

"I need a condom," he muttered.

Did that mean we were going to do it in the shower? Clearly, my internal question only highlighted how dull my sex life had been up until now. "I, um, have some in my suitcase," I offered. Oh, shit. What would he think with that admission?

Will must've read the panicked look on my face. "I have one in my wallet, too. Having condoms is safe, not a sign of being promiscuous. Okay?"

My mouth watered while I watched him put on the condom, and I wished my neurosis were easier to hide. "If I wasn't so turned on right now, I might be annoyed with your ability to read my neurotic mind."

He chuckled, pinning my hips to his and meeting my eyes. "This has been building between us for a while. We both knew you weren't going home with anyone but me. Even if neither of us were at the point of admitting it until tonight."

And here I'd thought it was one-sided the entire time.

He lifted me up to where I was eye to eye with him. "As much as I'd like to go slower with you, I think we're past that point. Wrap your sexy legs around me and hold onto my shoulders."

I shifted, allowing him to line up the tip of his cock with my entrance and then sucked in a breath when he drove into me inch by delicious inch. My body was primed for him, stretching when he moved deeper.

Oh. My. God. I was being fucked against a wall.

My fingernails dug into his taut skin while I felt him shift my weight and get a better angle before the next thrust. My head reared back with a resounding thump on the shower tile, but I barely noticed. Instead, I gripped him harder with my thighs, pulling him in closer. He set a rhythm, pounding me against the cool marble surface, handling my weight like it was nothing. He nipped at my neck and then peppered my chest with kisses and soft sucks while he hit a spot that had me chanting his name along with the Lord's over and over.

With one final thrust, he buried himself to the hilt and ground out his orgasm, meeting my mouth with the sort of kiss that sizzled its way into my bones.

I WOKE in the morning alone. When I felt the side where I thought Will had slept for a short time, it was cold letting me know he'd been gone awhile.

After our shower sex, which, incidentally, I was happily replaying in my mind, he had been attentive in ensuring I was washed from head to toe and then put me to bed. There, he'd pulled me into his embrace. It was probably a good thing he'd taken over because after the last orgasm, my entire body had felt boneless and exhausted from the combination of great sex, warm water, and jet lag.

Sitting up, I wondered if he'd returned to his own room because he'd wanted to sleep alone. Or maybe to emphasize that this was casual and not a relationship where he awakened me with breakfast in bed.

A glance at the clock showed it was mid-morning. I now recalled a conversation between him and his friends at the bar about surfing this morning. More than likely, he'd left in order to meet them, but maybe he'd wanted to stay?

Good grief. Sometimes I needed a vacation from my own thoughts and analyzing everything to death.

As I hopped out of bed, I found myself decidedly sore from last night. Obviously, my muscles were feeling the delicious effects of being used after a very long time.

A quick shower did the trick of waking me up and rinsing down the residual dirt on the shower floor long forgotten last night. After donning my workout gear, I threw my hair back in a low pony tail, and went about cleaning up the mess that I'd tracked into the room and which was currently all over the bathroom floor. Then I turned my attention to washing out my jeans and shirt by hand and hanging them to dry. I'd just finished rinsing out the towels I'd used to clean when I heard the click of my hotel room door. Peeking my head out, I saw Will coming in, balancing a coffee tray, his wheeling suitcase, and a brown paper bag.

"You're cleaning?" he asked incredulously.

"Hi, have we met? Of course I am. I can't help myself." I blew the strands of my hair that had come loose out of my face and wrung out the towels before hanging them up to dry.

He smiled at my retort. "I'd hoped I'd still catch you in bed."

I blushed, feeling inexperienced and unsure how to proceed now that I'd seen this man naked. Why, oh, why couldn't I be the type of woman who could roll with casual sex and be normal?

But evidently there was only one of us feeling uncomfortable, because he flashed his perfect pearly whites and crossed the room in four strides to cup my face. "Don't you dare start having doubts about this, love."

Love. Why did he have to call me love? And if his smirk was

any indication, he was reading me like a book when it came to my panicked thoughts.

"Relax, Cath, it's a term of endearment which I also call my sister. Now then, let's have breakfast and some coffee, and then we'll talk."

I nodded dumbly, relaxing some. But I knew inevitably he was about to say what I'd been thinking: last night had been fun, but it wouldn't happen again. Logical Catherine knew this was the best way to keep the lines from blurring any more than they now were. But the lower half of me was about to have a mutiny if I dared suggest this would be a one-and-done scenario.

We sank into comfortable silence at the small table, sipping our drinks and eating the muffins he'd thoughtfully brought. I noticed his hair was still wet. "Did you go surfing?"

He nodded. "Yeah. We met at six o'clock, but there was rough water, which is why I'm back early—not that I'm complaining. What was your ex calling you about last night?"

Hello, subject change. "It's anyone's guess this time around. He didn't leave a message." Since I was curious after last night's conversation, I performed my own subject change and asked, "What classes are you taking if you already went to college?"

"I have my undergraduate degree in psychology. I'm going for a masters in counseling."

"Do you, uh, want to stay working at Club T, then?"

"No. Not at all. I'd rather work with kids or families. Private practice or at a school. I'm not sure yet."

After a few minutes of silence and finally unable to stand his assessing eyes a moment longer, I blurted it out. "Look, I know what you're going to say."

He shook his head, a smile tugging at his lips. "No, you don't. And you won't until I tell you."

I gritted my teeth. "Fine, then what are you thinking?"

"I'm thinking I really enjoyed last night."

I waited for the 'but,' however, it didn't come. Instead, he reached over and clasped my hand. The tingle that came with his touch took me off guard.

"There's no but after that statement. It's simply the truth."

"You know what's in my head now?" I teased a little, unnerved again that I was so easily read.

"You weren't thinking just that?" He chuckled at my silence and then leaned in. "I knew I was in trouble the moment we walked into the bar last night. I took one look at my friends flirting with you, and I wanted you all to myself."

"You were jealous?"

He nodded. "Not only that, but I hated that what's-his-face was seeing this fake side of you. I knew he'd never appreciate who you truly are."

"The fake side is supposed to be my fun side, Will." That was my problem in a nutshell.

He stood and pulled me up with him into his embrace. "Did you fake anything last night with me?"

I smirked. "You know I didn't."

"Exactly. And I shouldn't have encouraged you to try to be someone else because I have news for you: you aren't boring."

I quirked a brow which made him chuckle.

"Boring people can't make people laugh. They have nothing to say and no opinions to offer. And they certainly don't love to be fucked against a shower wall."

My entire body heated with the thought, already craving an encore.

"And your ex-husband is a complete idiot if he ever made you feel like you were the one with a problem in the bedroom."

"He didn't say problem, but he did imply that was boring, too."

"There is nothing boring about the way you responded to me last night. How sexy and adorable you are when your body is saying yes, but your mind is second-guessing it."

The fact that he found my internal crazy adorable was, well, kind of adorable.

"So what if you're not wild and crazy? Embrace the fact that you're conservative and thoughtful, because that's what makes you unbelievably special."

I was speechless at his sweet words.

"So here's what I propose because the very last thing I'd ever want is for either of us to have any false expectations between us."

I swallowed hard. "Okay. Let's hear it."

"We both know I'm not what you're looking for long-term. The things on your list of criteria for a man make sense given where you are in your life. You should absolutely want those things, but I'm not there yet."

Of course he wasn't. He was twenty-seven years old, gorgeous, single, and not aiming to get married and have kids in the next couple of years merely because some woman's biological clock was ticking. He'd blown out of the water any other 'criteria' I'd thought I needed to be happy, like career and financial stability. But having kids wasn't something I could sacrifice. "I respect that, Will."

Now it was his turn to swallow hard. "I don't want to hold you back from the possibility of meeting the perfect guy, so I propose we enjoy one another for the short-term and always know that beyond that we'll remain friends."

Was it just me, or did his eyes fall flat at the mention of my perfect guy? "You don't think it'll make things awkward once we return to New York and, say, attend a group function together with our other friends?"

His thumb traced the outline of my lips. "We passed the point of no return last night when I was buried deep inside of you, don't you think?"

"Regrets?" I whispered and watched him shake his head.

"None. Why do you think I brought my suitcase in with me? It's because I'd hoped we were only getting started."

Okay, now it was official. I was abso-fucking-lutely clueless when it came to reading the lines, let alone in between them.

"And so long as we're both aware that time is limited between us and we focus on having fun and keeping our expectations in sync, we'll be fine," he finished.

"So this would be only for the time we're in Australia?" Could I do this? Could I have a fling without the emotional investment?

"If that's what you want. But in that case, you're definitely coming with me for the next week because we have some more items to get through on your list."

My face instantly heated when I thought about the sheet of fantasies I'd given Will, aka Calvin. "I thought you were shredding that document."

He cupped my face. "Nope. Your fantasy items are on my mind constantly, and especially after last night."

My eyes went wide. "What?"

He sighed. "I don't know how to explain this without it coming across creepy, but I'll try. When I first met you years ago during the interview for the model shoot, I thought you were absolutely stunning. I mean, who wouldn't? Then when I got to know you through our mutual friends at various events, I learned you were nice, classy, and I respected the hell of you. But I completely thought you were way out of my league."

"Why would you think that?"

"Because you seemed perfect, and it was intimidating as hell."

I scoffed. "Nobody is perfect."

He nipped the sensitive spot behind my ear and whispered huskily, "No, they aren't. But when I put the adventure-seeking Kat together with the Catherine I knew, I started to have ideas about you. You all prim and proper tied to the bed at my mercy, you on all fours while I pleasure you with toys you've never heard of, or you screaming my name while I have you for the first time here." His hands dropped and squeezed my backside.

Holy crap. My body's agenda overrode my brain and I was shaking with desire instead of mortified by his recollection of my written-down secret desires. I wasn't sure who moved first, but at once we were a collision of lips, tongues, and hands.

We couldn't get undressed fast enough, frantic for the skin-on-skin contact. It felt like we were starved for each other. My body didn't know how to respond to the overwhelming feeling of having him hold me, touch me, and kiss me with such unbridled passion. All it knew was I needed more.

He finally broke away to grab something out of his suitcase. I quickly realized it was a box of condoms.

It was on the tip of my tongue to tell him I was clean and on the Pill, but then I stopped myself. Get a grip, Catherine, this wasn't a relationship. This was short-term casual sex, which meant condoms. And judging from the size of the box he plunked down on the nightstand, a lot of them.

"Where'd you go?" he queried, meeting my eyes.

I shook off my relationship-esque thoughts and ran my hands down his chest. "I was wondering if you remembered everything on my list," I fibbed, trying to recall what all I'd written down.

"Item number four, I believe, said have a man eat you like he knows what he's doing."

He remembered the number? "Um, I'm reasonably certain it said for a man to go down on me like he wants to." Although I kind of preferred his version better.

"That's a matter of interpretation because I've thought of the taste of you for weeks. And now I have a new use for this little magic eight ball."

"What?" I squeaked and felt his shoulders shake in laughter before he could breathe enough to recover and talk.

"Damn, you have a dirty mind. I was simply intending to ask

it if we should scratch number four off your list. But don't you worry; appropriate sexual toys will be used at a later time."

I shivered with the promise and then watched him reach over to the table and grab the magic eight ball out of my purse.

Grinning mischievously, he shook it up. "Magic ball, I was thinking about spending the next hour devouring Catherine's pussy. Do you agree?"

I swore if the ball said no, I was chucking that fucker out the window.

WILL TOOK a languid approach of pulling off my thong slowly and then laying me out on the bed. But if I'd thought he'd get right to the point, I was wrong. Instead, he first lavished attention on my breasts, taking each nipple between his teeth. I squirmed under his touch, eager for more.

Holy hell, I thought, feeling his diabolical tongue travel south over my stomach. Then his mouth blew warm air on the most intimate part of me. If ever there was a lesson to be learned, it was that age did not equal skill because when his mouth descended, I had to grab the sheets with both hands to keep from bucking off the bed. He knew exactly where to suck and lick, firing all nerve endings clear down to my toes. But as soon as I would feel my climax start to build, he would pull back, turning attention on my inner thighs, then over my hips.

"You're torturing me," I panted and saw his face look up with a grin.

"Absolutely. But I promise it'll all be worth it, love. You taste incredible. So good, in fact, I may take the full hour."

I whimpered when his finger entered me, finding a balance between the soreness from last night and the exquisite pleasure he was inflicting now. Intense, delicious heat washed over me. "Will…"

"I love it when you say my name on a moan like you can't help yourself."

He inserted another finger, curling both up inside of me, finding the-elusive-up-until-now-spot which made my eyes roll back. Once his mouth joined the assault again, I was done for, completely toppling over the edge with the most powerful orgasm I'd ever experienced. Forget stars; all I saw was white heat that completely obliterated every thought in my brain along with the ability to function.

His smiling face hovered over mine when I finally opened my eyes. "You doing okay?"

I nodded. "Was I loud?"

He smirked. "Uh-huh, and I enjoyed every minute of it. And maybe the surrounding hotel guests did as well."

I covered my face with my hands. "Oh, God."

"I think that's what you said, over and over again." He laughed, a musical sound which was both husky and carefree.

Peeling my hands away, I realized that if he found it amusing, I could too. You know, being it was such a sacrifice and all. Tentatively, I leaned up onto my elbows and met his lips, enjoying the growl in his chest when I went all in with my tongue, not minding the sweet and salty taste of myself on his lips. If anything, it made the moment more erotic. By the time he rolled the condom on and entered me, I was already on the precipice of another climax.

As we lay there minutes after we'd both gone over the edge with our orgasms, spoon-like and catching our breath, I realized he was growing hard behind me.

"You're ready to go again?" I asked incredulously, not sure he'd ever softened.

He chuckled, running his hands down my hips. "There are some advantages to being with a man in his twenties, you know."

I heard the tear of foil and then gasped when he entered me

from behind. "I don't seem to remember that perk, even when I was in my twenties and dating guys the same age."

His breath tickled my ear while his fingers found my most sensitive spot. The combination of him deep inside of me while playing with my clit ignited my body. But he wouldn't let me move. Instead his one arm held me to him, ensuring I couldn't wiggle against him but could only be at his complete mercy.

"You were clearly with the wrong men, then. And we're only getting started. Now, tell me you're going with me tomorrow," he insisted, moving an inch.

"You're muddling with my decision-making powers," I mumbled, squirming with anticipation.

"Nope, I'm only ensuring we have a full week of this to look forward to."

CHAPTER ELEVEN

J'd never been a participant in a *sex marathon*. But considering that I'd lost track of the number of orgasms I'd been on the receiving end of and that we'd barely taken the time to eat room service over the last twenty-four hours, I could definitively say I'd now been properly inducted.

As I came out of the lust-filled haze in order to get in a rental car with Will for the two-hour drive, I started to have second thoughts about agreeing to meet his family.

He, on the other hand, didn't appear anxious at all about the prospect as he pulled out onto the highway. "I missed driving on the proper side of the road." He grinned, looking positively striking with his sunglasses on and sexy forearms on display.

"What makes the left side proper?" Not that I was particularly defensive of the American way of driving. I didn't own a car or drive all that often, living in Manhattan. But he'd resided in both countries, so I was curious.

He shrugged. "I guess it's because I only drove for a year in California before moving here where I drove for a few years. Being in New York, I don't drive at all now, and I miss it."

I nodded and then finally decided to blurt out what was on

my mind. "You know, maybe instead of staying with your family, I should get a hotel room."

"Why would you do that?"

"Isn't it a little heavy for you to be bringing someone home to meet them?" I wasn't an expert on casual sexual relationships, but wasn't one of the rules not to involve family?

Shrugging, he didn't seem fazed in the least. "I already told my mom you were coming. Plus, I met your parents, so what's the big deal?"

"We weren't sleeping together then."

He chuckled. "But they thought we were, despite you telling them we were only friends. Now we're still friends but with the added benefit of sex. At any rate, you'd be doing me a favor by coming with me."

I looked at him skeptically. "How do you figure?"

He let out a sigh. "Sometimes it's uncomfortable around my mum because I left when I was ten. Instead of going home, like most kids do, I'm visiting. Anyhow, having you there would help because she wouldn't insist I stay in their house, which would make things even more awkward for me. Plus, she wouldn't keep pestering me about settling down, either."

I could definitely relate, given my own mother. "Is California home with your dad?"

He shook his head, obviously not willing to talk about it.

It made me sad to think of him not feeling like he had an actual place to call home.

"And before you ask, we'll stay together in the same cabin. We're adults, and I'm not sneaking around as if we aren't."

Huh, I liked that he wasn't the type of guy who regressed while around his family. Instead, he was kind of acting all alpha which had me instantly hot and bothered. I forgot my original doubts for the moment. "Okay. So do they stay on the property?"

"Yeah, there's a caretaker's house about a mile from the cabins. That's where they've lived the last few years. It's small but cozy. Business is crazy during the summer months, which is winter for the US, but this time of year, they're mainly doing repairs and maintenance to get ready for the season. My stepdad does most of the manual labor whereas my mum cleans and does some of the cooking."

"And how far away does your brother, Thomas, live?" He'd mentioned he was in a facility, but I wondered if it was close by.

"I can't believe you remembered his name." He squeezed my leg affectionately. "He's twenty minutes north. Close enough my mum can go visit, but far enough where she doesn't fuss over him daily. He enjoys feeling independent. If you want, and only if you want, you could go with me to see him one of the days, but I'll warn you it's not always comfortable—he has a hard time speaking, and I haven't seen him in a year. But my mum said he's getting good care."

His vulnerability and insecurity about the situation was endearing, but before I could respond, he went on.

"And speaking of my mother, she obviously doesn't know about me working at Club T or that I had my appendix removed, and I don't wish to tell her because she'll worry about the money. And now I'm rambling. Sorry."

It was clear he was nervous. "I won't tell her anything, and although I'd be honored to meet your family, I wouldn't be offended if you don't feel comfortable with it." Our 'short-term-whatever the hell you'd call it' relationship was far from conventional. We'd started with sharing personal details and he'd already met my parents, but even so, the last thing I wanted to do was make things more awkward.

"If you come with me, I'll make it worth your while. Promise." His hand found mine over the console, and his baby blues glanced over.

But would I be able to keep things in the 'casual only' box while we slipped into this new territory? I wanted to, but I was anxious. I'd never been the type of woman to sleep with someone who I wasn't in a committed relationship with. My feelings between physical and emotional were so entwined that I worried about what this week might do to further the entanglement. But considering the alternative would have me giving up the best sex of my life, well, it might be a risk worth taking.

"Do you ever have a woman tell you no?"

"Not the smart ones," he quipped, causing me to shake my head and laugh.

We drove over the next couple of hours, chatting here and there, but both being content to enjoy the countryside as we proceeded out of the city and into more of a rural setting. I also took the opportunity to check my emails, not sure who I was more surprised to hear from: my ex-husband saying he needed to see me again or the matchmaker with two possible matches. I sighed deeply, not wishing to respond to either.

"Work emails?" he questioned, glancing over.

I'd been typing out responses to both of them, explaining that I was out of the country. "Uh." I'd always been a terrible liar, not that I attempted to do it a lot, but when I did, it was pretty much written all over my face. "Actually, one was from my ex-husband asking to see me. The other was from Melanie, who sent me a couple of new matches. I told them I was out of town."

"What does he want?"

His protectiveness on my behalf regarding my ex made me smile. "There was a reason I changed his contact name in my phone because who the hell knows? My guess is it's probably something else about the annulment, but I don't know what he could possibly ask me to do. I'm certainly not giving money to the church to expedite it for him, and I told him I'm not returning until next week." I refused to worry about it until then. I'd gone months without hearing from him, and suddenly I was on his speed dial?

"So what about Melanie? Did she send you anyone good?"

Talk about an uncomfortable question. I didn't want to

discuss possible matches with the man I'd been intimate with only hours ago. "I'm not sure. I didn't look."

"Because I'm here?"

He kept his eyes straight ahead on the road so I couldn't get a read on him, but I certainly knew my own thoughts on the matter. Why in the world would I look at any other man but the gorgeous one in front of me? "Partially, yes. It makes it awkward. Don't you think?"

He glanced over. "You'll have to get over it because I have every intention of helping you once we return to New York."

"That's so not happening." There was no way I was going out on a date and then, what, recapping with Will afterwards while in bed together? The vision made me sick to my stomach. Absolutely not.

"We had a deal."

And we were right back to him working off his debt. "Yes, and one of the reasons I agreed to come here with you was to be done with it by the time we returned."

"If you're implying having sex with you is working off the money, then I'm going to pull this car over."

I couldn't help it; I giggled. "I'm not sure that came across as the threat you intended." I watched him crack a smile. "Obviously, things have changed since we started sleeping together. Although, if we were moving down that route, it would already be paid off."

"Was that a weird sort of compliment?" He seemed amused at the thought.

"Probably better than telling you that you'd have a looooong way to go."

He chuckled.

I tried not to let it bother me that Will seemed more than fine, if not downright encouraging, to have me continue to date other men. I wouldn't have felt the same in his shoes.

"I understand paying me back is important to you, so I'm not dismissing it, but it's not going to be done by you helping me with dating any longer. And don't take this the wrong way or think I'm making what's between us more than what it is, but I'm not sure I'm all that anxious to get back to the dating world as soon as I return. I mean, can't a woman have the best sex of her life for a few weeks before returning to reality?"

Part of me couldn't believe I'd said that out loud, but then the other part was proud of myself. Open and honest communication to be certain our expectations were in sync. How was that for a novel concept?

"Best sex of your life, huh?"

It figured he'd hone in on that part. "As if you couldn't tell last night or again this morning."

He trailed a fingertip down the inside of my wrist, the motion both intimate and surprisingly seductive. "I can't wait to be reminded. As for your point, you call the shots. If you're okay with this once we return to New York, then we continue. But you'll need to be honest with me about your limits. The last thing I want is for you to feel bad because you wish to date someone who could possibly be part of your long-term future. Like I said, so long as we have the same expectations and are having fun."

I wasn't sure I could be honest with myself about my limits, let alone about him. But I didn't want to spoil our time together. After everything I'd been through, didn't I deserve to enjoy this?

"I am having fun."

He kissed my hand. "Good. Me, too, although I feel like a slacker only crossing one thing off your list so far."

"Uh, two by my count, actually."

He glanced over, clearly trying to recall what else.

"Multiple orgasms were on the list. Plus, you added some more items to it I hadn't known I was missing."

"Multiple orgasms shouldn't have been a desire; they should

always be a given. And what did we add? I'd like you to tell me all about it."

I turned toward him in my seat, smiling. "Are you trying to get me to talk dirty to you?"

"Depends. Would it work?" His hand came over and rested on my thigh. "Remind me: was there anything on your list about fooling around in a car?"

My face heated about the same time that desire pooled between my legs. It hadn't been more than a few hours since the last time he'd been inside of me, and yet right now here I was desperately wishing I'd worn a skirt or that we weren't in a moving vehicle. "Nothing I can recall."

"Pity," he murmured, stroking his fingers down the inside of my thigh and then pausing to take a long drink of water out of his bottle.

"You know, I do have an idea of what to add to the list. Here's a hint: I'm on my knees." I had the satisfaction of watching him nearly choke and patted him on the back while he coughed. "Are you okay?"

He laughed. "I think the only thing that would make me feel better is to have you scoot closer and tell me more. In detail."

Did I have it in me? And by me, I meant Catherine, not some version of myself trying to be somebody else. "Am I afforded a learning curve, teacher? Because you should know it's my first time." I tried to make my voice sound breathy, but it came out way cheesy.

He grinned at my attempt, taking my hand and placing it on his bulge. "The moment you mentioned being on your knees, I turned rock hard. Anything else is just a bonus."

I cupped him through the material of his jeans, enjoying the hiss of his breath at the movement. Shifting so I could whisper and kiss behind his ear, I went for it. "Sinking to my knees, I'd glance up at you, anxious to taste that first drop on the tip of your cock with my tongue. I'd lean forward, sucking gently, then—"

"Fuck." He closed his eyes, inhaling deeply before re-tasking my hand into his, away from his growing erection.

"Not good?" I leaned back, watching him struggle for words.

"Let's just say I'm trying not to pull this car over right now."

"What's stopping you?" Holy crap. Did that actually come from me?

The look on his face was priceless and the shock evident. "I —wow—I wasn't expecting that," he breathed out. "Although I want to, and believe me, I do—we're already on the property. They have cameras and probably already know we're here."

Right on cue, he turned on his blinker a quarter mile down the road and turned into a driveway.

"Huh. I never thought I'd be the adventurous one for a change."

My NERVES REPLACED all remnants of lust when we pulled up to the house three minutes later. Probably due to the fact that I hadn't met anyone's parents in this capacity since college. Of course it could also be because I'd been trying to convince him to pull off the road less than a half mile away from his family's home for a blow job. That would've been a great first impression on the resort camera. Glancing over, I watched Will shift in his seat, clearly still uncomfortably straining against his jeans.

"Sorry," I offered, not feeling the least bit so. He might not realize it, but knowing I had this sort of effect on him was quite a boost to my ego.

He grinned. "No you're not, but I look forward to continuing this conversation later."

"Okay, but it'll be tough to talk with my mouth full," I quipped. I watched his jaw drop as he clearly hadn't believed I'd say something so brazen. Evidently, the last twelve hours had queued up an insatiable sex brain.

"Cath, I'll warn you I'm about to throw this car in reverse and haul you down to our cabin before saying hello to anyone."

I waggled an eyebrow. "Promises, promises, but it I think you're too late."

As the front door opened, he growled and adjusted himself while taking a deep breath. Two large dogs came out and barked around the car, followed by a dark-haired, teenage girl who shouted at them to be quiet and smiled at Will. I assumed this was his sister.

"Good thing seeing my family is an instant deflator," he muttered, getting out of the car slowly.

Will hugged his sister while a woman who had to be his mother, wiping her hands on an apron, came out the front door. She was petite with brown hair pulled back and the same piercing blue eyes as her son. Both women regarded me curiously while I stood next to the car, trying to keep the dogs from jumping up in their excited state.

His sister called them to her and tried to settle them down.

"You must be Catherine. I'm Mary," Will's mother greeted me with a smile.

"It's nice to meet you." I was instantly engulfed in a hug.

"You, too. And this is Janet." She turned toward her daughter, who was eying me dubiously with green eyes.

"Hi," she said in that teenage way which left no clue whether or not she was happy I was here.

"Tim is out fixing some plumbing in one of the buildings, but he'll return in time for dinner. Did you want to go unload your things at the cabin, then come back for lunch? I wasn't sure if you, uh, needed separate rooms, but I have either a one or two-bedroom ready just in case." She cast a glance between the two of us.

"One-bedroom is good, Mum," Will responded without apology. "And we'll go do just that."

I didn't miss the flash of disappointment on his sister's face. She'd just seen her brother for all of two minutes, and he was already leaving. "Did you want to come along, Janet?"

She looked surprised but excited, and I hoped her brother was on board with the idea. I know we'd both been thinking about continuing where we'd left off in the car.

"Yeah, sure, let me grab my phone."

"She never goes anywhere without it," her mother said on a sigh.

"We'll be back soon," Will said, hugging his mom one more time and climbing into the car to join me.

"I hope that wasn't presumptuous, but she seemed crestfallen to see you leaving so soon."

Will took my hand and raised it to his lips, brushing my knuckles with a kiss. "Although I had other plans in mind for our 'unpacking'—" He did an air quote with his one hand. "It was worth seeing how pleased she was to be invited. The last couple of years I've come to visit, I haven't known how she'll be from one moment to the next. She's kind of moody."

I gave him a smile. "Teenage girls usually are."

On cue, Janet opened the back door and climbed in. "Mom said you two might want to be alone, so if you do, you know, I don't care. I can stay here instead while you settle in."

Will winked at me before turning around toward his sister. "We wouldn't have invited you if we'd wished to be alone. Plus, I haven't seen you in a year, love, so why don't you tell me what's been going on?"

She hesitated at first, but then launched into what she'd been up to with school and her friends. Although the cabin was less than a mile away, by the time we arrived I felt as though we'd been thoroughly dipped in the deep end of teenage-girl life. But the way her brother listened and also picked up on things and asked questions was impressive. Watching the affection he had for her was sweet.

While Will handled the suitcases, I stepped into the charming wooden cabin and immediately appreciated the rustic appeal. Off to the right was a small kitchen which boasted a stove, sink and countertop, and a small bistro table. The living area was made up of overstuffed, comfortable-looking furniture with a wilderness motif. A beautiful stone fireplace stood in the center of it all. The doors toward the rear I assumed led to the bathroom and bedroom.

"So you're from New York City?" Janet inquired.

"I'm originally from the Boston area, but I've lived in New York most of my adult years. Have you ever been?"

She sighed heavily. "No, but I really want to go. I asked Will if I could visit him, but he said not until I'm older. But how am I supposed to know if I could live there if I can't see it?"

"What makes you want to live in New York?"

"Aside from getting the chance to move out of this dreary town, I love fashion. And where better to go, especially when your older brother is a model in the industry?"

Will came in and rolled his eyes. "We've had the conversation, sis. And judging from your grades lately, there's no way Mum would let you come for a visit anyhow."

"What is it you wish to do with fashion?" It was in my blood to automatically ask this type of question.

Will flashed me a warning look that I didn't heed. If he wanted to talk to his sister about her grades or not visiting, fine, but I was a guest. That meant I got a free pass and didn't have to get into the heavy stuff with her.

"I want to design clothes. I sew all the time, putting together different fabrics and sketching outfits. Matter of fact, I made this." She ran her hands over her hip plaid jacket which she'd paired with leggings and Doc Martens boots to give off a cute punk meets classic lines style.

"Impressive."

She eyed my conservative jeans, boots, and cashmere sweater dubiously. "Yeah, well, most older people don't really get it."

Nothing like being called old and unfashionable by a teenage girl to make even the editor of a major fashion magazine humble. I couldn't help but laugh.

"To be fair, she thinks everyone over the age of twenty is old," Will said, coming back out from the bedroom where he'd dropped our bags. "And that was rude," he admonished his sister. "Believe me when I say if anyone gets it, it's Catherine."

"Sorry," she muttered, clearly embarrassed to have been called out in front of me.

"It's fine, really. Let me show you something you might like." I led her into the bedroom, taking in briefly the beautiful king-sized bed before setting the smaller of my two suitcases on top of it. When I unzipped it and flung it open, I had the satisfaction that I'd redeemed myself in her eyes when she gasped at the shoes inside.

"Are those with the red bottoms Louboutins?" She went to touch them but paused and glanced over as if to ask permission.

"Yes, indeed, and you can touch them. What size are you?"

"Size six." She frowned when she saw they were eights, but clearly admired the suede nude platform sandals nonetheless. "Are you rich?" She reached for the black Jimmy Choos, practically sighing with pleasure.

Will's voice came from the bedroom door where he leaned against the frame. "Really, Janet?"

She blushed. "Sorry, but these shoes are way expensive."

Will arched a brow, which conveyed a silent *you asked for this*, and backed out of the room.

"I do okay, but a lot of these were given to me by designers. I work at a fashion magazine."

Her eyes got big. "Which one?"

"Cosmopolitan Life."

"*The* Cosmo Life magazine?"

"That's the one."

She regarded me with a newfound appreciation. "Do they have internships there?"

I smiled and figured I'd be blunt. "They do, but they only accept the very best students."

"Did my brother put you up to this with the grades thing?" She eyed me skeptically.

"Nope. But if your goal is to get out of this town someday, the best way is to focus on school."

"All right. I get it. Can I see the rest of your clothes?"

How could I possibly say no to her request?

THE REST of the day went by quickly, with lunch and then driving to the next town over to see Will's brother, Thomas. The reunion between the siblings was touching to watch. When Will introduced me, I took Thomas's hand and answered his questions about how I liked Australia thus far.

Thomas was confined to a wheelchair and had a hard time with his speech, but was assisted by a computer that spoke for him. His blue eyes and dark hair were quite like his little brother's, as was the playful grin he'd sport when amused.

Will hadn't been kidding about the technology which allowed his brother an independent way of living. The impressive facility housed fifty residents with various needs and it was clear his brother was proud to have his own room, only using help when he needed it.

We met some of the staff while Thomas gave us a tour of the newest addition. This included a workout center, complete with a pool, and a team of physical therapists who worked with the patients daily to help with pain or physical limitations.

I wasn't surprised that Will was amazing, not only with his brother but also with the staff and other patients. He simply had a way with people. Didn't matter if they had a disability or not, he greeted everyone with a smile and an energy that was contagious.

After the tour, I wanted to give the brothers some privacy, so I said my goodbye to Thomas and then excused myself. I found a place to sit in the charming courtyard filled with flowers and benches. I could see now why Will was so adamant about keeping his brother here, but it was also evident that this didn't come cheap.

But the real reason I'd excused myself was because spending time with Will's siblings was only furthering an attachment to a man with whom I didn't have a future. Seeing him with his family and everyone here today only reaffirmed what an amazing guy he was. I was afraid I might already be in trouble when it came to wanting more than just the physical with him.

Hoping to distract myself, I checked emails, grateful to have an international phone so I could keep in touch with work. I thought it curious that I had a message from Colby Singer, Josh's younger brother. Even more interesting was the reason behind his email as it gave me an idea for putting Will's repayment of his medical expenses behind us once and for all.

He found me out on the bench almost an hour later and apologized. "Sorry, that took longer than intended."

I waved him off. "You should take all the time you'd like. I only wished to give you some privacy."

As we were about to walk to the car, one of the administrators caught up with us. He gave Will his card and told him the director would like to speak with him later this week.

"Everything okay with Thomas?" I asked once we were alone.

He put the card in his pocket. "Yeah, it's all good. They just want to talk to me about taking a job as a counselor. They spoke with me the last time I visited, too, but there's a new director who'd like to convince me. It's flattering, and I wouldn't mind working with people who have disabilities, but I can't see myself moving back to this small town."

I was relieved to hear it. Although he'd only been part of my world for a short time, I couldn't imagine him not in New York.

The return trip to the house was quiet. I imagined seeing his brother was emotional, to say the least. I took his hand, making him aware I was there if he wanted to talk but not peppering him with questions.

As we pulled up to the house, he turned toward me. "Thank you."

"For what?"

"For being so unbelievably genuine while you were there today. It's the first thing Thomas said to me. That you were sincerely happy to meet him, and then he told me you looked like Charlize Theron."

Ha, I wished. "Ah. He's charming, same as his brother, then. And I enjoyed meeting him." I hesitated, but thought it was worth saying. "I obviously don't know him like you do, but he seems happy there, Will."

He smiled. "He is. Tomorrow he'll come over to the house for the afternoon. The facility has a van service which can transport him, and it'll be nice for my mum to have all the kids under her roof."

WHEN WE SAT down for dinner that evening, I met Tim, Will's stepdad. He was tall and laid-back with an easy smile. He appeared to genuinely dote on his wife, which was sweet to see.

"Where's Janet?" Will inquired while helping his mom with the last of the platters filled with a delicious-smelling meal.

"She's been upstairs studying all afternoon. Janet, time for dinner," she called up the stairs.

She came down with exuberant energy and took her seat. "Looks good, Mum."

"What's inspired you all of the sudden?" her brother asked, passing around the chicken.

"Catherine told me about the internships at her magazine. And if I want a shot, I need to study more. By the way, would I get to go to a fashion show?" she questioned, glancing at me.

In fact, all eyes were on me, and Will's didn't appear too happy. "Uh, the interns often do get a chance to attend."

She practically squealed. The subject was forgotten when Will purposefully steered the conversation toward talk of Thomas, but there was no mistaking the set of his jaw. The subject of the internship and Janet wasn't sitting well with him.

Once we were alone in the car, I brought it up right away to clear the air. "Janet asked me if we had internships, and I took the opportunity to tell her only for those students who did well in school."

"I don't want her in New York," he said on a sigh.

"And what about what she wants?"

"She's fourteen and hasn't a clue what that is yet. Plus, she has the grand idea that I have some posh apartment in the city where she can sleep in the spare room while visiting."

And now his hesitation made more sense, given his current living situation. "We only accept college students, which means it would be years from now if she did come."

"Is there ever a time where you're not trying to get involved and do favors for people you just met?"

Ouch. And we'd come full circle to me paying for his medical expenses. I was torn between wanting to tell him to go to hell and my need to defend doing nice things for people. I decided I'd do neither and got out of the car, going directly into the cabin without waiting on him. I'd hardly stepped one foot inside before he pulled me into his arms.

"I'm sorry. That was uncalled for," he murmured into my hair before leaning back and meeting my eyes.

"I didn't say anything to her I wouldn't have said to any other young girl who loves fashion."

He swallowed hard. "I know. You're unbelievably generous, and I should be thanking you for motivating her instead of criticizing. So, thank you."

"You're pretty good with your apology, but it's still not addressing the real issue here."

He didn't bother to pretend he didn't know what I was talking about. "It bothers me to owe anyone, Cath."

"I may have an idea to remedy that. I received an email from Colby Singer earlier today. It was kind of strange, this coming from him, but anyhow, he's setting up a foundation for kids with cancer. He asked if I could possibly do a charity fashion show."

A smile stretched his face. "About time he did something to win the girl. So what's your idea?"

"That you model for the charity show and waive your fee. Maybe recruit some fellow models, too. Wait, what girl is Colby trying to win?"

"Kenzie. And that's something I'd donate my time to, anyhow. Plus, it's not paying *you* back."

"Yes, it is since I'd donate my own money to secure good models. Considering your asking price to do both a magazine spread and the show would be at least the amount owed, it works out. Hold up." What he'd said finally sank in. "Colby is in love with Brian's sister, Kenzie? But she's in love with—" I was about to say someone else, but now it clicked that I'd read it wrong in Vegas.

"Him. Always has been."

"Huh. I couldn't be more clueless about recognizing such

things. Seems I'm proven wrong yet again." I broke away and took a seat on one of the chairs to remove my boots.

He crossed toward me, taking my foot and unzipping the boot to remove it gently. One and then the other, he massaged my arches, which at this moment was not only a turn-on, but was absolutely sigh-worthy it felt so divine.

"The guy friend you told me about at Club T who you kissed and subsequently found out was in love with someone else— That was Josh, wasn't it?"

And just like that, my bubble of relaxation burst as I was reminded of something I'd confided to Calvin. I pulled my feet out of his grasp and sighed. "Way to ruin the moment."

He shrugged, unregretful about the subject change. "It's nothing to be embarrassed about. And if it makes you feel better, I kind of had a thing for Haylee for all of three seconds before I saw the way she and Josh were around one another."

"Yeah, but that's the difference. You saw it. I didn't. But then again, I didn't realize my own husband wanted out of the marriage until he told me he was leaving, either." I should dub myself: 'Clueless Catherine.'

He knelt down in front of me, placing his hands on either side of my face. "And you didn't see me kissing you in a muddy field in Sydney?"

His thumb caressed my lower lip before he dipped his head and kissed me softly.

"No, I didn't," I whispered.

"I think the lesson here is we always should be clear about what we're thinking, and right now I'm thinking it's time to cross another item off your list."

CHAPTER TWELVE

*S*imply put, I was in heaven. Will had drawn me a hot bubble bath in the gorgeous, claw-foot bathtub and was now stepping in behind me. The only downside was that I didn't get to feast my eyes on his delicious body by sitting in front of him, but there'd be plenty of time for that later.

The thing I was learning about the man was that he liked to vary the pace. One moment it was a frenzy, and the next he was taking his time. Although it would've been immensely satisfying to have him inside of me right now, there was something to be said for the unhurried way he went about foreplay.

"Penny for your thoughts." He soaped my shoulders and then reached around to cup my breasts.

"I was thinking you're very patient in your seduction."

"Mm. Is that what I'm doing? Seducing you?" His fingers trailed down my stomach, causing my breath to catch.

"If I'm misreading these signs, then I may need some serious help," I retorted dryly.

He chuckled. "I'd be happy to teach you. For example, if I were to reach down and touch you here—" His finger ghosted over my clit. "Then I think it's safe to say I'm seducing you."

"Oh, good. I got that one right, then." I arched my hips at his next touch.

With him behind me, he had absolutely full access to my body, a situation of which he was quickly taking advantage. "Are you wet for me?"

"I'm in the tub, so…."

He nipped my shoulder, a smile evident in his voice. "Smart arse."

I could feel him lean back, pulling me with him so I was practically lying on him.

"Open your legs for me."

I let my knees fall to the sides of the tub and then felt his fingers travel between my lips before settling once again on my clit.

"This kind of wet is definitely not from the water," he murmured while pinching one of my nipples and rubbing my clit at the same time. The two sensations caused me to suck in a breath and close my eyes.

"Tell me what inspired number seven on your fantasy list, to have someone talk dirty to you while you masturbated."

"Y-y-you did." Great, now I was stuttering.

"Me or Calvin?"

Was this a trick question? "Calvin, but your accent is even better." I'd thought his voice was made for phone sex from the moment I met him at the club, but add the Australian accent to it, and the level of heat went from hot to scorching.

"Mm, good answer. I want you to touch yourself, gorgeous."

The thing was I'd put that fantasy about phone sex on my list with the thought of doing so while traveling and away from my significant other. So Will wanting to do it in person was a lot more intimidating.

As if sensing my hesitation, he entwined his fingers with mine, moving them down to my heat. There he hooked a finger with two of his and put it up inside of me. "Feel how slick you are. This turns you on, doesn't it?"

I nodded mutely.

His breath came hot and husky in my ear. "Circle your clit, love. Yeah, just like that. God, do you have any idea how sexy you are like this? How much it turns me on watching you?"

The sound of his voice had me picking up the pace, searching for release as I felt his hands slide down my breasts, teasing the nipples, then smooth down to grip my hips.

"Do you feel how hard you make me?"

"Yes, and I want you inside of me." I tried to scoot back, wanting more, but he wasn't having it.

"Not yet. First you're going to come by your own hand."

"I don't know if I can." It had been a miracle to do it with the help of a device, but this I wasn't sure would happen even with his assistance.

"I know you can. Think of me sucking on your clit, licking down between your beautiful lips, then lower. Would you like that if I went lower?"

"Oh, God," I moaned, his words conjuring up such a dirty, delicious fantasy.

"That's it, Cath. You're close, beautiful."

I was beyond close, I was there, my orgasm taking me by surprise as it ripped through my body, causing my muscles to go taut and my hips to arch as I gave into the sensation.

My breathing was labored, and I practically purred when he whispered in my ear, "That was so fucking hot. I knew you could do it."

He suddenly stood up, the water sloshing over the side with the movement, and climbed out. But before disappointment could set in that he was leaving me, he pulled me up and helped me step out with him.

"Let's rinse, and don't be getting any ideas in the shower as I

163

have other plans." While evading my reach, he turned on the water.

"I don't think after our first time I'll be able to shower again without getting 'ideas.'"

His satisfied grin let me know how much he liked that thought. He made quick work out of rinsing us both and then took his time drying me from head to toe, kissing me along the way and in the process getting me completely worked up again.

At some point I realized that, although I was content with him leading this sexual progression, I was anxious to live out my earlier desire from the car ride.

"My turn to dry you."

I took the towel out of his hands and spent an absurd amount of time rubbing it over his chest and arms as an excuse to linger over his body. I then moved down, watching his hooded eyes track every move and go wide when I sank to my knees.

Wasting no time, I took hold of his hardened cock, never having wanted to go down on a man like I did in this moment. While sliding my hand down to his base, I mouthed the crown, enjoying his hiss of breath at the contact and licking the drop at the tip as I'd described in the car. As I ran my free hand up his strong thighs, I could feel his muscles quiver beneath my fingertips. This encouraged me in my ministrations to open my mouth fully so I could take him all the way in.

"Cath," he gasped, reaching down and running his hand through my hair and then pulling lightly as I started to bob up and down his shaft.

Hollowing my cheeks and pumping his length, I took him deeper, running my tongue up and down to supply more saliva. Pulling back a moment, I licked down further, lavishing attention on his balls. If his groans were any indication, he was enjoying this immensely. As I sucked them into my mouth, one by one, while I worked his length with my hand, I could feel his legs start to shake and knew he was close. Not wanting to miss a drop, I traded my hand for my mouth and swirled my tongue along the tip and underside.

"Fuuuuuuck," he whispered hoarsely, causing me to look up.

I wanted nothing more than to see him fall apart at my hand. The thought propelled me to increase the cadence and take him deeper into my throat. My eyes were starting to water, but I didn't care. I was lost in the giving of pleasure and his unfiltered response to it.

"I'm going to come," he ground out, giving me a warning that wasn't needed because I had no intention of denying myself the taste of him.

Instead, I made a moan of my own when I felt the first shot hit my tongue. The throbbing between my thighs had never been so intense. That's how much it turned me on to suck him dry and swallow every last drop, licking the tip for good measure.

He lifted me up and, much to my shock, met my mouth in the hottest kiss in the history of them. The taste evidently didn't bother him in the slightest, rather heightening the effect to beyond erotic when our tongues entwined. After walking me into the bedroom, he backed me up to the edge of the bed and pushed me lightly down onto the fluffy comforter.

He quickly grabbed a condom out of the outside pocket of his suitcase.

I watched with heavy eyes as he rolled it on while standing over me, hardly believing he was ready to go again as if I hadn't just made him come minutes ago.

"Get on all fours and play with your clit again," he instructed huskily and then watched me shift into position. "Do you have any idea how incredibly hot you are?"

"I didn't until you." No truer words had been spoken.

He moved behind me, but instead of feeling his hands, I was startled by the sensation of his tongue.

"I need a taste." Spreading my knees further, he didn't seem content with one and rubbed his tongue along the length of my slit, up and up, to exactly where he'd whispered in the tub.

I closed my eyes, giving myself over to the foreign sensation of first his tongue and then his finger, which trailed the wetness up to circle my back entrance.

"Of everything on your list, this is what I've been fantasizing about the most."

"I've never done that," I whispered, feeling an electric shock lance through me at the slight pressure of his finger coated in my arousal against the entrance.

"Me, neither, but I've always wanted to. Tonight, however, we'll just play."

He reached down, sweeping more wetness toward my rosette before pushing further with his finger at the same time he eased his cock into my pussy. The fullness coupled with the new sensation had me careening completely out of control. I was hardly able to support my own weight while an orgasm like nothing I'd ever felt before ripped through me. As the spasms overtook my body, I was aware of the slapping sounds of skin on skin and the feel of his one hand gripping my hip as he drove home, over and over. Then the sound of my name echoed around the room when he reached his own release with one last thrust.

SUNLIGHT STREAMED ACROSS THE BED, waking me from my coma-like sleep. Blinking, I let my eyes adjust to the light slowly before sitting up and taking a look around. Once again, I was naked in bed and Will was gone. But this time, instead of feeling weird about where we stood after amazing sex, I let the satisfaction from the previous night wash over me. Stretching like a cat, I wondered if I'd have time to do yoga today. I normally went three to four times a week and if I expected to keep up with a younger man, especially given the rate we'd been going, I might need to stay in shape.

Hearing the front door open, I pulled the sheet up to cover myself but then breathed a sigh of relief when I saw it was Will. He was dressed in athletic gear and, from the look of the sweat on his brow, had just completed a workout.

"I brought you coffee with one of your stevia packets from your purse, and a touch of cream."

It was exactly as I preferred it. "That's really sweet of you. Did you go to the gym?" I took the mug of java from his hands and took my first sip.

"There's no gym unless you travel twenty five minutes away, but I went for a run. Have to if I want to keep up with you."

"Ha, I was thinking the same thing when it comes to me keeping up with you, especially since you're in such amazing shape."

He leaned forward, peeking down my sheet. "Yeah? You like my body?"

"I'm not sure *like* is a strong enough word about how I feel about your body," I quipped and watched a slow smile spread across his face.

"How do you feel about joining it in the shower, then?" He stood up, lifting his sweatshirt over his head, showing off his delicious, glistening-with-sweat abs.

I flipped off the sheet and enjoyed the lust clouding his features when he took in my naked form. "What if I want your sweaty body on me here in the bed instead?"

He smirked. "You can't help but rhyme, can you?"

I shook my head laughing. I could definitely get used to this playful side of me which seemed to come out with Will. It was obvious it had its benefits when he pounced on top of me.

By the time we finally got around to showering and then hopped in the car to drive up to the house, I was absolutely famished. "We're not late for anything, are we?"

"No. My mum doesn't keep a schedule. Plus, I told her you were still sleeping."

"I feel bad having her do all the cooking."

He shook his head. "Good luck trying to get her to do anything else. She isn't happy unless she's feeding someone, I promise."

We walked in and, as predicted, Will's mom wouldn't hear of me helping out. Instead, she insisted I take a seat at the kitchen table.

"Would you care for some vegemite and toast?" Mary offered.

Not having a clue what she was asking, I looked at Will's smiling face.

"Mum, most Americans haven't heard of it, and the ones who have don't really enjoy the taste."

She directed her gaze on me. "What do you mean? You know the vegemite jingle, yeah?"

I shook my head, trying not to appear rude. "Sorry, no. I'm afraid I don't." Frankly, any food item which sounded like "termite" didn't exactly inspire me to chow down.

"We're happy little Vegemites, as bright as can be. We all enjoy our Vegemite for breakfast, lunch, and tea…" she prompted.

"No, sorry. But I'm happy to try anything. What's it made from?"

"Fermented yeast," Janet offered, scrunching up her nose with distaste.

"Don't let her put you off, Catherine, as she's the only Aussie for miles around who doesn't like it," Mary said.

"Then go ahead," Janet returned. "Let her smell it and take a big old spoonful and see."

"Nope, no smelling it, and you can't eat it alone. You wouldn't go putting a spoonful of ketchup in your mouth. Vegemite is meant to be spread on toast."

Okay, not being allowed to smell it wasn't a good sign. Coupled with the word "fermented," and I started to worry. When I saw the thick brown substance being slathered on toast, I looked toward Will, waiting for him to say "just kidding."

Instead, he only said, "Go light with it, Mum."

She smiled and put the slice on my plate. "I know she'll love it."

No pressure. I lifted it up to my mouth and watched Janet giggle. She apparently suspected something amusing was about to happen.

"Don't put it too close to your nose," she warned.

I took a bite and chewed slowly, taken aback with the salty, almost meaty taste. For some reason, it reminded me of beer, maybe because of the yeast. "Um, it's not terrible," I offered and reached for my coffee to wash it down. Oh, no, the coffee was a mistake. The sweetness and creamer did not mix well with the strong taste of the toast.

Will chuckled. "Probably should've warned you about that combo with the sugar. You want some water?"

I stood up from the table, trying not to lick my napkin like a little kid in order to get the taste off my tongue. I managed a nod and took the water gratefully.

"Who is *why the hell is he calling me now*?" Janet questioned, glancing at the phone I'd placed on the table, which was now vibrating.

Will rolled his eyes. "Catherine's ex-husband again. I thought you told him you were out of the country."

I couldn't answer right away because I was too focused on the way Will's mother's face soured. I'm sure she was none too happy to have her twenty-something-year-old son involved with a *divorced* thirty-something-year-old woman whose stupid ex-husband still called her.

"Yes, I did." I walked over and grabbed the phone, silencing it and then ate some plain toast, anxious for breakfast to be over.

. ***

After our meal and helping with the dishes, Janet coerced me into taking her into town to the local fabric shop. I was thankful for something to get out of the house after the awkwardness of the morning. Later I'd need to bite the bullet and return Michael's call, when I would give him a piece of my mind. He clearly wasn't getting it. For now, though, I was too pissed at his stupid timing to deal with it.

Will tossed me his rental keys and quipped, "Remember, drive right, stay left."

I wasn't so confident about this whole driving on the right of the car and the left of the road. We were about to leave when I realized I'd forgotten my coffee and ran back inside to grab my travel mug.

As I walked into the kitchen, I came smack into the scene of Will's mother yelling at him. She appeared very upset.

"I don't want one dime from him, Will. Ever. He doesn't bother to acknowledge his oldest son, and now I have the other one suggesting that he help pay for his care. Honestly, if you really loved your brother, you'd tell your father to piss off and never speak to him again."

Both turned to see me, frozen with a big deer-in-headlights look on my face.

"Sorry, I forgot this—" I grabbed the mug. "—and, um, we'll be back later."

I flicked a quick glance at Will and was out the door in a shot. Once in the car, I sighed deeply and put it into reverse, self-ishly thankful that at least she hadn't been reading him the riot act about me.

"Everything okay?" Janet asked, studying me.

"Yeah, fine. Sorry, I was just thinking about work."

"You're a terrible liar."

She grinned and then so did I. At fourteen, she was annoyingly perceptive. "So I've heard. The truth is that I walked in on your brother and your mom discussing something personal that I probably shouldn't have overheard."

She didn't seem surprised. "So what if you're divorced and older? As I told my mum, it's none of our business who Will dates or if you have money. It's not like you're old enough to be a cougar. Plus, I think you're cool."

That was a lot to process, especially since it wasn't the topic I'd walked in on. Undoubtedly, my suitability had been discussed at some point after breakfast, most likely when I'd used the restroom. Out of the mouths of babes. I gave her a small smile. "Thanks, Janet."

"At least they're not fighting about Will's dad this time. Will left early on his last visit because of it."

My father wouldn't even hear of letting me pay for a meal in a restaurant. So the fact that Will's mother would rather have her son than Thomas' biological father pay for his considerable care didn't sit well. This was especially unsettling for me since it was such a heavy burden for Will to shoulder. However, I told myself it was none of my business. After all, I was merely the temporary, divorced, not-quite-a-cougar in Will's life.

By the time Janet and I returned from the fabric store with a few new pieces that had the young girl excited, Thomas had arrived, and the house was full of laughter and food. Whatever argument had been fought earlier between mother and son seemed to take a backseat to the pleasure of having everyone here now. I was grateful Will was the type of guy to let it roll off of him and not affect his mood.

Of course, that meant I needed to do the same. What did I care if Will's mom liked me or not? Not only was I past the point in my life of trying to please parents, but also, frankly, I'd probably never see her again. Yet the reminder that I was only temporary was depressing.

Later that evening as I stood in the cabin bathroom, removing my makeup, I could feel Will's gaze on me. Turning, I saw him leaned up against the door jamb, shirtless. That picture alone was enough to distract me from anything negative.

"Don't stop on my account. I find it fascinating to watch you."

He stepped behind me, meeting my eyes in the mirror and smiling before leaning down, where he swept my hair to the side and kissed the back of my neck.

A shiver ran through me with the heat of such a simple gesture. "Today was nice with your brother here."

"It was, and I think it made my mom really happy. Look, about the argument you walked in on earlier with my mum and I..." He seemed tense, almost like he was bracing himself for the conversation.

"I'm sorry I barged in on such a personal discussion. If you don't wish to talk about it, it's okay; I won't take offense."

"It's not much of a discussion when only one person is doing the yelling. More like venting her frustration, I suppose." He paused as if he'd revealed too much. "But no, I don't want to talk about it."

It had been a long time since his parents' divorce and thus surprising that his mother was still so angry, but if he didn't wish to get into it, then I needed to respect that. "Okay, then we won't." Deciding to lighten things up, I quipped, "So do you honestly enjoy the fermented veggie stuff?"

His fingers tickled my sides, causing me to laugh. "Vegemite. And it's a comfort thing, I suppose. Eating it on toast reminds me of when I was young. When my dad moved us to the States, it was a bit of a culture shock at first with so many changes."

And because he had opened the door, I decided to tiptoe through it. "Did you like living in California with him?"

"For the most part. Played soccer, as you yanks call it, and surfed. My dad started a business, so he worked a lot, but he always made sure he came to my games. I also had a good group of mates."

"What made you decide to move back and go to college in Sydney?"

"It allowed me to be closer to Thomas and help out when I could on university breaks. Then, once I signed with the modelling agency, I moved to New York, and the rest you know."

"I take it your mom resents your father for taking you away?"

He nodded. "I think she could've gotten over him forgetting about her. But that he didn't have anything to do with Thomas is something she can't forgive. She hates that I maintain a relationship with him and balancing the two of them is sometimes hard."

I turned around to touch his shoulder, now understanding more about what drove him in wanting to support his brother and take the burden off his mother. "That would be rough. Do you think your father would help out if you asked?"

He shrugged. "Maybe, but it would send my mom off the deep end. So much for not talking about it, eh?"

I smiled, happy he felt comfortable enough to do so. I kept to myself the thought that Will was working himself to the bone to try to spare his mother's feelings and his father's responsibility.

He met my gaze and stroked my cheek. "So, do you want to discuss what Janet thinks you overheard? She spilled the beans when you got back."

Ah, the divorced cougar comment she'd thought I'd walked in on. "Not really. It's no big deal, and I can do a lot worse than being called a cougar." It was a reminder that Will and I couldn't be in more different places in our lives.

"I believe the proper term would be puma. You're not old enough to be a cougar."

"Well, that's good to know. But I feel like either one may be an invitation to scratch the hell out of your shoulders tonight."

He grinned, pushing his hips against mine and leaning me back onto the shelf vanity. "In other words, you're ready to change the subject."

I nodded, throwing my arms around his neck. "I think we both are."

WILL'S voice permeated my dream until I realized he was actually speaking to me. "Wake up, beautiful."

I opened an eye and realized he was standing next to the bed, fully clothed. Glancing toward the window, I saw it still appeared dark. The two facts combined weren't computing, especially since I was currently naked under the blankets. "Why are you up?"

"We have plans."

"What time is it?" My brain wasn't yet firing on all cylinders, and my body was protesting the thought of getting out of a warm bed.

"Early, and although it's tempting to join you again under those blankets, we have a drive, so we need to get moving."

"Mm. To do what?"

"It's a surprise. Wear your workout gear."

"Do I have a few minutes for a shower?"

He grinned. "Only if you hurry. Come on."

By the time I was dressed and in the car, I'd begun to wake up and the sun had started to rise. Will had been thoughtful enough to pack both protein bars and my precious coffee, prepared just the way I liked it. "No hints?" I prompted.

He shook his head. "Not even one. Now tell me, were you a wait patiently to see what Santa brought you as a kid, or did you snoop for your gifts?"

"Neither. I didn't trust that Santa wouldn't get me something silly, given how my mother thinks. The fact I clued in that he wasn't real by the time I was six meant I had a list prepared by the end of October with several price points so my mother could give ideas to my grandparents and anyone else who might ask. I shudder to think what level I would've taken it to if I'd had Pinterest available at the time."

Glancing over, he chuckled. "That's adorable."

Now it was my turn to laugh. "You're crazy to think so, but how about you?"

"Snooping is what ruined Santa when I was eight because I found a toy under my parents' bed and when the same toy was under the tree on Christmas morning, it let me know the truth. The lesson was: unless you want to ruin the fantasy, don't go looking for a reason to do so."

Although there appeared to be no intent to place a double meaning in his words, I thought of the applicability toward our situation. I hoped I could keep myself from overthinking things and thus popping this virtual bubble we'd created.

As we pulled into a dirt parking lot, I wondered if we were going on a hike. But then I caught sight of some people on a bridge and, more shocking, one diving off. Oh, my God. My wide eyes met Will's twinkling ones. "We're bungee jumping?"

He leaned in and kissed my shocked face. "I'm showing diversity by crossing off things on your nonsexual list, too. Let's go have some fun."

"PUT ON A DRESS and some comfortable shoes for dancing. I'm taking you out on a date."

Will announced this once he'd returned from spending the afternoon with his brother. After my morning high from the adrenaline rush of diving off a bridge, I'd come back, napped, and then caught up with some work. I couldn't remember the last time I'd taken a nap: of course the long sexy shower which had resulted in two orgasms might have had something to do with it.

"Really?"

He waggled his eyebrows. "Yes. And if you play your cards right, you might get lucky tonight, too."

I laughed, enjoying the novelty of it. For the first time in forever, I was going out on a date without stressing about what to say, how to act, or how it would end.

Our evening started with a romantic dinner in town where we both enjoyed beers and steak while weaving between small talk and more personal things.

After the meal, Will took my hand and led me two doors down to an upscale bar with a band. It felt natural to be in his arms on the dance floor where he held me close and we swayed to the slow song. It felt the same way when he put his hand on the small of my back while ordering drinks at the bar. He leaned in and whispered the things he couldn't wait to do to me later this evening.

Even as his words left me breathless, a kernel of fear set in. I couldn't remember ever having so much fun as I'd had today with any other man, either in and out of the bedroom. So, what would happen once I tried to return to the real world of dating? I had already been disappointed when the expectations had been low, but now that the bar had been set sky high with a guy like Will who was the total package, panic was starting to bloom, despite my best efforts to damp it down.

He paid the bill at the bar just the same as he had at dinner, obviously not entertaining the idea of my doing so. Then he wove his fingers with mine and walked me out to the car. The sound of my cell phone broke through on the way, and while I was content to ignore it, my date wasn't.

"Is that your ex-husband again?"

I shrugged, taking the phone out of my clutch and showing him it was, indeed.

"I could nip this right now. Do you mind if I take it?" He held out his hand for my phone.

Huh. I was fascinated to see what he'd have to say, so I held it out for him and watched.

"Catherine's phone," he answered. "I'm sorry, but she can't talk at the moment as she's in the shower."

I quirked a brow, enjoying his passive-aggressive attempt to make my ex aware he was interrupting.

He stopped and listened a moment. "Yes, I know who you are, but the question is why do you keep calling your ex-wife when she's made it clear she's on vacation and doesn't wish to speak with you?"

Add this to the list of items that surprised me about a man Will's age as he had no qualms about taking charge of a situation. I watched his eyes flick to mine while he listened to whatever explanation Michael had.

"I see. I'm sorry for your loss. Hold one moment." He sighed deeply and handed over the phone, mouthing the words, "His mother died."

Oh, shit. "Hello," I answered and then listened to Michael break down about the unexpected death of his mom a couple of days ago.

Will opened my door and sat patiently while I apologized with my eyes for the unplanned conversation, but I knew he understood. He rubbed my back while I tried to pay attention to the details Michael was telling me.

"The wake is on Friday evening and the funeral on Saturday morning at Saint Marks. She'd want you there."

My mother-in-law and always been kind to me even if we'd never had the closest of relationships. But, selfishly, the first thing that came to mind was that I'd have to return to the church in which I'd married where I'd have to see all of my ex-relatives and my ex-husband's new pregnant fiancée. But then when I looked over at Will and felt my heart in my throat from the feelings I'd already developed for him, I realized this was my out. I had better grab it like a lifeline before I got in in any deeper.

"I'm in Australia, but I'll try to get a flight out tomorrow."

He sighed. "Okay, good. Um, who was answering your phone?"

"We're not talking about that. I'm truly sorry for your loss, Michael and I'll see you Saturday."

After saying goodbye and hanging up the phone, I sat there in the passenger seat, absorbing the news that his mother had died from a heart attack after a brief hospitalization. She'd only been in her late fifties. And here I'd been dodging his calls, irritated with his intrusion while he'd been losing his mother. Will's voice broke my thoughts.

"Don't go feeling guilty, love. You couldn't have known. He could've told you in a text or voicemail, and you would've contacted him sooner. And I wouldn't have been a dick on the phone to a guy who'd just lost his mum."

I met his eyes and took his offered hand. "You didn't know, either, and I was appreciating the whole knight-in-shining-armor thing up until he broke the news. Thank you for being so understanding."

He started up the car. "You're traveling back for the funeral, I take it?"

"It's the respectful thing to do. I need to find a flight for tomorrow."

He sighed. "If the funeral is Saturday, then you could leave on Friday. The time difference works in your favor on the return trip."

I glanced over, feeling like a chicken about my impending white lie. "I may try to go to the wake, too. She was my family at one time, and I don't want to take any chances on a delayed flight."

He started up the car, and we drove in silence. Once we arrived, I moved quickly inside. "I'm going to call my travel agent and then pack." I flitted around the room, gathering my things, only to have him tug on my hand.

"What if I go with you? That way you aren't alone seeing your ex and his family."

It was incredibly considerate for Will to suggest this and not at all surprising since he was such a caring guy. Unfortunately, his offer only drove home my fear that I was already too late to prevent myself from falling for him. "I appreciate the gesture, but you should stay and spend time with your family. Besides, it's probably better I go home and get a jump start on all I need to get done in preparation for Fashion Week."

He studied me for a minute as though he could see through my bullshit. Then he kissed my cheek. "Okay. Whatever you want."

CHAPTER THIRTEEN

J arrived ten minutes before the funeral service for Michael's mother and took a seat in the rear of the beautiful cathedral. I'd chosen not to attend the wake yesterday evening simply because it would've been too much of a hassle to go straight from the airport. Plus, one ex-family event was enough to pay my respects.

My last evening with Will had been bittersweet. We'd spent the night in each other's arms and hadn't spoken of when we might see one another again. Although I'd panicked, running as fast as I could from Australia, now that I was back in New York and off vacation, I knew reality would inevitably change our dynamic. Hopefully that would allow me to put things firmly back into the casual bucket and not leave me with the same emotional risk.

Surveying the hundreds of people sitting in front of me in the pews, I wasn't surprised to see the great number in attendance. Michael's mother had been heavily involved in the church and various charities throughout the years. What was shocking was to see my mom and dad walk in and take a seat next to me. My mother answered my unasked question.

"Michael let us know about his mom and that you'd be coming for the funeral, so we thought we'd come to pay our respects and be here for you."

Parents of the year, right here, I tell you. Their presence and unwavering support meant the world to me.

Michael's eyes met mine when I went up for communion, but I had no intention of staying to speak with him or anyone else. This was a day for family. So when the service ended, I slipped out the back door with my parents. But he must've made a beeline for me the moment they announced refreshments would be served next door because there he was hurrying down the front steps of the church after us.

"Catherine, hold up."

He caught up to me as I was texting Sherman to bring the car around. My mom said some comforting words to him and gave him a hug. My father did the same before Michael turned to me.

My parents stepped away to afford us some privacy.

"It was a beautiful service, Michael," I murmured and was then startled when he engulfed me in a lingering hug. Then again, he'd just lost his mother, so I returned the embrace. In his moment of grief, he probably needed support from everyone.

"I'm so glad you came. It would've made her happy." When he pulled away, I could see the unshed tears in his eyes.

"Your mother was always kind to me." And she had been.

"Why don't you stay for a while? After refreshments in the church hall, we're having family and friends over to my father's home if you guys want to come."

Uh. Awkward. "Thank you, but I think it would be better if it's only your family." I didn't say it with any bitterness; it was the truth. We weren't part of that family any longer, and our presence didn't seem appropriate.

He sighed. "All right. So, maybe I could call you later this week?"

"I'll be busy prepping for Fashion Week and all the shows

coming up. Oh, I think someone's looking for you." I saw a pretty girl coming down the steps and assumed she was his fiancée although I'd never met her in person.

"Brittany, I told you to wait inside," he snapped impatiently.

I don't know who was more shocked by his sharp tone: her or me.

"I, oh—okay." She turned around with her head down and retreated up the stairs and into the church.

"I'll let you get back," I murmured, not liking the way he'd spoken to her. But now wasn't the time to judge him for it considering he'd just lost his mother. Frankly, it wasn't any of my business.

"I have time." He dragged a hand through his hair, almost appearing nervous.

What in the hell was going on with him? Thank goodness for my mother cuing in on the discomfort and helping me navigate out of it. "Actually, we have plans, Michael. But please give our respects to your father and the rest of your family. Again, we're very sorry for your loss."

Luckily, Sherman had pulled up, and my dad was opening the car door for us to get in.

Once the door closed, my mom sighed. "Good grief. I know you probably don't want to hear this, Cathy, but I can't believe he spoke to his fiancée in that manner. In all the years you were married, I never heard him use that sort of tone toward you."

No, I hadn't either, but to be fair, I didn't know the man who once was my husband any longer.

"Give him a break, Liz. He's grieving. Besides, it's no longer Cathy's problem." My father focused his attention on me. "How you holding up, kiddo?"

I gave them a soft smile. "Okay. Thank you both for coming."

"Of course we'd be here for you. It's very sad. She was the same age as me." My mom exhaled heavily before looking at me curiously. "Now then, would this impromptu trip to Australia you flew in from have anything to do with the extremely hot British guy?"

I rolled my eyes, aware my mother had only started with the twenty questions. "He's Australian, and we're only friends." As the words left my mouth, I wondered if I was trying to convince my mom or myself.

NEW YORK FASHION WEEK was in full swing. Although I looked forward to it every year, it came with the price of a grueling schedule of events. This involved multiple daily wardrobe changes and social engagements, including the gala my magazine was hosting tonight at the Westin Hotel. I glanced around the beautiful ballroom, recognizing quite a few faces, from both the magazine and the designers in town for the week.

As far as I knew, I was the youngest major fashion magazine editor in the business today. But what I didn't have in experience, I made up for in my people skills. These last couple of days presented a prime example. In my opinion, sitting at the shows for this annual event, mingling with the workers, and networking with the designers, most of whom were the who's who in the fashion world, was what had catapulted me to the top. I didn't take any details for granted, from remembering names to taking the time to thank people for their hard work.

I'd seen Will briefly on the runway yesterday, and the sight of him had propelled my heart up into my throat. I doubt he'd noticed me considering he'd had to maintain a thousand-yard stare while walking, but the sight of him had made me realize how much he'd been on my mind over the last week.

Checking my phone for the millionth time, I promised myself that I wouldn't be the first one to send a text. We'd both had a busy few days with little time for anything outside of work-related tasks, but this was only an excuse. The real reason I hadn't texted him was because I didn't trust my words wouldn't reflect how terribly I'd missed him since leaving him in Australia. Talking with him, sleeping with him, and being with him, period. It was a confirmation of my epic fail in the attempt to keep things casual.

Moving around the room, I mingled among the growing crowd for an hour before gratefully taking a glass of champagne and sipping it out on the balcony. The fresh air was a welcome respite, if only for a minute, before I needed to get back in there.

"Hiya Cath," came the low voice from behind me, instantly recognizable from his accent.

Once I turned, setting my gaze on him, I had to restrain myself from physically touching him because the urge was so strong. "Hi, Will." He was dressed in a tuxedo, and I found myself breathing in the scent of him, wanting to get closer.

"You look beautiful. I thought red was your color, but the blue really brings out your eyes," he complimented.

"Thank you. You, too. I mean, not beautiful, but handsome. I saw your show yesterday. You did a great job." Awesome, I was talking in short, silly sentences as if I'd never spoken with a member of the opposite sex before.

He smiled with humor in his eyes at my lousy attempt at conversation. "Thanks. I have to say I prefer magazine shoots over runways, but it was still a good experience."

"I'm sure you'll get quite a few bookings after this week."

"Yeah, luckily I already have. So, how's your week been?"

Terrible because I've missed you. "Busy, but good. Yours?"

"Same. Uh, do you—?"

He was cut off when a German designer by the name of Claus von Loch came up to greet me. "Catherine Davenport. I swear you get more stunning every time I see you, darling." I turned toward him and he made a show out of kissing both of my cheeks dramatically.

"Claus, how nice to see you. This is—" As soon as I turned, I realized Will had excused himself quietly and quickly. I tried to ignore the pang of longing I felt with his absence. "Sorry. I'd thought to introduce you to Will MacPherson. He was in the Calvin Klein show yesterday."

"Ah, yes, the Australian with those stunning blue eyes."

I wanted to gush and give him a recommendation. Getting signed by Claus would be a huge paycheck for Will, but knowing how sensitive he would be to a *favor*, especially now that we'd slept together, I chose to keep my mouth shut and leave it alone.

Three glasses of champagne and two hours later, I was heading into the home stretch of the party and spending way too much time scanning the crowd for Will's face. That's when I saw a beautiful redhead cozied up to him. She looked like she was a model, too, and whatever he was saying to her was making her laugh.

When his cool gaze met mine, I could feel my face flood with hot embarrassment that I'd been caught staring. Swallowing hard, I purposefully walked toward the other end of the room so I wouldn't be tempted to torture myself further by gawking.

And this, in a nutshell, was why I couldn't do casual. He was free to sleep with her or anyone else, for that matter. It should've been my wake-up call, for if it stung now, it would only get worse if we continued sleeping together. But then his text message came in.

"Meet me on the second floor by the Mayfair Conference Room in 5 min."

Well, that was unexpected. With butterflies in my stomach, I tried to appear nonchalant while strolling to the elevator, but then decided the stairs would be easier. Considering most of the guests had rooms in the hotel, it wouldn't be out of character for me to be heading to mine if I'd booked one.

After stepping onto the second landing, I followed the sign

for the Mayfair. As I came around the corner, I felt a hand grab my arm and tug me into a nearby room.

"It's me."

Will's voice relaxed me immediately as he closed the door. "You startled me. Where are we?"

It looked to be a large storage closet stacked with chairs and folded-up tables. The only light came from Will's illuminated phone.

"Storage closet. Sorry about that."

"It's okay. Did you need to speak with me about something?"

"I'd rather not talk." He put a hand behind my neck; the other gripped my ass, pressing me against him. "How long before you have to return to the party?" He kissed behind my ear, on a quest for the sensitive spot he knew drove me crazy.

"A few minutes. Why, do you have something in mind?" I was unable to deny myself this moment with him, despite my earlier thoughts about this making things harder in the long run.

When he tucked his phone in his pocket, the small space was plunged completely into darkness. He turned me around and put my hands on the wall and then skimmed down my bare arms with his fingertips. "Yes, I have number twenty-two on your list in mind."

"I can't remember which fantasy that was," I whispered, feeling his hands traveling up the outside of my thighs, taking the material of my dress with them to bunch around my hips. The sensation of his fingers working my thong down came next. He made short work out of helping me step out of it entirely.

"It's the one where you said you'd like the thrill of potentially getting caught. It's making you wet to think about it, isn't it?" His fingers reached around and slid directly into my heat.

"Yes," I murmured, having missed the feel of him. I protested with a whimper when he removed his hand.

"Give me a second, love," he whispered.

I heard the sound of his belt, the rustle of clothing, and the distinct sound of the foil packet. The sensation of having my lower half exposed like this inside of a closet one floor above my magazine's party was feeding both a sense of fear and adrenaline. But once he touched me again, I couldn't think of either as I became so lost in the sensation.

"Keep your arms up, palms on the wall. I'm going to fuck you hard and fast while you try to remain quiet, and then I'm keeping your panties while you go back downstairs to your fancy party."

Was it possible to orgasm with words alone? Because when he entered me on one stroke, crowding my body closer to the wall and lifting me up with every thrust, I was already close. No warm-up, no slow teasing, just him burying himself deep. "Yes, oh God, yes." The darkness was only heightening my senses, with every touch feeling electric. The heavy sounds of our breathing provided the erotic soundtrack to the primal way he was taking me against the wall, unapologetic in our coupling.

"Come for me," he demanded, cuing into the fact that I was on the edge and triggering my orgasm. His followed shortly after.

We stayed like that for a couple of minutes, him deep inside of me, both of us trying to steady ourselves before we moved.

I winced as I felt him pull out, already missing the fullness of him inside of me. When I turned around, his hands lingered while they straightened my dress before tending to himself.

He took out his phone, illuminating it just enough that we could see one another again. "I've thought about you all week long, wanting to contact you and find out how you were doing after the funeral."

"Why didn't you?"

He chuckled. "Because you practically bolted from Australia, using the phone call from your ex as an excuse."

That might be the truth, but I certainly didn't like him noticing my panic. "I needed to go to the funeral."

He tucked my thong into his pocket, and my eyes went wide. He was serious about not giving it back. "Are you really keeping my panties?"

"Absolutely. Maybe I need a souvenir since you seem to be in a hurry to escape."

"It's hardly escaping when I have a party I need to return to." I hated my defensive tone.

"Talk to me, Cath." His hand stroked down my face.

"It's not you. It's me."

He broke out into a smile. "Eliza Winters said the same thing to me in the fourth grade when she dumped me on the playground."

Being compared to a fourth-grade girl in this situation wasn't helping my self-esteem. "I'm sorry, but you, of all people, know how badly I suck at this part."

"Which part?"

The part where I was already at risk of falling for him. "I need to go." I squeezed past him into the hallway, grateful there wasn't anyone around.

He tugged on my wrist. "I'm a grown man. You don't need to let me down easy. Like I said in Australia, you're in the driver's seat. But don't make me guess. Just be honest."

I sighed, deciding perhaps the best method of self-preservation was to put it all out there, after all. Once he heard I couldn't do casual, the Band-Aid would be ripped off, and he'd run far, far away. "Okay. How's this for honestly. I'm getting way too attached to you considering we'd only agreed on fun and casual."

His eyes widened in disbelief. Before he could say anything, I decided to get the rest out. "I know there are some women who can do casual sex, but I'm not programmed that way. Just seeing you downstairs with that redhead made me crazy with realizing I have no claim over you, no expectations that we're exclusive. I have no regrets whatsoever. Matter of fact, thanks to you, I've learned a great deal about myself in the last few weeks. But I need to be honest."

He started to speak. "Cath, I—"

We both jumped when a woman's voice called out. She approached us, dressed up and looking familiar with her long blond hair and big brown eyes. "Excuse me, Catherine?"

Recognition dawned as she walked closer. It was Michael's fiancée, Brittany. Will must have sensed my shock because he stood close to me.

"Yes, and you're Brittany? Michael's fiancée?" I added the last part for Will's benefit.

She appeared nervous. "I am, or at least I was." And just like that, her face crumpled and she burst into big fat, ugly tears.

Will and I shared a 'holy shit' look before he stepped forward, taking charge of the situation in his compassionate, effortless way.

"Deep breaths, Brittany." His voice was soothing as he tried to comfort her.

She took one and then apologized profusely. "I'm so sorry. I went by your office today to talk to you because I wasn't sure who else to speak to. They told me you were at Fashion Week, but then I read that your magazine was having a party in this hotel, so I thought I'd come here. I followed you upstairs thinking maybe you were in the restroom, but I couldn't find you. And now here you are, and I realize this was a big mistake."

"No, it's okay. But why did you want to see me, of all people?" That was the million-dollar question.

She sniffed. "Michael is having a midlife crisis or something. He doesn't want our baby now." This statement launched a fresh wave of tears, which were morphing quickly into full-on sobs.

And yet still she hadn't answered the question. But what struck me the most about this bizarre situation was that I experienced no satisfaction in her distress. Not that I was the type to relish someone else's misfortune, but even I wasn't above hoping my ex-husband's newfound happiness would crash and burn—as if this would prove that he'd made a mistake in leaving me. But in this moment, all I could feel was gratitude that this wasn't my life.

Will took her arm. "Don't cry; it's not good for the baby." He turned toward me. "Cath, why don't you return to your party, and I can speak with Brittany here. And we'll talk later." His eyes made a point with his last sentence before he surveyed the space. He seemed to be scouting out the best place to move the overly emotional woman.

I felt terrible for putting this burden on Will and was growing more and more pissed off that my ex-husband had once again caused me drama at the expense of his very pregnant and emotional fiancée. Wondering if I'd regret it later, I made a quick decision. "What if I have Sherman come around, and you can talk in the back of the car? Give me twenty minutes to say good night to everyone, and then I can join you."

He arched a brow. "Are you sure?"

I mouthed, 'Are you?' I was grateful when he nodded. "Okay, let me text him, and he'll be out front shortly."

I RETURNED DOWNSTAIRS, distracted by the situation that I'd just had sex in a closet, blurted out my feelings to Will, was wearing no underwear, and now had my ex-husband's pregnant, emotionally distraught fiancée in my car with the guy who had my thong in his pocket and was probably thinking about all the ways he could let me down easy. How was that for an evening so far?

As I said goodnight to my guests, I contemplated whether or not to call Michael, but opted to speak with Brittany first.

Will got out of the car as I approached and then closed the door to speak with me privately on the sidewalk.

"I'm so sorry and owe you big time," I started out saying, but he only shook his head.

"You have nothing to apologize for, but your ex sure does. She's calmed down, but the CliffsNotes version is he's been treating her like shit since the funeral and staying out late. He missed the baby checkup today which is what set her over the edge. He also accused her of trapping him."

"That's ridiculous. He'd already proposed to her before she got pregnant. Where is she staying?"

"With a friend for now. What do you want to do?"

"I'll talk to her. Thanks again. You definitely have a knack for doing this for a living someday."

His baby blue eyes didn't waver. "I'm staying with you."

"Look, if you think I'll kick her when she's down—"

"Of course I don't. But I want to be there for you. Okay?"

I let out a breath, not knowing what I'd done to deserve someone like him coming into my life, but very grateful for his presence. Giving him an appreciative smile, I nodded. "All right."

Brittany seemed incredibly young and sad when I slid into the back seat. "I feel so horrible about this, especially if I interrupted your party."

I handed her a tissue out of my clutch as more tears tracked down her face. "It was already winding down. Are you doing okay?"

She went on to tell me much the same story Will had recapped for me a few minutes ago. At the end of it, I still felt no joy in her misery. But I also didn't know why she'd come to see me, of all people. I wasn't uncaring, but the man she was engaged to was my *ex*-husband. For the first time since the divorce, I could honestly say I was ready to put him completely in the rearview mirror.

I chose my words carefully. "I'm terribly sorry that you're going through this, Brittany, but I'm not sure what it is I can do."

She sniffed. "I don't know. I thought maybe you'd have some advice. If maybe he'd ever flaked out with you like this?"

Will's eyes met mine, and I knew what he was thinking. Yep, he definitely had. But when he'd freaked out with me, he'd told me he was leaving and wanted a divorce. However, sharing my marital and subsequent divorce history with an emotional, pregnant woman wasn't going to do her any good. Maybe the thought of becoming a father, regardless of with whom, was a freak-out point for him.

"If I were to guess, losing his mother has a lot to do with what's happening right now. As for advice, the most important thing you need to do is take care of yourself and your baby. Can we drop you off at your friend's house?"

She nodded. "I guess so."

"What about your parents?"

"If I told my father about the way Michael has been acting, he'd never forgive him, and I really do want to work things out."

I sighed, deciding to give her the best counsel that I'd once followed. "Brittany, I don't know you or your family, but let them be there for you. You don't have to tell them anything other than that Michael is going through a difficult time with the loss of his mother and that you need to give him some space to be alone with his grief."

"I know you're right. They live in Queens, so maybe I'll catch a taxi and go home to them instead. The bed is sure a lot more comfortable there than with my friend."

"My driver can take you."

"Oh, no, I couldn't," she protested.

"I'd feel better if you'd let him."

"I'll ride with you since I live in Queens, too," Will offered.

I should've been relieved by the respite from our earlier awkward conversation. And I should've been more grateful that he was offering to see Brittany home. But instead I was left on the curb, feeling both unsettled and emotional as I watched the

man I'd confessed I had feelings for accompany home the
fiancée of the man I no longer did.

AFTER TAKING A TAXI HOME, I stripped out of my beautiful gown
and, on a whim, took my engagement and wedding rings out of
my drawer, setting the opened box which held both on my nightstand. I had no clue why I'd hung onto them longer than my
wedding photos, but for some reason, tomorrow didn't seem
soon enough to ban them from my life forever. First thing in the
morning, I was calling about an auction house and then donating
the money I received to charity. It seemed only right.

Feeling good about taking that step tomorrow, I climbed into
a warm bath. The only thing missing was a glass of wine. But
considering the headache I was already nursing from the
evening, not to mention the few glasses of champagne I'd
already consumed at the party, I opted for water and two Motrin
instead.

Although I wasn't happy with the way the evening had gone,
I was proud of myself for having the guts to tell Will how I was
feeling. The very last thing I wanted to do was avoid questioning
the elephant in the room for fear that he'd get up and leave. I'd
come too far in my emotional awareness to go back now.
Becoming attached to someone as quickly as I had become to
him wasn't something I'd planned on. However, now that I was
aware of my tendency to become so easily involved emotionally,
I would be better prepared for the future.

Hearing my phone ring where it sat on the bathroom vanity, I
ignored it. But whoever was calling wasn't giving up because it
started to ring again. Stepping out of the tub, I steeled myself for
talking to my ex, but I saw Will's number instead.

"Hello."

"Hiya. Can you call down for your doorman to let me up?"

My heartbeat shifted into overdrive. "You're downstairs?"

"About two minutes away."

"Uh—okay. I'll call down."

"Good. See you in a couple minutes."

Once I rang the front desk, I threw on a nightshirt, panties, and donned my long robe, pulling it tight. I wasn't sure what he had to say, but I certainly wasn't going to dress up to get the 'I hope we can still be friends' speech.

Hearing the knock on the door, I took a deep breath and promised myself that whatever happened, one, I would be okay, and two, I wouldn't cry. At least not until later when I could do so in my bed alone.

I pulled open the door, but instead of being greeted with what I assumed would be an awkward-looking Will trying to figure out how to let me down easy, he stepped inside, reached for me instantly, and shut the door with a kick of his foot. He hauled me flush up against him with his free hand. I vaguely registered him dropping his duffle bag with his other hand before it gripped my ass. Then he backed me up to the edge of my sofa.

His fingers tangled in my hair while his mouth descended and his tongue found mine, coaxing it out and sending heat straight through me. My hands trailed down his muscled back, grabbing his waist and pulling him further into the apex of my thighs. I was hungry for the feel of him despite the inevitable emotional fallout. His grunt of pleasure only fueled me to move faster before my brain caught up and potentially overruled my body. But he beat me to it by pulling away slightly, putting his forehead to mine so we were eye to eye, both of us panting to catch our breath.

"I'm attached to you, too, Cath."

CHAPTER FOURTEEN

*M*y response was a moan when he reached under my nightgown and a finger hooked into my lacy thong and swept it aside. He slid a finger, then two inside of me. I clenched my inner muscles, hardly believing my impending orgasm was upon me so quickly. When his thumb pressed on my clit, it sent me over the edge, incoherent words spilling from my lips.

Wasting no time, his hands tore at my robe and nightgown, taking them both off within seconds and pulling down my thong to leave me completely bare to him. His lust-filled gaze tracked up my body as he ran a palm between my breasts and over my stomach. Bending down to my breast, he circled his tongue around my sensitive nipple, bringing it to a peak before switching to the other.

I swore I could come again with the sensation on my breasts alone, but he wasn't done with his magic fingers, slipping two inside of me again and curling them up to demand another orgasm in that fashion. Only this time, I wasn't content for him to do all the touching.

Reaching out, I cupped his bulge through his slacks and then fumbled for the zipper, finally freeing him to lie heavily in my hand. His groan spurred me on to wrap my fingers around him. As I stroked back and forth, I could feel him grow harder.

His lips traveled up, fingers grasping my hair and exposing my neck to his tongue and teeth nipping my skin. Then his hot mouth was on mine, his tongue delving inside with the most seductive kiss I'd ever experienced. He swallowed my cry of release as it ripped through me.

Taking my hand, he tugged me down the hallway toward my room, shedding his shoes along the way and attacking his clothes as if he couldn't get naked fast enough. "Get on the bed, gorgeous."

I lay on my back in the center of the sheets, propping up on my elbows to watch him crawl up the length of me. His hot skin coming into contact with mine lanced a shiver through my entire body.

He produced a condom from somewhere, ripping open the foil packet with his teeth and rolling it over his cock with his eyes never leaving mine. Aligning his tip to my opening, he sank into me slowly, as if he was savoring every inch. His hips rolled into mine, setting off a new spark of sensation, curling my toes with the magnitude.

"Oh, God, Will," I whimpered, grabbing his ass and arching up to meet his thrusts, never having felt so unbelievably possessed. It was almost too much—this raw physical coupling.

"I'm right there with you," he groaned into my mouth as if confirming he was feeling the overwhelming connection, too.

His kiss turned wilder now as did his thrusts, and we both clawed at one another until he pinned my hips to the bed and buried himself to the hilt, rotating his pelvis to hit a spot that took me over the edge and owned me completely. I felt his entire body stiffen as he growled my name and emptied himself inside of me.

I WAS unable to sleep even into the wee hours of the morning and lay with my head on his chest, his hands splayed on my back to hold me close. My body was sated. My mind, on the other hand, was not as fortunate as I wondered what this new development would mean.

"Are you making a mental list of why or why not we should keep doing this?" Will whispered in the dark.

Propping myself up on my elbow so I could see his face, I trailed my fingertips down his bicep. "I'm resisting the urge because this feels too good to stop. How was Brittany when you dropped her off?"

His smirk and arch of the brow came instantly. "Nice change of subject."

"It's my specialty if you haven't noticed. I think it's probably better than, the 'where does this leave us' talk."

"I meant what I said about being attached to you, too."

I wasn't sure what that exactly meant, but wanted to clarify one point. "If we're both attached, does that mean there won't be any other attachments to anybody else?"

"I would've thought that'd be a given, but if you want it spelled out, you're not sleeping with anyone but me."

His possessive words surprised me. "Uh, and what about you?" Considering he was the one with more of an opportunity, I thought it an important question.

"There's no one but you, Cath." As if to prove the point, he rolled me onto my back, sealing it with a kiss.

"Did we just agree to be exclusive?"

"My little alpha way of phrasing that fact wasn't clear?" he teased.

A giggle escaped my lips. "It was kind of unexpected for sure."

He laughed. "Hm, I was shooting for hot. The answer is yes,

and maybe I need to work more on my caveman approach." He moved us both so we were on our sides, legs tangled up in one another.

"You're still young, so you have time to perfect it. And considering before you came along, my life was boring— Ow," I squeaked when the flat of his hand spanked my ass, loud and firm. "What was that for?"

"I've decided in the interest of improving my alpha male behavior which, admit it, we both know turns you on, and the fact that I'm vehemently opposed to you calling yourself boring, that whenever you say the word *boring* from now on, I'm going to smack you on the arse."

Now I was in a full on giggles, and he was making it impossible to stop by tickling my sides, now straddling my legs and looming over me. "I dare you to say the word again."

"Boring," I breathed, quite excited for the consequences.

"Something tells me you're not at all intimidated by your punishment," he chuckled, turning me over on my stomach and moving down my body before sinking his teeth playfully into the muscle of my backside, then sucking hard.

"What are you doing?" I squirmed, feeling his mouth leave me and two hands massage my cheeks.

"Since you seem to think I'm so young, I thought I'd demonstrate a lack of maturity by giving you a hickey on your arse."

We both started laughing, but then I sighed in pleasure when his hands moved up and started massaging my shoulders. "Point taken. And the only problem I have with your age is that it reminds me of mine. I'm turning thirty-five soon."

"Better to be thirty-five and look like you're in your twenties than the opposite."

"Your charm is undermining your alpha goals, but I'll take it. So now that we've established exclusivity by you marking my ass, do you think it's safe to say we're playing the rest by ear?"

"Are you comfortable with doing that? At least for now?"

He was sincere in his question and not mocking my tendency to desire things tied up in a package with a bow. Although I'd love a guarantee, there simply weren't any. Not when you said *I do*, not when you thought you were trying for a baby with your husband, and certainly not when you were still getting to know someone. But what I did have was something I absolutely wanted to explore further.

"Yes."

He nuzzled the back of my neck. "And if you start to feel like you might not be, will you talk to me about it instead of making assumptions again?"

"I think I can do that."

"And as far as the matchmaker is concerned—"

I flipped over and held a finger to his lips. "Unless the last half of that sentence is something along the lines of telling Melanie no more matches, don't finish that sentiment."

His smile could've lit up a room before he kissed me thoroughly. "So no more lessons?"

I shook my head. "Now, that would be a shame. We'll just have to find other topics for you to teach me."

"Oh, I can think of a few." He chuckled, pinning me to the bed and kissing me thoroughly before snuggling me into him, spooning me from behind.

"Not to change the subject back to the subject that I wanted to change it to earlier, but did Brittany seem better after the car ride home?"

"Definitely. Telling her to go see her family was the right call."

"Good."

"How are you with having to deal with her tonight, with the whole, you know...?"

"Pregnancy thing," I finished for him. "Surprisingly fine. I feel bad for her, but I didn't get any satisfaction over her misery. If anything, I'm sympathetic, yet at the same time grateful I'm not in that life expecting a baby with him. Although the divorce was brutal, it would've been way worse to share a child and custody."

"Very true. By the way, I gave Brittany my number. That way, if she feels compelled to talk to you again, she can go through me instead of showing up at your office or at another party."

"I don't want it to become your burden, but you're a complete saint for doing that." To be honest, I wasn't sure I liked her having his number at all. But I reminded myself it was in Will's nature to be helpful, and I did, in fact, trust him.

"I think that title probably belongs to you. I don't know many women who would've been so kind to their ex-husband's new pregnant fiancée after she ambushed them at a party."

"Yeah, well, let's hope in this case a good deed can actually go unpunished."

THANKFULLY, my first fashion show wasn't until one o'clock, which allowed me to sleep in. Considering the last time I'd glanced at my bedside clock it had been after three am, I easily snoozed until ten. As I got up, I wondered where Will was and if I would ever wake up with him in a bed. Yawning, I pulled on a robe, liking the way the silk felt against my bare skin, and puttered down the hall. I smelled something good coming from the kitchen.

Seeing him standing at my stove shirtless, with only flannel bottoms slung low on his hips, stole my breath. I wasn't sure what was sexier, the way he looked or the way he was effortlessly flipping an omelet in my kitchen. When he turned to notice me standing there staring, the playful grin he gave me would've melted my panties if I'd been wearing any.

"Hope you don't mind me making breakfast."

It took me a moment to recover from his delicious accent topping the erotic sensory overload that was Will MacPherson.

"Uh, no, I'm impressed."

And because I had free license, I stepped behind him, putting my arms around his waist from the back, splaying my hands on his chest and kissing his golden skin.

"Mm, I'll make you breakfast every morning for a greeting like this." With a flick, he turned off the stove, slid the omelet onto a plate to the side, and turned around, suddenly slanting his lips over mine. His hands slid beneath my robe and froze. "Oh, I'm liking this. A lot."

He lifted me up and set me on the granite island, opening my robe and running a hand down my body straight to my heat. Laying me down gently on the cool stone, he lavished attention on each of my breasts with his tongue before spreading my legs wide and diving into my pussy.

"Ahh, Will, I haven't showered." My mild protest was more of a disclaimer because there was no way I actually wanted him to stop.

"As if I care. You taste amazing, and I can't get enough of you," he mumbled against my cleft. Inserting two fingers, he curled them up to the right spot while running his tongue down the length of my slit.

Once he fasted onto my clit, I detonated, barely aware that instead of easing his attention, he was increasing the pressure. "I can't," I moaned. It was too much, I was too sensitive, and yet he moved his fingers and tongue faster, sending me careening out of control with a second orgasm roaring through my body.

I lay there coming down off my high and only mildly conscious that Will had stepped away and was now back between my legs, pulling me closer to the edge before sliding into me. I tried to sit up, but he wasn't having it.

"No, like this with your sexy body on display." His hands

lifted my hips to meet his thrusts, angling me so that a third orgasm was already brewing.

I wasn't sure my body could survive it, but if I had to pick a way to go, this would be a good one. And the look of pure pleasure on Will's face when he hit his own climax made it all worth it.

He helped me up, kissing me deeply before disposing of the condom and washing his hands.

"Kitchen counter sex wasn't on my list, but it should've been." Of course the OCD in me had the bottle of cleaner out scrubbing the surface as I said it.

He leaned over, giving me another peck before making me a fresh omelet and reheating his. "What's with the rings in the open box on your nightstand?"

I'd completely forgotten I'd left them there last night. "My wedding and engagement rings. I took them out of my jewelry box last night with the intention of calling someone today about either auctioning them or consigning them."

He dished up our plates, and we both sat down on stools at the kitchen island to eat.

"Closure?" he asked softly, his eyes meeting mine.

"Long overdue, especially considering I never really cared for the engagement ring, truth be told."

"It wasn't big enough?" He teased, knowing full well since the box had open that the engagement ring was obnoxiously large.

"Six carats, so no, it wasn't the size that was the problem."

"What was?"

"I felt like I was wearing his ego on my finger. He'd brag about how it was Neil Lane and ensure I showed everyone— almost as if it was more about what he could afford than the sentiment behind it. I would've preferred a band with a sweet inscription rather than the largest diamond."

I thought it interesting, the difference between ego and pride.

Will had pride when it came to accepting a handout, but Michael had an ego when it came to how much money he made and the way that would make people view him. It only highlighted the fact that it came down to the man, not the job, paycheck, or age.

Will looked contemplative. "Yet you listed you want a man who makes more money than you."

Had I? "I believe I said financially independent. My hope was to find someone who isn't competitive about my salary or who wouldn't just want me for my money."

"How's your omelet?" Now it was his turn to change the subject.

"Really good." And it was. Fluffy, with the right amount of cheese. "All I can seem to manage is to scramble them."

"When you eat two dozen eggs a week, you get creative."

It was clear he worked for his body, but I realized I hadn't a clue about his diet or routine. "What else do you eat?"

"Protein bars or shakes through the day, a veggie and chicken typically for dinner. But by Friday night, I'm typically bad with pizza."

"Any chance you want to be bad together tonight?" The moment the words left my mouth, I blushed at the assumption he'd wish to see me again so soon. We might be playing things by ear, but that didn't mean all of a sudden we'd start spending every minute together.

Will only grinned. "It's a date, but I have to work first. I can bring pizza by afterward, but it'll be past midnight."

Right, he had his job. At the sex club. Although I hated him working where he was talking to other women about sex, I absolutely respected that he did so in order to pay for his brother's medical needs. "Sure. I'll put you on the front desk's list so you can come right up."

He got up to clear the dishes, but I beat him to it. "You cooked. I'll clean, and I may need to stock up on breakfast fixings for tomorrow. My culinary efforts are quite boring compared to—" I screeched when his palm smacked my backside and realized I'd said the B word.

He chuckled, rubbing the spot with the offending hand and pulling me toward him. "Something tells me I'm gonna enjoy this bit of fun. How much time do you have for a shower?"

My hands roamed down his back and shoulders, exploring his defined muscles before I trailed kisses down his neck, the dishes long forgotten. "Plenty."

As he took my hand, my intercom buzzed from downstairs.

I pulled away reluctantly, pressing the button. "Yes."

"Michael St. Clair is here for you Ms. Davenport."

Will arched a brow while I shook my head.

"Told you. No good deed... Shit."

"I can go if you want to speak with him in private. Or stay."

"Why should you have to leave when it's him who's intruding?" I pressed the button, determined to get this disaster over with once and for all. "Send him up." But then I realized I was still naked under my robe.

Will chuckled. "You go get dressed, and I'll let him in."

Now it was my turn to arch a brow. "Well, that ought to make quite the statement."

He grinned. "I'll even put on a shirt as not to make it sting quite so much."

I DRESSED QUICKLY. By the time I walked out to the living room, Michael was standing by the door while Will was in the kitchen scrubbing dishes. He threw me a wink over his shoulder.

"Michael, your unexpected visits are growing tiresome. What do you need?"

My unusual, less-than-cordial greeting took him off guard, and he glanced in the direction of Will. "Sorry to have interrupted you, but you're the one butting in where you're not welcome by driving Brittany to her parents' home last night."

I held up a hand, feeling the sum effect of the last two years bubbling up. I'd been gracious, I'd been fair, and most of all, I'd always remained polite. But no longer. "Your fiancée took a page out of your book and decided to crash my party yesterday evening. I made sure she made it somewhere safe for the night, not liking that she was so upset and knowing she's pregnant. So if you aren't here to thank me for it, then get the hell out."

His eyes widened.

Although I didn't look at Will, I could feel him silently cheering me on.

"I'm sorry. She's just so damn sensitive at the moment with the pregnancy hormones and I'm—"

"No, no, no." I shook my head, feeling de ja vu all over again where he took ownership of nothing.

"What?"

"I said no. I'm not listening to this. I'm your EX-wife. And do you know what benefit that affords me? It gives me the right to tell you I don't have to listen to you absolve yourself of a mess you helped create. Your fiancée is pregnant with your child and crying her eyes out, so your selfish excuses are bullshit. It's not her being overly sensitive, it's you being insensitive."

"I thought that you, in particular, would understand."

"Believe me when I say I do. I understand that in the ten years we were together, I've never heard you speak to me the way you did to her on the church steps after the funeral. That despite how shitty your timing was for calling an end to our marriage, I couldn't ever truly call you an asshole. But the man I'm looking at right now is exactly that. Hell, you stalked me, then dragged me in to get an annulment weeks ago because you wanted to hurry up and get a ring on her finger, and now you're saying she trapped you. Grow the fuck up, Michael."

"That's rich coming from you with your boy toy in your kitchen."

Oh, no, he didn't. "First of all, you don't come into my home and insult my guests. And secondly, Will has more class, more maturity, and more integrity than you've ever shown. And the fact that you stand there insulting him says way more about your character than his. You're going to be a father, so whatever is happening with you, I suggest you get it together. Because, like this, you aren't the man I once respected or someone your mother would be proud of."

If it hadn't been true, it might've sounded like a low blow, but I knew it resonated when tears sprang to his eyes. "I—shit— I'm sorry. I don't know what to do now. I screwed up, and it might be too late."

Finally, I stole a look at Will, who was sliding a mug of coffee over the kitchen island toward my ex. "Here. Start with some coffee, yeah?"

If ever there was a measure of a real man, Will was it. Watching him extend an olive branch to someone who'd not two minutes ago insulted him was something to behold. I realized in that moment none of the criteria I'd thought I wanted in a mate could hold a candle to those held by the man who was standing in my kitchen.

I watched Michael hesitate only a moment before taking the offered cup.

"I'm sorry." Michael moved closer, extending his hand over the countertop.

Will took it. "Apology accepted."

Next, Michael turned toward me. "This was all done in really poor taste, and you're right. I should've thanked you for last night. I need to man up and not only be a father, but also figure out how to make amends with Brittany. But I can't marry her properly until after the baby gets here."

I wasn't sure where all this advice was coming from, but

apparently I'd tapped a well of wisdom. "Then take her to a courthouse or a beach or Vegas and marry her improperly. You can marry her a second time once the annulment comes through, but do something to show her that you want to be with her and that you're committed to starting this family together."

Will handed me a cup of coffee with an approving smile. Although Michael was going through a personal crisis at the moment, the very real fact remained that he was cutting into my shower time with Will. As though he could read my thoughts, the object of them smirked.

We were both brought out of the moment when Michael took a seat on my kitchen stool, clearly seeking counsel, oblivious to his interruption.

"You think? You think we should go elope?"

Yes, like right this very minute.

Thankfully, Will was a bit more diplomatic than my thoughts had been. "Yes, and maybe get the nursery ready, buy some baby clothes and surprise her. Something that makes her believe you're excited for this baby."

The sound of a cell phone came from the bedroom, and Will excused himself to go answer it, evidently recognizing the ringtone.

"You've changed," Michael commented, looking at me strangely once Will left the room.

"I'll take that as a compliment." And I did. I'd always been able to go after what I desired within my career, unapologetically, with a combination of determination and hard work. But with my marriage, I'd been content to act as little more than a spectator. Now, I was no longer content to let life pass me by. Instead, I wanted to be in the driver's seat and put my own personal happiness as a priority.

"It was. I just never pictured you so, I don't know…"

"Blunt?"

"I was going to say confident."

In other words, not boring. My lips curved into a smile. "Confidently chewing you out?"

He shrugged. "It was deserved and probably long overdue. I thought maybe—after my mom was in the hospital that I'd call you, and you'd come and be there. You were always so good at stuff like that, and I found myself needing you. That's why I kept calling."

Ah, yes, the safe-in-a-crash Volvo edition I used to be. "You only felt that way because you were reaching out for what was comfortable in a time of crisis."

"Is that what we were?" His brown eyes looked sincere with the question, and I didn't hesitate with the answer.

"Yes. Comfortable, but not really happy. Not toward the end, anyhow."

He sighed, clearly knowing I was right. In fact, he'd had the guts to see it before I had. And maybe that truth had been harder to face than him actually leaving.

"You seem happy now?"

"I am." I turned, watching one of the reasons come down the hall with his bag over his shoulder and his shoes on.

Will turned toward me. "Sorry, I have to go, but I'll see you later tonight with a pizza, yeah?"

"Sounds good."

Having my ex sit there watching us made our goodbye awkward. It pissed me off, but obviously Will didn't care. He cupped my face and leaned down for a lingering kiss, not at all concerned about our audience.

He turned and offered his hand one last time to Michael. "Good luck to you."

"Thank you and again, sorry for earlier."

"Water under the bridge," Will said before walking out of my condo.

Iт тоок another ten minutes to get Michael out of my home, but not before I made him promise not to show up unexpectedly at my door, at a party, or to cause his fiancée to do the same. I felt good about closing that chapter of my life. Finally.

The last two fashion shows and subsequent party made the remainder of the day go by quickly. But once I'd returned to my apartment, time ticked by slowly. I finally decided to crawl into bed and save some energy for Will's arrival and woke to the sound of knocking.

Not bothering to throw on a robe, I answered the door in my silk nightie and enjoyed the way Will's tired face lit up when his gaze landed on me.

In addition to a duffle bag, he was carrying a pizza box. Judging from the smell, it was freshly made.

He shut the door behind him, flipped the lock, and set the box on the counter before tugging me down the hallway toward my bedroom.

"What about your pizza?"

He glanced back, giving me an incredulous look. "The day I pick food over sex with you, you're welcome to kick my arse."

Ah, one more reason I was quickly becoming a fan of men in their twenties.

It was almost two o'clock in the morning before he brought a now-cold pepperoni pizza to bed, unapologetic in scarfing it down while naked. "Want a piece?"

I shook my head, barely able to keep my eyes open after two orgasms. I felt as though every part of my body, even my mind, was completely contented at the moment.

"Sorry I had to leave when I did earlier, but the call was from my agent about a gig in Miami in a few weeks. Did Michael stay long after?"

"No, thankfully. And I hopefully made it clear that I'm done with impromptu visits, phone calls, or interventions."

He chuckled. "You were something today."

"Mm, something good or bad?"

"Something amazing. At the risk of sounding condescending, I'm proud of you. Did it feel good?"

"Thanks. I think closure always does. Although two years ago it sucked going through a divorce, now I know it's better for the both of us."

He swallowed hard. "Uh, what you said about him not being half the man that I was, it meant a lot."

"I meant every word. Michael was always so jealous of any success I had and never truly supportive. Clearly, he's also still struggling with the thought of responsibility."

"He should've been proud instead of competitive. No one who loves you the way you deserve should ever ask you to diminish yourself so they can shine brighter."

If I wasn't already falling hard and fast for this man, I would be now with that statement. "Your maturity and class are definitely well beyond your years."

He trailed his hands down my arm. "So, I take it you're a fan of being with a younger man now?"

I grinned, liking the way we were able to remain playful even after serious conversation. "For more than one reason."

He slid a hand up my thigh. "How about I give you a couple more?"

OVER THE NEXT FEW WEEKS, Will and I continued the pattern of spending our weekends together, starting with him standing outside of my door after midnight on Friday with a pizza in his hand and not eating it until much later when it was cold.

This weekend, however, was the first time we'd be attending a party together with our mutual friends. It was an event up in Connecticut for Colby's charity foundation to raise money for kids with cancer and would consist of a cocktail party on one evening and a luncheon the next day. Although I would've been okay in telling people about our relationship, I didn't know if he felt the same.

Considering today was Friday and I'd see him tonight, I figured it might be a good time to discuss it.

I was sitting at my desk at work when Erin patched Claus von Loch through. I picked up the phone immediately. "Claus, how are you?"

"Fantastic, darling, but I need a favor. Do you remember the Australian from your party last month, uh, William something? Modelled for Calvin Klein."

Talk about a loaded question. My heart beat faster simply from the sound of his name dropping from my lips. "Will MacPherson. Yes, I remember."

"Good. I may be looking to sign a fresh face, and I heard you've worked with him before. Can you recommend him?"

I hesitated briefly, knowing this was tricky territory, and proceeded with the safest possible answer. "Of course. He was on my cover. But I'll tell you up front I'm biased because he's a friend of a friend, which is how I found him. So for an impartial recommendation, you should contact Bart Chesley. He's worked with Will a number of times."

"You're always so diplomatic, my dear. I'll give Bart a call, then. But if he still works with young William, that in and of itself earns him an audition."

Bart was a very exclusive photographer who only worked with people who were professional. Simply put, he didn't allow or entertain bad behavior. His endorsement would go a long way.

"I look forward to seeing you in Milan in February then, my dear."

"Yes. I can't wait. See you then." I hung up, feeling good about the way I'd navigated that situation without overstepping and causing Will to freak out because I'd done him a favor.

I arrived home later that night after my regular Friday night yoga class. There I showered and packed my suitcase for the weekend up in Connecticut, checking things off a list, of course. I wished Will and I were traveling up together, but he wouldn't be able to leave until after his shift at Club T tomorrow night.

Ugh. I hated the reminder of that place. Not because I had anything against it. Obviously, that would've been hypocritical as I'd gone there as a client myself, but because the thought of him talking to other women about sex made me uneasy. God only knew the types of conversations he had, ranging from women like me who were trying to find their confidence to very adventurous types telling him their ultimate fantasies without reservation.

Although I absolutely had no complaints about our sex life—considering I'd had more and better in the last few weeks than I'd had—well ever—I did feel an urge to be more adventurous. Maybe more Kat-like by taking charge for once. The thought gave me an idea of a way to greet him when I opened my front door this evening. Maybe in nothing at all.

An hour later, I'd put the finishing touches on my bedroom, having set out candles and massage oil for Will's surprise, when his text message came in. Checking the time, I realized he was about to start his shift. He'd probably already scarfed down dinner and done his laundry, his typical routine for Fridays.

"I have an audition with Claus von Loch tomorrow."

I was about to type congratulations when his next message came in.

"But you probably already knew that considering he mentioned he spoke with you today. I'm not sure what part of 'I don't want any favors' wasn't clear. I'll take a raincheck on tonight."

I sat there for a moment, staring at my phone in disbelief. I immediately dialed to speak to him, but after one ring, he sent it to voicemail.

I started to type out a text message to explain but then erased it, pissed off that I had to defend myself in the first place. Why should I feel guilty when I'd told Claus to speak with Bart for an unbiased opinion? Plus, even if I had gotten involved directly, reputation and who you knew was a vital part of this business. For example, if I hadn't been doing Haylee a favor years ago, I wouldn't have interviewed Will and landed him on the cover of Cosmo Life, which in turn had got Calvin Klein to sign him.

If he wasn't coming over tonight, that meant I wouldn't see him until tomorrow night at the party. And then what? Hope we could hash it out over a weekend amongst friends? Ugh. And of course, as fate would have it, he was flying out from there to Miami for a week-long shoot.

I wasn't much on arguing, period, but I especially hated a disagreement via text. In my opinion, this was nothing but a way of miscommunicating your feelings while misinterpreting what was said in return. No, thanks. This discussion needed to be face to face.

After pacing for an eternity, I pulled out the magic eight ball from my bedside drawer. I'd known from the first night I'd gone to Club T that they rented rooms by the hour for couples since Brian had surprised Sasha there. If I got a room, not only would it allow me to apologize in person, but it could also fulfill my desire to become more adventurous when it came to sex. The thought of him sneaking into my room and me taking charge gave me confidence in my decision, but because I was a big ole chicken, I consulted the ball.

"Should I go to Club Travesty tonight?"

'My reply is no'

Stupid ball. Wasn't it aware I just needed it to agree with me and override my rational thoughts? I shook it again. It took three times, but I finally got the answer I'd wanted. *'Yes'*.

CHAPTER FIFTEEN

*I*t seemed strange to return to Club Travesty after all these weeks considering so much had happened between the first time I'd met Calvin and now.

When I arrived this time, instead of being greeted by my concierge as in my previous visits, I was ushered to another part of the club. This was more like a hotel check-in where they handed me a key. I guess this was the difference between renting a room and paying for any type of service. As part of the package, I was offered a choice of goodie bags. Thinking it a sign regarding my earlier thoughts, I bought the *Takin' it up a Notch* bag. Honestly, I wasn't sure what it entailed, but it certainly sounded interesting. Of course, I had to remind myself that my first priority was to speak to Will about the model shoot and Claus. Then after….well, maybe we'd be taking it up a notch.

Rolling my eyes at myself, or at Kat, if you will—unfortunately my only way into the private club had been to use my previous alias—I smoothed my wig and was shown to the room I'd rented for the next few hours. Oh, God. That thought alone left an anxious feeling in my stomach.

I, Catherine Davenport, queen of all things proper, who'd

never done anything remotely scandalous, had rented a room by the hour. Insanity had to be the reason I was suddenly in a fit of giggles when the door closed and I surveyed the small room. Either that or I'd experienced a surge in sexual confidence attributable to a certain gorgeous Aussie.

For a sex room or, as they officially called it, 'a couple's suite,' it was classy, with a lush carpet and hues of purple and black. The chandelier with dim lighting in the middle of the room hung over the centerpiece, a small bed. I stepped closer with my heart racing. The bed was essentially more of a table, with various types of restraints on either end as well as the sides.

Checking my watch, I sighed at the fact it would be at least two hours before Will finished with his last appointment and would be able to join me. I'd arrived early to make sure he'd receive the text in plenty of time. I could only imagine his face when he read that I was here in room two-nineteen waiting.

I crossed over to the small table next to the bed and bit my lip as I studied the things included in the goodie basket. Evidently, the 'taking it up a notch' staples included a blindfold, a couple different battery-operated devices, and two bottles of what I guessed was lube. The one with the strawberries on it caught my interest first. I wondered if it smelled or tasted like the berry, or maybe both.

Knowing I had plenty of time to find out, I slid my thumb under the seal and tried to uncap the bottle, but it wasn't budging. As I attempted to add more force, the sound of the door shutting behind me made me jump, resulting in me squeezing the tube too hard and squirting strawberry-smelling lube all over the front of my black Zac Posen dress.

Absolutely freaking perfect.

Turning, I put a hand to my chest and saw that it was Will, or Calvin, since he had his mask on. "Holy crap, you scared me. I thought you weren't off for another couple of hours, and I was positive I'd locked the door." I removed my hand, now coated in the same lube which was sliding down the length of my dress and glopping onto the floor.

Will crossed the room, taking in the scene with a heavy dose of bewilderment bordering on amusement when he realized what I was covered in. "I have a master key and one client cancel. What the hell happened?"

He handed me a towel, which I used to get the goop off of my hands and dress the best I could. "Would you believe I was attacked by a bottle of strawberry lube?"

I'd thought it was funny, but Will didn't even crack a smile.

"I'll finish cleaning it up, but you need to go."

My eyes went wide at his abrupt dismissal, not believing I'd heard him correctly. "You mean, leave?"

"Yes. Look, I don't have time to explain it, but you can't be here. I can't believe you'd waste your money like this."

Was that why he was so upset? "I wanted to clear up the misunderstanding about Claus, and since you wouldn't accept my call—"

"You paid cash, right?"

"Yes, of course. I want to start by explaining the Claus phone call—"

"We can talk about it later." I could see his patience running thin. Agitation was practically rolling off of him in waves as he took my arm and led me to the door. "I just need you to go home. Right now. Got it?"

I bristled at his tone. "You're spelling it out pretty clearly, so yes, I have it."

And with all the dignity I could muster, smelling like the strawberry lubricant still spotting my dress, I turned on my heel and did the walk of rejection all the way out the back door to where Sherman was mercifully parked curbside.

WILL TEXTED me within minutes of my getting into the car.

"I'll come by later and we'll talk. Okay?"

"Please don't," I responded.

With the one-hundred-eighty degree turn he'd given me, I remained in shock, unable to process any emotion. I'd thought it might be a fun surprise and a nice way of making up after I explained his assumption had been wrong. But evidently, he was still angry and not even willing to listen to what I had to say. It wasn't like going to the club tonight had been a comfortable gesture on my part. I'd done it because I'd wanted to ensure we didn't go into the weekend with unresolved issues. Plus, I'd wanted to maybe show him I wasn't afraid to try new things. A fat lot of good that had done me.

After saying goodnight to Sherman and ripping off my mask and wig, I went up to my condo and promptly threw both items in the trash. Never again would I return to Club T. I slipped off my shoes and then my dress, putting some stain remover on the latter in hopes the spots would come out.

Note to self: do an article in a future edition of my magazine on the best stain removers for everything, including lube. Glad something could come out of this night that was useful.

Heaving a big sigh, I glanced at my phone where I saw no reply from Will, not that I'd expected one. I then climbed into bed, not bothering to remove the red lingerie I'd worn under my dress or put away the candles I'd set out earlier. What I needed was a reset button for tomorrow. The best way to get there was to fall asleep and be done with today.

I was woken from a deep sleep by a knocking on my door which was getting increasingly louder and my cell phone buzzing. Glancing at the clock, I noted that it was well after midnight. I went to the door without bothering to put on a robe. When I peered out the peephole, I saw Will standing there with a damn pizza. Opening it a couple inches, I decided to be candid.

"I'm really not in the mood to speak with you this late."

"Open up, Cath," he beseeched, looking tired.

"Go home, Will. The last thing I need is you here feeling guilty."

"What did I tell you about making assumptions?"

I quirked a brow. "I can't remember since you can't seem to follow your own advice."

He had the decency to blush. "I know, and I'm sorry. Now, can you please let me in so I'm not forced to eat this pizza in your hallway with your neighbors eavesdropping on my apology?"

I could picture him doing exactly that, so I swung the door open, letting him pass by.

His eyes did a slow perusal of my red lingerie and, by the time they reached mine, were full of heat.

"I'm going to throw on a robe." I only got one step before he snagged my hand, set the pizza on the counter and pulled me to him.

He breathed in my scent, skimming his hands down my back. "I'm so sorry about tonight, and there's a lot I need to say to you, but for the moment, I just want to hold you."

My entire body released the tension I'd been carrying, and I wrapped around him, needing to be held. We stood like that for a few minutes. Instead of the anxiousness I'd normally feel to rush into talking, explaining, or sharing my side with him, I was content to simply stand there in the moment.

"Come on. Let's talk." He led me down the hall and quickly stripped down to his boxers in my bedroom. He then sat on the bed and patted the space beside him where I ended up taking a seat.

"Are you purposefully trying to distract me by being half naked?" Because a magnificent distraction it was.

He chuckled, giving me another once-over. "It's only fair, considering what you're wearing." He leaned in and cupped my face. "I should've asked instead of jumping to conclusions about Claus when he'd said he'd spoken to you about me."

"I did speak with him. He called me in the office, and we have a longstanding professional relationship. But when he asked about you, I told him I was biased because you were a friend of a friend and referred him to talk to Bart Chesley. I knew you wouldn't appreciate me telling him he'd be crazy not to sign you. I'd hoped to explain that to you in person tonight instead of waiting into the weekend when we were around our friends."

He took both of my hands and sounded sincere in his apology. "I'm sorry. For the text message where I was pissy, for not taking your call, and to my reaction to you being at Club T tonight. The more I started to think about it, the more I realized I was jumping to conclusions and had planned to come by later to apologize."

"If you'd started to realize that, why were you so angry with me when you saw me at the club?"

"Because you checked in as Kat, my former client."

He waited a beat as if something should've dawned on me. "It's not like I could've given them my real name or gotten in tonight with a new one. It takes at least a week for a membership."

He sighed. "I realize that, but after checking in as Kat, you then rented a room and sent me a text to come meet you. Yes, it was on my personal phone, but there are cameras everywhere, so there was no way they wouldn't have seen me go into your room. In the club's eyes, I had a client trying to pay me for sex off the books."

My face must've shown my astonishment. "Wait. What?"

He turned pink with the next admission. "I'm embarrassed to say it's not the first time. Some of my clients don't like the fact I won't do the physical stuff, so I get propositioned. In a couple cases, they've rented rooms and hoped I'll join them."

I had no words as no part of me had even considered this possible construction.

"And the thing is the management at the club has been pushing—well, not really pushing but strongly suggesting—I take it up a level during the last year because my clientele keeps requesting it. I've refused, not wanting to cross that line. That's why tonight I needed for them to see me enter the room and you leave right away so they'd know I'd turned you down."

"Holy fucking fuck."

His eyes got big and he grinned. "I never thought I'd ever hear those words from your pretty mouth. If I'd been thinking straight, I would've simply sent you a text explaining it all instead of barging into your room. Instead, I reacted because I couldn't believe you were actually there. It's like I had to see for myself."

"I didn't—I mean I wouldn't have—" In a million years I couldn't believe I'd been that stupid.

"I know, and I didn't handle it well, but between getting your text and then seeing you with lube all over your chest, I wasn't firing on all cylinders. Plus, I don't want anyone to ever associate you with Club Travesty. That could be devastating to your career. So I panicked and was a dick. I'm sorry."

"I should be the one apologizing for not realizing. Clueless Catherine certainly outdid herself this time around. And now I'm sitting here jealous over these women, which I know is stupid. Plus I'm even more irritated to hear people are pushing you to have sex for money."

He kissed the inside of my wrist. "You weren't clueless, just not thinking about it from that perspective. As far as the club is concerned, it's all about money to them. If I did more services, they could charge more."

"And you would make more, which sucks. Is it tempting?" I'd wondered since meeting him as Calvin if it was a moral objection or something else.

He sighed heavily. "Earning more money always is tempting, but I promised myself a long time ago I wouldn't go down that rabbit hole. I'm not judging the people who choose to have sex for money, but it absolutely doesn't work for me."

"I'm so sorry I put you in that position tonight."

"If I hadn't sent you a shitty text message full of assumptions or I'd picked up the phone when you called me, none of it would've happened."

True, and it felt good to hear him acknowledge that, but there was something else which needed to be discussed. "In this business, people ask me almost daily for recommendations. They know you were in my magazine, and I gave you a glowing endorsement for Calvin Klein in the past, not to mention others, so—"

"That was different."

"How? My opinion on your work ethic is the same."

"I don't want the favor."

"From me," I finished, watching his frustration mount.

"It's not personal."

"It feels personal, but more than that, it feels like something that won't ever change."

Although we were talking about professional favors, it was the personal side which started to sink in. While it was true that Will was not the type of man who'd ever use me for my money or resent my career or success, would I ever be able to have a future with him? Would his pride ever allow me to pay for a vacation, gifts, or anything regarding money? And since it was in my nature to be generous with people I cared about, how would that work? But the most important question I had burning in my mind was why it was so important to him to do everything on his own.

"Would you want a man who used you for your money or to get ahead in his career?"

"Of course not, but it's obvious you're not that guy."

"You're right, I'm not."

"But if we both know that, why are you so adamant against accepting any help? Are you afraid of what other people might say or think?"

He shook his head. "I worry about someone linking you to me and then to a sex club and what it could potentially do to your career."

"No offense, but that's my choice to make. I was the one who took that risk when I showed up as Kat the first time. My only regret about it is the kind of position I put you in tonight."

"It's not like it's a job I love. If this Claus thing works out tomorrow with the audition and I can get some more steady modelling work, I could finally quit. At least that's what I want. Especially now." His eyes were laser focused on mine. The implication that he desired a future away from the club, with me in it, appeared to make him nervous.

I didn't hesitate with my response. Maybe after he stepped away from it and was more secure in a modelling career, his pride over accepting help would become a moot point. "I want that, too. A lot."

His smile lit up the room before he reached for me. "You still smell like strawberry."

"That little bottle kicked my ass."

He threw his head back and laughed. "Mm, so were you trying to tell me something by ordering the 'take it up a notch' goodie bag?"

"Maybe—wait, where are you going?" I watched him get up and go down the hallway back toward the living room.

He returned with his bag and took out some items. "It would've been a shame to have wasted your money entirely, although we're down one strawberry lube."

"Really?"

"I felt kind of like a thief taking them, but figured you'd already paid for everything." He crawled up the length of my body and, much to my surprise, put the blindfold over my eyes.

"Mm-kay. And although I'm not arguing, it was my plan to seduce you for once this evening."

"FYI, you seduced me in a muddy field in Australia with those big blue eyes ready to murder me. I haven't yet recovered. But if you want to take charge, I won't complain...although I'm having a vision of tying you up."

"I think I can take a raincheck on being in charge." Cuz the thought of him taking control and tying me up was further up on the fantasy list.

"Good, then give me your hands, gorgeous." He took each of them in his own and pulled them up over my head, binding them together. "You okay with this?"

"Uh-huh." It felt so strange to lose the ability to see or touch him, but when his mouth fastened on one of my nipples through the lace of my bra, I nearly bucked off the bed. His fingers unclasped the front and then his hands palmed each breast while his lips traveled down my stomach. Thumbs hooked on either side of my thong, sliding it down slowly and leaving me completely naked and at his mercy.

Hearing a buzz, I tensed, but then let out a low moan when the vibration settled on my clit. Will wasn't content, however, to let the device do all the work as his tongue traveled the length of my slit before spearing inside of me. "I—Oh." I'd been stripped of the ability to do anything but feel, and the dual sensations were about to send me over the edge. But he wasn't done. Another device replaced his tongue, entering me slowly before he started working it in and out.

"You are so beautiful, so unbelievably sexy like this. I want to watch you come for me," he demanded, moving quicker and upping the power of the vibration.

My body answered in kind, convulsing with the orgasm that consumed me.

I was barely aware of his fingers working my wetness until he worked it further down, teasing my pucker. But before he proceeded further, his lips found mine, kissing me until I was breathless. "I need you to be sure," he whispered in my ear, ghosting a finger over that taboo place.

"I am. I want it all with you." With him, I had no reservations, no insecurities, and absolutely no hesitation over experimenting sexually.

Sucking in a breath when he inched his finger inside, I forced myself to relax while he stretched me slowly, first with one, then with two fingers. The initial burn gave way to pleasure. I could tell by the labored way he was breathing that he was just as turned on as I was. Hearing the sound of lubricant and having him pause—I assumed to put on a condom—I waited with anticipation. I nearly came undone when his fingers returned, and I felt something larger pushing at my rear entrance.

"So fucking sexy," he said, moving a fraction and letting me adjust to the new feeling. As if that wasn't enough, I felt the cool sensation of something else slide into my pussy followed by his finger circling my clit.

I moaned, feeling as though he was about to send me over a cliff with every conceivable way of making me orgasm at once.

"Relax, love, and let me in."

I took a deep breath and felt him push in further. "I need to touch you," I pleaded.

He paused and untied my hands, allowing me to touch his arms.

But I wanted more. "I need to see you, too."

He didn't hesitate in flipping off my mask, locking his eyes on mine with nothing but heat between us. He slid in another inch, gritting his teeth. "So tight."

I expelled a breath and shifted my hips, pulling him into me deeper.

The look of surprise mixed with pure, undiluted lust filled his features. With one final thrust, he was home. There he stayed unmoving, allowing me to adjust to the foreign sensations of having him buried inside my ass and also being filled in both places.

My body was shaking, and I realized I wasn't the only one. We both fought not to lose control. But suddenly I didn't want to fight it any longer. More than that, I needed to strip him of all restraint. "Fuck me, Will."

He leaned up and smirked. "You don't have to ask me twice." Pulling out slightly, he then filled me to the hilt, moving the dildo in the process, providing dual sensation. Once his finger rubbed between us, I was done, as in completely eviscerated with the climax that consumed me.

When I regained cognitive ability, I found Will's body weight pressed upon me and his heavy breathing in the crook of my neck. "That was incredible."

"I'm glad you thought so because I have to be honest: I don't remember much past the point of my orgasm."

He chuckled after easing both himself and the device out. "Come on, let's shower."

We made quick work out of doing so, and I climbed into bed exhausted. When I didn't feel Will's weight join me, I glanced up and laughed.

He was eating cold pizza, standing nude next to the bed.

"Now that's a sight," I joked.

He shrugged. "I need it to keep my strength up. You want a piece?"

I shook my head.

"What time is your train up for the party tomorrow?"

"Eight am."

"Why so early if the party isn't until the evening?"

"Since Sasha is coming up, we thought we'd do a spa day with Haylee. What time do you think you'll arrive?"

He frowned. "I'm off early, but still won't get out until nine.

So maybe I'll get there sometime after eleven. Haylee said the party should be going until after midnight."

The party was for those who would be intimately involved with the foundation to include friends, family and some of the hospital staff they'd be working with. The following day would be the charity luncheon which would announce some of the fundraising activities planned over the next year.

"I'm assuming they put us all in the same hotel. Any chance I can tempt you to sneak into my room?"

He took a seat on the bed, running a hand down my side. "I don't think you could keep me away."

"You're going to be tired, though," I teased, running a hand down his abs, simply because I could.

He chuckled, wiping his pizza hands before settling down in the bed. "We should go over the order of things again when it comes to men. Sex, then food, then sleep."

I curled into him. "What if we went sex, then food, then sex again with very little sleep?"

His response was to press his already growing erection against me. "Now you're catching on, but I don't have any more condoms. Do you still have the ones you brought along to Australia?"

"Somewhere, and maybe this isn't the best time to discuss it, but—" I took his length in my hand, stroking gently and feeling it harden further. "Since we're exclusive, and I'm clean and on the Pill—I'm not sure how you feel about the possibility of—I mean, I don't want to pressure you if you're not on the same page, but I was thinking—"

He didn't let me finish my rambling thoughts, instead capturing my lips, throwing my leg over his and shifting so he could push inside of me. "God, Cath—I'm clean, too. And I've never been with a woman bare, but I've been thinking about it with you and wondering how you felt."

I kissed him, finding his admission both endearing and a

turn-on, and moved to allow him a deeper angle. I was taken completely off guard by how soon my body was craving him again. More than that, though, I was surprised by how natural this felt to be with him like this, making love slowly after the intensity of earlier.

Will took his time, proving sleep truly didn't matter to him. He was languid, with his hips rolling into mine, finding my sweet spot steadily before building and taking me over the edge with a slow wave of pleasure that took over my body from head to toe before I felt him find his release.

There was something that felt incredibly right and immensely satisfying about having him fall asleep inside of me after this new level of intimacy.

CHAPTER SIXTEEN

*A*fter a sex-filled morning with a promise to see me later that Saturday night at the party, Will left for his model shoot. He insisted that Claus had wanted a just-out-of-bed look and our sleepless night would only help him with the audition. I wasn't sure about that, but neither could I keep my hands to myself to let the poor guy get some rest.

Once I arrived at the station in Connecticut after the two-hour train ride, Sasha greeted me on the platform with a big hug. A spa day with my girlfriends was long overdue. It had been since Vegas since we'd gotten together.

"I feel like it's been forever since I've last seen you," Sasha remarked, leading me out to where she was parked.

"Me, too. How are things?"

We both got into the car and she gave me the summarized version. She liked her new job, which was still with the same company but now involved delivering new-business pitches. She was hunting for a larger house and planning a wedding, for which she was letting Brian take on most of the tasks. "You know me; I get overwhelmed with details and dealing with people."

Only last year Sasha had shared that she managed an anxiety disorder. This had been a complete shock to me as she'd been very good at hiding it. But it had also opened my eyes. Everyone had their own battles to fight. In the end, I think her revelation made us even closer as friends. "Knowing Brian, he's probably ecstatic to take on some of those things anyhow."

She laughed. "He totally is."

"Who's all meeting us at the spa today?"

"Haylee should already be there, and Kenzie is arriving in the next hour. My friend Juliette is coming, too."

"I recognize her name." I was always happy to meet new people, especially if Sasha called her a friend considering the title didn't come easy for her.

"She's the office manager from Charlotte and has been close to both Brian and me for years. But she's going through a terrible divorce. For the protection of herself and her son, she temporarily moved up to New Haven a couple days ago and is living in the same building as Haylee. I think it'll be good for her to get out and meet some people. She's amazing. Although she'll put on a front, this whole business has seriously shaken her self-confidence. She could probably use the post-divorce perspective, if you don't mind sharing some."

Show me a breakup that didn't wreak havoc on a person. But everyone dealt with things differently. At least I'd never had to worry about custody or protection. I felt instantly sympathetic to the woman. "If she opens the door and wishes to talk about it, I'd be happy to."

She smiled. "Thank you. You're always so good with people and know just when to say something and when not to. So what's been happening with you?"

Oh, boy. My normally boring—oh, great, now I was thinking about Will spanking my ass with that comment—life had been quite eventful since the last time we spoke. But I realized Will and I never had gotten around to discussing whether or not we felt comfortable telling our friends about us. So I filled Sasha in on Fashion Week and then dropped the bomb of Michael and his fiancée drama, which made her eyes go big.

"Holy shit. I'm in awe of how classy you kept it. So how did the matchmaker work out?"

Since I'd dragged Sasha on a whim to a speed dating night and also to Club Travesty in my quest to figure out what the hell to do with being single again, I thought it would be crappy to completely withhold information. "I only had one date, and that went terribly because he knew my ex-husband. But then I went to Australia and had a lot of fun. I closed a chapter with Michael and now, for once, I don't feel pressure about dating or marriage."

Considering I'd been in a panic over the last two years, this was an important turning point for me. Yes, I definitely still wanted to have a family, but for once, I was more concerned about *who* that would be with rather than *when* it would be.

She glanced over with perceptive eyes. "Did you meet someone?"

I sighed, knowing I was terrible at keeping secrets. I also thought back to the fact that she'd confided in me alone the very first night she'd realized she might have feelings for Brian.

"How about I take a raincheck on that question and talk to you tomorrow when we have more time?" We'd just pulled into the parking lot of the spa, and the last thing I wanted was to have Haylee overhear at this point. She and Will were good friends, so I definitely needed the chance to speak with him first.

Her smile was quick, and she turned off the ignition. "Whenever you're ready, I'll be here to listen."

We went inside. After I hugged Haylee, who already had her feet in a pedicure basin, a petite blonde said hello from beside her.

"Hi, I'm Juliette, and I promise I'm not nearly as obnoxious as Sasha has probably told you I am."

I couldn't help but laugh. It was obvious at once that Juliette was the polar opposite of Sasha. Yet the affection was clear between them when Sasha shook her head and laughed.

"I'm Catherine, and it's a pleasure, although Sasha has never once referred to you as obnoxious."

Sasha grinned. "She's not. But to be fair, she's been influenced by Brian for many years, so there's most likely potential."

Juliette nodded with her brown eyes sparkling. "It's true. He's corrupted me, although the redneck was there long before he came along. Now then, ladies, after the pedicure, I'm game for anything with the exception of hot wax coming anywhere near my lady bits."

Haylee and Sasha both laughed while Sasha spoke.

"One of these days, I'll convince you. But for now, I think a nice facial, mani, and pedi will break you into your first spa day properly."

Juliette looked relieved. "Considering my hoo-ha hasn't seen action in years, it's not exactly my priority for making pretty." She turned to me. "Sorry. I'm kind of the girl who doesn't have much of a filter."

I smiled, finding her refreshing. If this was her way of dealing with a nasty divorce, well, I had to give the woman kudos for the ability to appear like she had it together.

An hour later after my facial, I was seated next to Juliette in the manicure chair.

She glanced over smiling. "I feel like we've been set up on a divorce prep talk date. I love Sasha and Haylee both, but I'm sorry if it makes things awkward for you."

I laughed at her perception of the ladies' good intentions. "It doesn't at all. But I also respect that not everyone goes through the same things or wants to talk about it the same way. Nor do I think I'm an expert on divorce."

She sighed heavily before speaking again. "I wish I could fast forward a year where, hopefully, I'll have full custody of my son, the divorce is final, and I'm able to move on with my life."

"I wish I'd had that ability, too. But the thing is you can wish it to death, and it doesn't change a damn thing."

"So what's the secret to getting yourself back?"

Two months ago, I wasn't sure I could've answered this question. "For me, it was embracing who I was, for better or worse." So what if my ex-husband had thought I was boring? Maybe I had been boring when with him because he didn't inspire me to be anything else. But I certainly wasn't dull to my friends or to Will.

"And sometimes the things you may not like about yourself are there only because of who you were with. You need to find someone who brings out the best version of yourself, imperfections and all."

Now that I was with Will, I could honestly say I'd never been more secure with myself. I truly believed that my divorce, although painful, had not been all about me. I wasn't the reason Michael had been unhappy and wanted out of the marriage. He was. No amount of perfection or work on my part would've ultimately changed the outcome. In fact, we were both happier on the other side of the relationship and I was finally at the point where I'd started to look at the last two years with a different lens.

"I worry that I lost who I was somewhere along the way."

"You'll find her again. She may be different than when you last saw her, but it'll be a stronger, more mature version, I promise. But sometimes getting there requires hitting rock bottom first."

"You hit rock bottom?" She looked surprised.

"A couple of times, in fact. But this last one turned out to be the beginning of only going up from there."

I was suddenly overwhelmed with impatience to see Will

again. He'd become so important to me in such a short amount of time. Not as a crutch or a rebound, but rather as someone who brought out this side of me I hadn't believed existed. He'd seen me at bottom, and yet it had only made our bond stronger. I felt fun, sexy, and even silly around him without ever worrying about putting on a pretense or that he might think less of me for it. I didn't have to hide my lists, my over-analysis, or OCD tendencies because, contrary to what I'd assumed, he thought they were adorable.

"Juliette, this is just a chapter of your life—a rough one, but it's not the whole story. I promise."

"I'm really glad I met you."

I took her hand and squeezed. "Same. And you make sure you call me anytime. I mean that. Rock bottom doesn't feel good alone; just remember it's not a one-way ticket. If it wasn't for my friends and family with their support throughout, I wouldn't be where I am now."

AT THE PARTY later that evening, I wore a blood-red dress with matching lips, having Will in mind. I hoped like hell his train was on time, and he'd be here later tonight as he'd planned. Now that the notion of telling our friends about us had taken root, I was anxious to discuss the idea with him.

The rooftop of the apartment building Haylee called home while attending Yale Law School was decorated beautifully. Twinkling lights were strung about the space that was dotted with high-top tables and potted trees. Waitstaff passed around appetizers and drinks. Josh had bought the building and had renovated the top floor into a nice living quarters for the two of them plus baby. He'd also fixed up several other apartments of the building, in one of which Juliette was staying.

When Colby, the one responsible for starting this charity foundation, walked toward me, I smiled. Without sounding condescending, I was proud of him in this impressive endeavor to use his family's business to start a cancer foundation for children.

"Nice to see you, Catherine. And thank you for offering up the fashion show." Colby gave me a kiss on the cheek.

"It's my pleasure, and I've got quite the lineup." So far, I had obtained fantastic models, including Will. Also Bart Chesley, one of the best photographers in the business, had volunteered his services. I hoped to feature the entire charity show in my magazine.

"Ah, speaking of which, nice to see you, Will," Colby greeted over my shoulder.

"You too, Colby. Hiya, Catherine."

I had to take a moment before turning because my need for him took my breath. After rotating around slowly, I did a slow perusal of the man. He looked amazing dressed in dark slacks and a cobalt blue dress shirt.

"Hi, Will. How was your trip up?" He was here at least two hours early and I wondered why.

"Good, thanks."

We both stood there for a moment, eyes locked, until I realized something was off with him. I wasn't sure what, but now, unfortunately, wasn't the time to ask. As if serving to remind me of that, Kenzie's voice broke through, and we were both swept up with other people.

I mingled at the party for the next thirty minutes, wishing I could get Will alone to ask why he was here so soon. I became distracted from these thoughts when Haylee crossed the room with a handsome gentleman by her side that I didn't recognize him.

"Catherine, I'd like to you to meet Doctor Trevor Patterson. Dr. Patterson is one of the oncologists that the charity is working with at Memorial Sloan Kettering Cancer Center in New York."

He smiled warmly before taking my hand. "Pleasure, and please call me Trevor." The good doctor was handsome, with salt-and-pepper hair and nice brown eyes.

"Nice to meet you," I said.

We made small talk, and I noticed Haylee give me a wink behind him before walking off. That's when it dawned on me that this had been a setup. A few months ago, I would've been thrilled, but now I feigned naiveté when Trevor, who was new to the area, hinted at needing someone to show him around the city. How was that for irony? For once I wasn't clueless when it came to getting the cues.

Excusing myself when my eye caught Will heading downstairs, I hurried to catch up with him.

"Hey," I said from behind him, slightly breathless.

"Heya," he replied and waited for me.

"You're here earlier than I'd expected."

He grabbed the back of his neck in a nervous habit I'd never seen from him. "Yeah. Unfortunately, my appointments cancelled. You look incredible, by the way."

Stress was apparent in his features, but maybe it was because he wouldn't get paid for his no-show clients. Attempting to change the subject to something more pleasant, I moved closer and placed a hand on his chest. "I maybe wore the red for you."

"Mm, it is my favorite color on you, although I'm also a fan of blue, which brings out your eyes—or nothing at all," he murmured.

"Come on, I have an idea." I walked by him and crooked a finger, loving the unfiltered look of hunger that came over him.

He followed close behind, and we went into Josh and Haylee's condo. This was essentially four apartments remodeled to be their living space. I led him to the bathroom furthest away from the front door and flipped the lock.

His brow arched when I turned. "And what is it you're going to do with me now that you've got me alone?"

I hadn't yet revealed this sort of sexual confidence, but in this moment, I was definitely feeling it. I reached for his belt and unfastened the buckle. "I'll give you a hint. I think it may relieve the stress you have reflected on your face." Whispering this, I reached for the next button of his slacks.

"Jesus, Cath."

"Oh, you think you've figured it out, have you?" I pushed his slacks and boxers over his hips and down his legs to reveal him hard and ready.

"I can only fucking hope so…" His hands tangled in my hair while his breaths came out ragged. "Those red lips will be etched in my mind forever as wrapped around my cock."

I wished we had more time, but unfortunately we might be missed at the party at any moment. So there was no place for teasing and only time for rocking his world. Which I proceeded to do in five minutes.

Then he returned the favor in three.

WE SNUCK out of the bathroom giggling like teenagers who'd just gotten away with fooling around without the parents noticing. This reminded me of my earlier thought this evening.

"Hey, one question real fast." I stopped in the hall before we returned upstairs.

"The answer is yes." He was all smiles.

I quirked a brow. "You don't know what I was going to ask."

He winked and lowered his head to whisper. "After a blow job like that, I'm not very likely to say no to anything you request."

My face heated, but I played along. "Good, then we'll go tell people we're together. Or maybe it would be more fun to have you pull me close, lean in, and kiss me breathless to see who notices."

His face morphed from smiling to shock to horror in three seconds.

"Okay, based on that expression, I'm guessing it's a no, then." I attempted to walk by him only to feel my arm pulled back.

"Please don't walk away. You took my off guard. I mean, why now?"

"Why not? Unless I totally misread how you feel about me." Shit, had I really managed to be off base again when it came to reading him? Old insecurities were starting to well up in a hurry.

"No, no, of course you didn't. I'm absolutely crazy about you, Cath, but you have your career to think about. I'm a part-time model who moonlighted at a sex club, so either you're incredibly naïve about that, or reckless."

My temper flared. "I'm going with neither of those options since both are insulting. A simple no, you weren't ready would've sufficed."

"I'm sorry. That was uncalled for. I just don't want your association with me to cause you any fallout." His eyes appeared burdened with raw insecurity.

I decided to be clear about something I wished I'd said way sooner than this. "Will, I'm proud to be with you. I thought maybe this would be a natural next step, considering we have mutual friends. But if it's freaking you out, then it can wait." Maybe he needed more time to believe I meant it, but then something struck me about the way he'd phrased *moonlighted*. "Wait, why did you say you moonlighted at the club, as in the past tense?"

He swallowed hard. "I quit tonight when they gave me an ultimatum to change what I offered. That's why I was up here early for the party."

My face drained of color. "Oh, my God. It's all my fault because I showed up last night."

He hurried to reassure me. "No. It's not. It's been brewing for months. Honestly, there's a large part of me that's relieved to finally walk out of there for good."

"But what are you going to do?"

"I'll figure it out. But I don't want you to worry about it. At all."

"Okay." My anxiety was growing by the second over the fact that I was partially to blame.

"And as for you wanting to tell people we're together, I'm at a loss for words—in a good way. But can we hold off for now?" He squeezed my hand, his eyes intense on mine, pleading for me to understand.

"Yes. Of course. I didn't mean to make things complicated." Here he was whirling with what he'd do for income to pay for his brother's care, and I'd been busy plotting ways to have him grope me in public.

He leaned in and kissed my neck. "Don't you dare apologize. Just know it means—well, a lot. But let's discuss it later. Yeah?"

I nodded, wishing there was a fast forward button for the party.

THE KNOCK CAME on my hotel door ten minutes after I arrived in my room. After opening the door, I tugged Will inside—barely—before pulling his head down for a kiss.

He didn't hesitate to reciprocate, his hands coming up to frame my face.

"I'd love nothing more than to fall into bed with you right about now," he murmured in between kisses.

"Why do I sense a *but* in there somewhere?" I felt his lips trail down my neck to the base of my throat.

He pulled away hesitantly. "Because we need to talk."

"That's what Johnny Taylor said before he broke up with me in eleventh grade," I tried to joke, but he wasn't smiling.

Giving me a heavy sigh, he took my hand and pulled me over to the bed where he tugged me onto his lap. "I didn't get a chance to tell you earlier that the audition went great. I think I might have a real shot at the contract with Claus, which would be quite lucrative."

"That's amazing." But noticing he wasn't excited about the prospect cued me in that I was missing something. "But you're not happy about it?"

"The job with Claus would mean moving to LA."

My breath caught in my chest. "What? Why?"

"He photographs primarily in Cabo San Lucas and the events over the next few months are mostly in LA and Las Vegas. If I still had a job here in New York, then I'd contemplate flying back and forth, but without one, it doesn't really make sense."

"Maybe you could look for another job in New York, then. One that you'd actually enjoy."

"I wish, but the likelihood of finding one which both pays well and I enjoy is pretty low."

"Right." What else could I say? He'd made it clear time and time again he didn't want my help. Besides, he might not even need a second job if he moved to LA for the modelling contract.

"It wouldn't be an easy decision, but it would allow me to finish up my last semester of school for my Masters and make enough money with modelling to keep Thomas where he is for at least the next year. After that, I'll have to figure out something else."

I didn't know what to say as this seemed like the best decision for him. Who was I to keep him from such an opportunity?

"It sounds too good to pass up. Uh, what time do you leave for your shoot in Miami tomorrow?"

"Right after the luncheon. I wish you could sneak down to be with me for a couple of nights."

I felt like I was on autopilot with my answer, still reeling over the thought of him moving to the West coast. "Yeah, me, too, but unfortunately I have meetings all week that I can't miss."

He smiled, stroking my face. "I understand."

THE FEELING of waking up in Will's arms the next morning was one I realized I wanted every morning. Unfortunately, it was also a reminder that if he moved away, I'd miss it greatly.

His arm pulled me in closer, and I could tell he was awake. Or at least part of him was. I shifted and wrapped my fingers around his arousal, moving them up and down his length slowly.

"I could get used to this kind of morning," he murmured, sleep still in his voice.

"Me, too." I moved so I was straddling him, loving how this position allowed me complete access to his chest and the ability to watch his face, which was looking more awake by the second.

After riding him to mutual orgasms, I collapsed on top of him, breathing into his shoulder because—morning breath. I basked in the feel of his strong hands rubbing my body.

The sound of his stomach growling intruded on the descent from our high. "Breakfast?" I questioned, hungry myself.

"Depends. What time is it?" He moved me carefully, dropping a kiss to my nose and hopping out of bed in a hurry, like he'd suddenly remembered something.

"Um…." I rolled over, checking the clock on the nightstand. "Eight. Why?"

"Golfing. I'm supposed to meet the guys at Josh's place at nine."

"You golf?" I slipped out of bed, grabbing the phone and dialing down for room service.

He shook his head. "Terrible at it, but none of them are competitive, and it's normally a good time."

We ordered omelets, and after Will downed his, he gave me a kiss at the doorway. "See you at the luncheon."

CHAPTER SEVENTEEN

With the guys doing their thing on the golf course and me up early, I texted Sasha to see if she wanted to meet for coffee. I didn't think twice about the state of my room until she walked in and looked at me with wide eyes.

"Catherine Davenport, did you have sex last night?"

My entire body flushed red with her question. "Oh, my God. How could you tell?" I was mortified and quickly tried to usher her out the door.

She started laughing. "Because your room looks like the one Brian and I are in, with tangled sheets and room service plates for two on the table."

"I completely forgot about the plates," I muttered, cracking a smile. I'd intended to confide in her about Will anyhow, but not quite this way. At least she hadn't told me the room smelled like sex, although it probably did.

We walked down to the coffee shop on the corner, each chose our latte of choice, and then we meandered to a park a block away, stopping to sit on a bench. "I love fall up here," I commented, taking in the leaves that were turning color and the crisp morning air.

"Yeah, yeah, it's beautiful. Now, spill it. Did your mystery man travel up here to surprise you last night?"

I laughed at her impatience. "Uh, not exactly. He was at the party. As a guest."

Her brow furrowed as she obviously took a mental inventory of the people in attendance. "It couldn't have been the doctor because you hadn't met him before. So who?"

"Will."

Her expression was priceless as it morphed from confusion to shock to a huge grin. "Holy shitballs."

I chuckled, having said the same thing to her when I found out she was seeing Brian. "Indeed. And you're the first I've told, so I'd appreciate it if it stays between us for now." Based on Will's reaction last night to the idea of people finding out about us and his possible plans to move to LA, I didn't want everyone knowing now.

"Of course I won't say anything. I don't know him very well, but he seems really sweet and, not that I have to tell you— gorgeous. Haylee and Kenzie can't say enough nice things about him."

"He's incredible." Not just as my lover, friend, or whatever other label I'd put on it, but as a human being.

"So when did this happen? How?"

My version of the story focused on our return flight from Vegas when he'd had appendicitis and I'd helped him. I omitted the Club Travesty connection altogether and went on from there.

"Wow, so you weren't kidding about having a good time in Australia, then."

"No, I wasn't. Only one big problem."

"What's that?"

"He just found out he may be moving to LA for the next year if he gets this big modelling contract."

She sighed, looking sympathetic. "Not sure how you feel about long distance or him, for that matter, but Brian and I did it for months, and Josh and Haylee are managing it. So I'd say it's something to think about. California is a long ways, but it's not impossible."

No, it wasn't.

———

AFTER THE CHARITY LUNCHEON, which was being held at our hotel in one of the ballrooms, I knew that Will had to go straight to the airport and fly to Miami. This meant I wouldn't get a chance to be alone with him. Clearly, he'd been thinking along the same lines because he texted me:

"Meet me on the third floor next to the Roosevelt room."

I immediately smiled. The last time I'd received a message from him asking to meet like this had been during my magazine's gala. Only now when he came out from a door next to the designated room and pulled me in with him, I wasn't surprised and met his kiss with one of my own.

He nipped my neck. "Like the thought of a supply closet these days, do you?"

"With you, absolutely."

"I just wanted to get you alone for a proper kiss goodbye. I'll be in Miami until Friday."

"Only a kiss then?"

He pulled back smirking. "God, I wish I had more time, but Haylee is literally waiting downstairs to drive me to the airport."

I begrudgingly let him go, giving him one more kiss for good measure. "When do you think you'll find out about the contract and LA?"

He sighed, tucking my hair behind my ear. "With any luck by the end of the week. And I hate the idea of hoping for it because it would mean moving away from you."

It was on the tip of my tongue to ask him how he felt about

long distance relationships, but his phone buzzed and he grimaced. "Time is up. I'll see you Friday."

Right. Friday.

———

By Monday night I was restless. I had a list of reasons, including my meetings this week, against hopping on a plane to Miami to see Will, but one big one that had me booking the flight anyhow.

Because I was in love with him.

And for once in my life, I didn't want a list of pros and cons to dictate my happiness. My gut was saying to go for it and tell him. Once upon a time, I'd hoped my husband would come back to me. But at the end of the day, I'd never made a grand gesture to go after him because I didn't have it in me. Nor had he been worth making such an effort. Somewhere in my subconscious, I'd known that even back then.

So with all rational thought put aside, an email to my assistant to reschedule all of my meetings for tomorrow, and a host of rehearsed things that I was sure would fly out of my head the moment I saw Will, I booked myself on the next morning's ten am direct to Miami flight.

The following day, however, as I dressed for the airport, I started to have second thoughts. Traveling down to see Will to declare my love was so far out of my comfort zone; I didn't know if I was prepared for the possibility he might not feel the same.

Insecurity was a tricky bitch. The moment you thought you'd put her firmly in a box and stopped giving her the power, she'd figure out a way to undermine your confidence.

That's why my mind started working overtime. Maybe Will had been letting me down easy while in the meantime secretly looking forward to living it up single in LA. Perhaps he was glad to be rid of the boring ball and chain back in New York and had absolutely no intention of ever coming back.

I wheeled my suitcase downstairs and let Sherman put it in the back. I then sat in the back seat, completely undecided.

His eyes met mine in the rearview mirror, and he asked where to.

Shit. I should've brought my magic eight ball.

"Um, maybe I should just go into the office, Sherman. Thanks."

His gaze didn't leave mine. "I think you'd be better off going to the airport or train station or wherever you intended when you packed that suitcase, Ms. Davenport."

I was stunned. Never in the six years he'd been driving me had he shared an unsolicited opinion. "Why's that?"

"Because life is short, and sometimes you have to take chances."

Even now, he was a man of few words. Yet the ones he said held maximum impact. "I'm curious. Would you have given me the same advice while I was married?"

Wisdom in spades was reflected in his eyes while his one simple word spoke volumes. "Nope."

"To LaGuardia, please."

"Yes, ma'am," he returned with a smile.

THANKFULLY, an email to Will's agent telling her I happened to be in Miami and would like to speak with her client was answered by the time I landed and she was helpful enough to let me know his hotel. Sometimes it paid to be the editor of Cosmo Life and pull some strings.

Will had indicated he'd have evenings off, which gave me enough time once I arrived at the hotel to get checked into my room and showered. But then what?

Going forward with half-baked plans hadn't exactly paid dividends for me previously if my debacle of showing up unannounced at Club Travesty to rent a room was any indicator. This meant a text message letting Will know my room number was out of the question.

Been there, not doing that again, thank you very much.

So I did what any other perfectly sane woman, trying not to look stalkerish while, in fact, stalking the man she loved, would do. I waited in the lobby bar of the Fontainebleau hotel for him to come in, drinking a glass of wine as though I was supposed to be there. Yep, that was the extent of my grand plan.

Which would've been fine had he actually been alone when he arrived. But instead he climbed out of a van with the entire crew from the shoot and also two gorgeous female models.

My heart beat into overdrive, and self-doubt threatened to take hold. I contemplated leaving, but not before his blue eyes seemed to laser in on me and he stopped mid-conversation, looking shocked to see me.

Tempted to wave, instead I made myself sit there, watching as he hesitated and then proceeded to the far side of the hotel as if he hadn't seen me there at all.

I think I sat stunned for a full three minutes before I could feel my heart start to beat again and air fill my lungs. The jolt from having him ignore me was so acute that it took me another moment before I could function. I put down a twenty, more than covering the glass of chardonnay I'd been sipping, and stood up on shaky legs, determined not to lose it in the middle of the hotel lobby.

Putting myself in motion, I strode toward the towers in the opposite direction of Will and company, cursing my choice of the four-inch Jimmy Choo heels and long, fitted navy skirt that didn't allow me to move any faster than the small steps allowed by the slit.

I'd stayed at this hotel once before, and it was absolutely

stunning with its modern architecture and a happening dance club, which was already starting to draw a crowd. But I didn't notice any of that now. Instead, I focused on one thing.

The sanctuary of my room.

Although I could faintly hear my name getting louder coming from behind me, I didn't register it was Will speaking until he stepped in front of me just as I found my elevator. I reached around him to hit the up button, not making eye contact, thankful when the car lit up and the doors to my right opened immediately.

"Cath, wait. It's not what you think."

Thankfully, it was only the two of us in the small space as I hit the twenty-ninth floor and the doors closed. I turned toward him, meeting his eyes. "So it wasn't you completely ignoring me in the lobby."

"I did that for your own good."

"My own good?" I couldn't believe what I was hearing.

The doors dinged open and I walked out with him hot on my heels. "Yes. I was with seven people from the shoot, half of whom probably know who you are. If I'd gone over to see you, they would've wondered what was going on."

I put my key card in the door's slot and walked in, already taking off my shoes with the intention of packing them up and getting the hell out of here. "So, what? Why would I care if they saw you with me?"

"The last thing you need is for people to know—"

I held up a hand, something dawning on me for the first time. "No, you did it for you. Because you're the one embarrassed to be seen with me."

His eyes went wide. "Why the fuck would I ever be embarrassed by you?"

Sighing deeply, I realized from his stunned expression that he didn't have a clue about his own internal reservations. "Because you don't want people to think you're with me for the money or because of my connections."

"What?"

"You say it's about protecting me, which I believe you think is important, but it's also about your pride. That pride won't allow anyone to think for a second that you're getting help from someone. So not only will you not take it, but you also don't want even the perception that someone is giving you a hand up."

He stood there staring at me, absorbing my words. "I—" He scrubbed a hand over his face. "I never consciously thought about that." He stopped and sighed. "But I guess when it comes to you, I'm sensitive to it."

"But why?"

He stepped closer, cupping my face. "Because one of the very first things you did was give me money."

I closed my eyes, annoyed with myself that I hadn't seen that sooner. I'd hit his trigger from the beginning by paying his medical expenses. Now he didn't trust me not to go behind his back and do it again. It explained why he'd jumped to the conclusion that I'd given the recommendation to Claus and his general distrust. "If I'd had any clue we would've become involved, I would've thought twice before doing it."

He kissed me softly. "Your generosity is what makes you, well, you. And I'm sorry. I could never be embarrassed to be seen with you."

"It's ironic because if the donation for your surgery had stayed anonymous as planned, we might never have gotten together."

His lips curved into a smile. "I would've never brought you to Australia to work it off or found out you have a killer mud ball aim."

I laughed, needing the humor in the conversation to remind me of our connection. "God, the expression on your pretty-boy face that night was so worth it."

We both smiled at the memory before he asked, "I thought you couldn't come down here because of your big meetings this week?"

"I rescheduled today, but need to be back by tomorrow morning."

"Why would you do that?"

Putting all the doubts to the side, I went for it. "Because I've been thinking about this California thing if you get the contract with Claus. I'd be up for traveling out there. Maybe not every weekend, but every other one. Or if you're modelling in other places, we could try to meet wherever they are."

The hope on his face quelled any doubts I might have had that he'd been using this as an excuse to end what we had.

"You'd be open to doing the long-distance thing?"

"Yes. Absolutely."

His face looked full of optimism before he sighed regretfully. "Cath, I can't let you do that. I mean, you have a whole life in New York and would get tired of the travel, not to mention the expense. It just wouldn't make sense."

My heart was in my throat, but I didn't travel twelve hundred miles with the intention of not putting it all on the table. "I came down here because, for once in my life, I'm not taking the safe route and sitting at home keeping my feelings to myself. I want to be all in with you, Will. No safety net. No regrets. Even if that means getting my heart broken for the effort."

He stood there staring for the longest moment. "Are you saying what I think you are?"

"You're the mind reader, so I'm surprised you didn't already know."

His hands framed my face. "Say it," he demanded softly.

"I'm in love with you."

"Really?" He looked as though he couldn't believe it.

"Yes, really. And although I know this isn't exactly 'playing it by ear'—"

He cut me off with a kiss. "You should've stopped at your first word because I love you, too."

I felt the adrenaline flow through my veins with his declaration and launched myself at him. Unfortunately my skirt wasn't allowing much movement, but Will took care of that by unzipping it. Freed, I jumped up and wrapped my legs around his waist. Mouths clashing, he walked us over to the bed.

"Jesus, Cath—" He appeared half amused and half in shock once he'd deposited me on the bed and followed me down.

"Is that a 'Jesus, Cath stop,' or a 'Jesus, Cath, *don't* stop'?" I wasted no time in going for his buckle.

"Don't you even think about stopping."

So we didn't for two whole hours.

"I'M STARVING," I whispered, watching the light disappear with the setting sun in the hotel window.

"Room service okay?" He stroked my back as if he couldn't touch me enough.

"Perfect. What would you like?"

"Meat of any kind and veggies would be good. And make sure I'm paying. You can charge it to my room."

I slipped out of bed and grabbed the robe from the closet. "No."

He sat up, quirking a brow. "What?"

After tying my sash, I reached for the menu and dialed the phone. "You heard me. I said no. I'm paying for dinner."

He looked like he wanted to argue, but I was busy speaking into the phone to order two steaks with veggies and wine.

After I hung up, he crossed over, still completely naked, and pulled me to him. "What was that about?"

"I paid your hospital bill back before this getting naked business —" I motioned between us. "—for which you're paying me back with Colby's charity event in January. But once that's done, I refuse to walk on eggshells or keep apologizing for it. You're going to have to learn to trust I won't overstep those boundaries again. And when I travel out to LA, the last thing I want to do is fight about money."

"If you're paying to fly out there and probably for a hotel room, then I'm paying for dinner while you're there."

"Okay, that's fair."

He laughed. "So you really want to go for it?"

"Are you changing your mind now?"

His grin confirmed his answer before his words. "Never, although I feel selfish in saying it. Of course, I still need to hear back, but my agent said it was looking good, so I'm hopeful I'll get confirmation soon."

"What's selfish about it? I want to be with you, and if you feel the same way…"

He caressed my face, keeping his gaze locked on mine. "I hate that you have any doubts about it. That means I haven't done a very good job of convincing you how much you mean to me."

A relieved smile spread across my face. "You just did, but I'd be lying if I said I didn't have a small reservation that you might desire a new life out in LA."

He shook his head, dropping a kiss on my lips. "Not even a little bit."

BACK FROM MIAMI and walking into the office a little after ten o'clock on Wednesday morning, I couldn't keep the smile off my face. I was under no illusion that maintaining a long-distance relationship would be easy. Quite the contrary. But the fact that I'd rather put in the work and effort with Will than have it easy and convenient with anyone else told me all I needed to know.

Plus, I was proud of myself for putting it all on the line. I'd come away feeling confident that without risk, there's no reward. Of course, the fact that I was already missing him presented a challenge if we were to spend weeks at a time apart. But we'd cross that bridge when we came to it.

Funny how I'd once used work to distract myself from a crumbling marriage, then from the sting of divorce, and then to make myself feel fulfilled in life. But right now at my desk with twelve things I needed to do, I was instead distracted by a replay of this morning and how sweet Will had been while kissing me goodbye.

Unfortunately, these meetings weren't going to run themselves, so for now I'd need to move on with reality.

By Friday evening, I was about done with the real world, where I'd been obliged to pack all of my missed meetings into three days. But more than that, I was excited about seeing Will tonight. It wasn't lost on me that missing him would be the norm once he moved to LA. Nevertheless, when his name illuminated on my cell phone and I smiled more than I had all week, I knew staying together would be worth it.

"Hiya, Gorgeous."

I'd never get tired of that greeting. "Hi, yourself. Did you just land?"

"Yeah. Long day. How about you? You still in the office?"

"About to leave. You want to come over?"

"Uh, yeah. It might be a bit, though, as I have some errands to run."

"Everything all right?" There was something in his tone that sounded off.

"We can talk about it once I get to your place in a couple hours if that's okay."

"Sure." I tried not to feel anxious about his words. Maybe he'd just had a bad shoot in Miami, or something was going on with his family. But even as I tried to convince myself not to worry this would affect us, my gut already knew it would.

———————

TWO HOURS later I opened the door to Will after hearing his knock. I'd barely shut it before he was on me.

Lips met mine while his hand wasted no time cupping my sex. "God, I fucking missed you. Only two days away, but it feels like weeks."

"I missed you, too," I gasped, feeling his hand slide in past the waistband of my yoga pants. Two fingers shoved inside of me and found me already wet for him.

"I'm a selfish bastard, but I need you too much right now to stop."

That sounded strange for him to say, but I didn't question it considering this felt too damn good to ruin the moment.

Wasting no time, he backed me up into the couch and pushed my pants down past my hips. He didn't bother to shed any more clothing before kneeling in front of me and devouring me completely. His tongue ran the length of my slit before focusing in on my nub. He took my over-sensitive clit between his lips and sucked while his fingers continued the havoc they were wreaking by curling up inside of me to the perfect spot.

"Will…" I let out on a hoarse moan and allowed the climax to annihilate me. My legs no longer supported my weight, but he was attuned to my inability to stand, thankfully, and supported my body while lifting me up to sit on the back of the couch.

As his lips met mine, he unzipped his pants and thrust inside of me fully on one stroke, the slight burn causing us both to gasp. This carnal, almost frenzied coupling was so different from his usual slow workup, yet it was no less of a turn-on.

Wrapping my legs around his hips, I pulled him deeper, fueled by the taste of me on his lips and the wild pace he'd started to set. His hand pulled on my hair, forcing my head back and exposing my neck to his lips and teeth. He nipped his way down, rougher than normal and practically inviting my nails on his skin. I raked them over his ass, and his grunt of pleasure only spurred me on further.

This time when my orgasm bore down on me, I took him over the edge with me, my intimate muscles gripping him to the point where he had no choice but to grind out his climax deep inside of me.

We lay there on the sofa afterward, catching our breath and tangled together. He spoke quietly. "I didn't hurt you, did I?"

Propping up on his chest, I met his eyes. "Not at all."

He sighed in relief. "I didn't mean to make it so rough."

I couldn't help smiling. "I'm not complaining. In fact, I really liked it."

At least that pulled a grin from him. He stood up, took my hand, and proceeded to lead me into the bedroom where he removed the remainder of my clothing methodically, in between kisses. He made love to me slowly then, almost as though he was trying to show me the complete opposite of our earlier frenzy.

LATER, I watched as Will got up out of the bed and went into my bathroom. Feeling his weight back on the bed, but not his warmth, I opened my eyes again to see him sitting on the edge of the bed, his head in hands. "What's wrong?"

He turned, his blue eyes meeting mine with something I'd never seen reflected in them. Defeat.

"I didn't get the modelling contract with Claus."

I expelled a breath, knowing the timing of this news had to be devastating for him, coupled as it was with quitting his job at Club T. "I'm sorry."

"It was presumptuous for me to think I would."

In the back of my mind, I thought it might've had some impact if I'd been able to give him a recommendation, but considering it was a moot point, I kept quiet on the subject. "We can figure something else out."

He shook his head. "*I.* I will figure something else out."

I took a deep breath and thought this, right here, would be the reason we failed as a couple. Because I wanted a partner for better or worse. Not someone who shut me out the moment things got tough and tried to bear the burden alone. "Why is it so important for you to do this on your own?"

"It just is." He offered no further explanation, instead walking out into my living room where I found him staring out the window at the city nightscape.

When I joined him, he took my hand and curled me into him on my sofa. Although he was holding me, I'd never felt less connected to him.

Maybe if he wouldn't take help from me, he would consider it from someone else. "What if you spoke with Josh, or better yet, Bart could know of—"

He leaned back, his temper snapping. "No. Absolutely not."

"Do you know that I wouldn't have received my start at Cosmo Life if it wasn't for a mentor of mine? While I was interning during college at a Fashion Week, she called in a favor and got me the interview at the magazine because she wished to give me a chance."

"It's not the same."

"Why won't you consider my help?" For someone who seemingly wanted a future with me, he was discounting both my assistance and my support, acting as thought we weren't in this together.

"To do what? Write me a check? Is that your answer for everything? Or were you planning to call in a favor to get your boy toy a job?"

My eyes narrowed. He was hurting and therefore lashing out,

but I didn't deserve it. I stood up, needing my robe. Being naked while fighting left me feeling vulnerable. "You insult both of us by implying I've ever treated you that way. If you've been thinking this way the whole time, then we were done before we even began."

His anger evaporated just as rapidly as it had ignited, and he followed me back down the hall to my bedroom. "Shit. I'm sorry."

"I know you are," I said quietly, slipping on my robe.

Will didn't apologize unless he meant it, but this was bigger than his comment.

"But...?" he prompted, evidently sensing I was holding something back.

I turned toward him. "But a couple consists of partners, two people who share both the good and the bad. It wasn't like I was planning to get you a job or give you money, Will. I was only going to suggest calling around to see who might be holding auditions. You want to be there for me, but in turn won't reciprocate and let me in. Instead, you resent any advice or support I try to give you."

He ran a hand through his hair, his eyes reflecting sadness. "You're right. And what I said was completely uncalled for." He sat down on the bed, sighing heavily. "I'm leaving on Sunday."

"For what?"

"To take the counselor job at the facility where Thomas lives in Australia. Besides a salary, I get a discount on his care. Thirty percent the first year I work and up to fifty percent the longer I stay. And I'll still have the Calvin Klein contract and possibly some local modelling jobs out of Sydney."

I tried to keep my voice calmer than I was feeling with the shocking news. "When did you decide all this?"

"After the club first suggested I step up my services last year and, coincidentally, Thomas's rehab center offered me a job, it became my contingency plan. I called the center yesterday, and they made me an offer."

"So all along you knew you were moving to Australia if the contract in LA didn't work out?"

He nodded, looking guilty.

"Was this breakup sex tonight?"

"I didn't mean—"

"You didn't mean *not* to tell me about your plan to move to the other side of the world if you didn't get the Claus contract. Or mention it as a possibility while I was down in Miami telling you I loved you. Or before you were deep inside of me tonight? What were you going to do: leave a note, text me that you weren't coming back?"

"I was planning to tell you tonight. And I don't want moving to Australia to be my only option. But for the moment, it is."

My frustration with him hit a breaking point. "It's not, though. Can't you see that? I respect you for working hard. Although I'm not sure I fully understand why you need to be the only one responsible for paying for Thomas's care, I even respect that you would bear the burden. But what I don't understand is you cutting off all other options simply because of your pride. You have a ton of friends and colleagues who'd move mountains to help you get auditions or interviews if you simply tell them you're looking for work. You're not asking for a handout, only a chance."

"I don't want that."

"But why? Give me a reason here, Will."

For a moment I thought he'd open up to me, but instead the walls came down.

"I'm sorry I wasn't completely honest. Selfishly, I'd not only hoped it would work out, and I wouldn't have to tell you at all, but I wanted to spend any time I had left with you. I'll still plan on coming back for the charity show in January. You should know—" He paused as if the words were difficult to get out.

"That I've never felt this way about a woman before you. I only hope you understand I hate this as much as you do, if not more because it's my fault."

A tear broke free in spite of my best effort. Although part of me wanted to be angry with him for not telling me until now, sadness was overriding all my other emotions. I couldn't stand the thought of him walking out of my life permanently.

"What if you give it a couple weeks to explore more options before you make this decision?" It seemed like everything was happening in fast forward; maybe a few extra days would give him some other alternatives.

He was already shaking his head while getting dressed. I clamped down on the urge to argue with him as I wasn't about to act desperate to keep him. It wouldn't make a difference, and my self-respect wouldn't allow it.

"I can't," he whispered hoarsely.

Two simple words had never sounded more devastating. Emotion clogged my throat and I knew I was moments away from breaking down, but I refused to let him see it. "So this is it, then?"

He finished putting on his shoes and grabbed his bag. "I'm sorry. Walking away from you is the hardest thing I've ever had to do."

He leaned over, kissing my cheek before leaving.

I swallowed the words until I heard the front door click shut: "Then don't."

CHAPTER EIGHTEEN

*I*t wasn't until I stood under the warm water beating down from the shower an hour after Will had left that I let the tears really flow. What was it about a shower and crying that seemed to go together?

After drying myself off and slipping on pajamas, I sat on my bed and stared at the wall. I refused to start down the beckoning rabbit hole of self-doubt and insecurity.

This was not about me.

This was *not* about *me*.

That sentence, although simple, bore repeating until I absolutely believed it. Will choosing to move away wasn't because I'd been too boring, too wrapped up in my career, or because I should've done things differently. This wasn't about me any more than my divorce had been about me.

I was imperfect, at best. But on the other side of a failed marriage and with hindsight as my ally, I was done shouldering the insecurity that I hadn't been good enough to hold onto a man. I knew this was true despite watching Will walk out in a cruel rehash of an old scene.

Two years ago, I'd been devastated and completely caught

off guard. This time, although it hurt like hell, I knew I'd ultimately weather the storm. Not today, maybe not tomorrow, but eventually. I'd learned I was stronger than I'd ever given myself credit for. So for right now I might feel like my heart was aching, I might be disappointed about those things I couldn't control, but at the end of it, I could at least say I didn't have any regrets about the relationship itself.

I didn't even regret making myself vulnerable and putting it all out there in Miami. As much as I was frustrated that Will hadn't confided his contingency plan to me all along, I knew it was because he'd been waiting for a miracle before he made his final decision. I only wished I could offer that miracle and not have him resent me for it.

Unfortunately, sleep was elusive after I crawled into bed after midnight. I kept coming back to one question I wished he would've answered: why was he so hell bent on refusing help?

My cell phone cut through my thoughts about a half hour later as I was still tossing and turning. Rolling over, I grabbed it and hit talk when I saw Will's name illuminated on the screen.

"Hello."

"Did I wake you?"

Although it was tough to tell on the phone, I swore I could hear an unfamiliar slur to Will's words. I'd never known him to drink much, let alone get intoxicated. "No. I was still up. Where are you?"

"At my place."

At least he was safe even if it was a mattress on the floor. "Everything all right?"

"No, it's not. I told myself I wouldn't call you. That I'd walk away and leave you to live your life with a guy who can give you those things from your list."

Sighing, I cursed that stupid list. I then slipped back into my old habit of assumption. "Meaning you don't want the same type of commitment I do."

"What are you talking about?"

"The part about wanting to settle down and—"

He interrupted. "It's not that. More like making more money or being established in my career—"

Now it was my turn to interject. "For the record I never said I wanted someone who made more money. I said I wanted someone financially independent. Meaning they're secure enough in themselves not to compete or resent my success. And as for the career thing, I want to be with someone passionate about what they do regardless of money. So maybe I didn't artic-ulate my list then the way I would now, but Will you are every-thing I could ever want."

"But you still deserve more than I could ever give you."

"Not possible." But then his words turned on a lightbulb of awareness. "Is that why you won't let people help you? You don't think you deserve it?" I could tell I'd hit a chord with the way he cursed under his breath.

I was met with silence, so I pressed on, feeling I was on to something. More than anything, I needed to understand. "Is it the guilt over your father taking you with him to LA and leaving your mother and Thomas?"

He sighed heavily. "I can't do this."

Feeling my frustration bubble up, I sat up in bed and was blunt. "No. You won't do this. And there's a difference in those two statements. You *can't* implies there aren't any other options. You *won't* means you refuse to take them."

"Cath, you don't understand."

"You're right, I don't. And although I've asked you to explain it to me, you won't. Are you sensing the theme here, Will?"

He was so quiet on the other end that for a moment I thought he'd hung up. "Are you still there?"

"Yes."

"Then tell me why you don't think you deserve to accept

anyone's help. Please."

It took a minute before he began talking, his voice quiet and tortured. "When my Dad left, my mum had nothing. Not even a job because caring for Thomas was a full time one in and of itself. So she had no way of supporting herself. She had to go on the US equivalent of food stamps and sell the house, moving them both into an apartment. I'm not sure if they would've made it if it wasn't for my stepfather coming along when he did. He moved them in and took care of things financially, but that was after two years of suffering on their own."

He paused, and I had to keep myself from judging his mother for having shared this information with her son. She knew he'd had absolutely no choice at age ten, either to help her or to control his father's actions.

"My dad in the meantime started a successful business, took us on vacations, and bought me a car when I turned sixteen. It wasn't until I traveled back to Australia for a few weeks over the summer when I was a teenager that I realized what my mother was sacrificing for Thomas and his care. That's when I grasped what my father had done."

"Because your mother told you all this?"

"Yes. She wanted me to understand why she was still angry with him."

"That's why you decided to return to Australia and go to college in Sydney?"

"Yeah. I told my dad I didn't want his money and funded it through loans and working part time. How could I possibly accept anything more from him, knowing he'd abandoned his duties to the other part of his family?"

So not only did Will feel guilty, he was also out to prove something.

"Did you ever ask him why he didn't offer assistance?"

"Does it matter? He disappeared out of their lives

completely, taking me with him. And despite him offering to pay something now, it doesn't make up for it."

"I'd say it does matter very much. In fact, if you flip your argument around, I'd go so far to say that he owes your brother. With or without Thomas's disabilities, your father didn't meet his responsibility toward him. I'm sure there's a great deal of pride in telling him to shove his money up his ass, but I think you're letting him off the hook at your own expense."

"My mother is adamant against accepting his help."

I remembered walking in on their argument too well. "I know this is going to sound harsh, but as the person who isn't paying, why does she have the decision-making power? This is affecting your life, Will. You warrant having some say in it. Plus, no offense to your mom, but there are always two sides. Talk to your dad and ask him what happened."

He was quiet. I'd probably said more than I should have, but if I were in for a penny, I might as well be in for a pound.

"I see you shouldering a burden out of guilt and misplaced obligation to make up for a decision that was made by others when you were ten years old. In you not asking for help or accepting that people want to support you because you don't think you deserve it, you're doing a disservice to yourself and to those individuals around you. Doing things for people you care about feels good. It especially feels good for people to do something for someone who is constantly sacrificing for others. It's like you're punishing yourself. I know I'm probably overstepping in saying all of this to you, but please understand I'm doing it because I love you, if that counts for anything."

"It counts for everything. And I love you too, Cath. So fucking much."

I closed my eyes, absorbing his words and trying to quell the threatening sob over the unfairness of it all. We felt so strongly about each other, and yet it still wasn't working.

"I'm sorry I called you so late."

I swallowed hard. "I'm not. It's the first time you've opened up to me."

"You aren't wrong, you know. I do have a ton of guilt and trouble accepting help because of it. I don't know; it's like I don't feel worthy, as I'm sure any shrink would say."

For the very first time I had a spark of optimism. If Will realized his problem, there might be some hope he could address it. "You deserve good things in your life, Will. Whether it includes me or not, I hope someday you'll believe that."

After a couple minutes of silence, his breathing was the only thing proving he was still on the line. Frankly, I had no idea how much he'd remember tomorrow if he was, in fact, too drunk for my words to sink in. But it did mean a lot that he'd finally revealed his deep-rooted reason for his actions.

"I should go," he said finally.

"All right. I'll let you go then."

"Bye, Cath."

The call disconnected about the same time my heart broke.

I BARELY SLEPT after Will's call. I wished that he'd consider a different course of action or at least think about what I'd said. But given that he'd been drinking, I had no way of knowing if he'd even remember the conversation today.

By the time afternoon rolled around, I decided at least to shower and put on some clothes. But I had the intention of doing absolutely nothing with the rest of that Saturday until I realized I hadn't eaten since the day before. The beauty of living in Manhattan was you could order pretty much anything to be delivered. In my case, this included an entire cheesecake, which later that evening sat half eaten on my countertop.

There was a part of me that hoped Will would come by on

his final night, but then again, I wasn't sure I had it in me to watch him leave again.

The sound of my intercom buzzing from the front desk surprised me. But not as much as the name of the person who'd come to see me.

"Ms. Davenport, I have a Mr. Josh Singer here to see you."

"Uh. Okay, send him up please."

Considering Josh had never done more than meet me in my lobby, even when we used to attend functions together years ago, I was completely shocked he'd be here now—and would ask to come up.

I was in sweats, without makeup, my hair back in a low ponytail, and with a half-eaten cheesecake sitting unapologetically on my countertop. It was ironic how time and perspective had changed me. Today I didn't give a crap that the man I'd once had a crush on was seeing me this way.

Josh's arched brow when I opened the door, making it obvious he was taken aback to see me looking this way as well. He didn't beat around the bush. "You okay?"

"Is that your way of asking why I look like shit?"

He chuckled while following me inside. "I'm not touching that question."

"Smart man. What brings you by?"

He studied me as I turned to face him. "Will came over for dinner tonight. Matter of fact, he's still with Haylee and Abby right now."

"That's nice." I wasn't so much concerned about keeping our relationship a secret as I was curious about what Josh was fishing for.

"Haylee is pretty upset he's moving to Australia."

"I'm sure there will be a lot of people who'll miss him."

"You know, I don't quite have Will's gift for being perceptive or Haylee and Brian's knack for saying the right thing to people. But I didn't think it was coincidence that he asked if I'd spoken with you today and how you were doing and that he isn't happy about moving. So I took him aside and asked him what was going on."

I raised a brow. "And he told you?"

"Not in so many words. But considering the half-eaten cheesecake on your counter, I'm assuming he's not the only one miserable right now."

I cracked a smile that he still wasn't touching the fact that I probably looked like hell after my restless night. "I need coffee before I can talk about this. Didn't sleep much last night. You want a cup?"

"Sure."

I moved to the kitchen, taking down two mugs and using the Keurig to brew coffee quickly. Once it was ready, I slid a cup to him as we stood across the island from one another.

He sighed heavily. "Catherine, we've been friends for many years and have seen one another go through some pretty rough times with our divorces. So believe me when I say you deserve someone who makes you happy. Matter of fact, once I realized the possibility of you and Will together, I couldn't think of someone better suited for you. He's a good guy."

"You don't have to tell me that."

"So then, what's the problem?"

It dawned on me that Josh seemed to think I was the one responsible for Will leaving. "Did he tell you why he was moving to Australia?"

"He mentioned his brother and a job there, but I assumed part of it might have to do with you. He went on about how incredible you are and that he wished things could work out differently. He seems absolutely shredded."

I had to bite down on my frustration considering I very much wished they could, too. "I love him, and I want to be with him, but unfortunately, he has some things he needs to deal with. In Australia which isn't exactly conducive to a long distance relationship. As far as working out differently, he must be referring to the choice he's making to move, a decision I have very little say over."

"I'm sorry. I'd thought perhaps I was on a mission to convince you to give him a shot."

I shook my head. "I wish you were. Just as I wish he believed me when I say how much I love him. I want nothing more than to help him find other options that'll allow him to stay, but we're at a catch twenty-two considering he'd resent me if I so much as made one phone call."

"You know, Haylee had some things to work out when she moved up to Connecticut last year. Hell, she basically broke up with me."

My eyes got big with disbelief. I'd always thought that he and Haylee had struggled at first with the long distance thing, but then had found their rhythm without too many bumps. "So what did you do?"

He sipped his coffee and sighed. "Almost fucked it up by letting her go completely, hoping she'd figure it out and come back to me."

"But she did, right? I mean, obviously you two are together and happy."

He shook his head. "No. Matter of fact, if it hadn't been for Will letting me know how miserable she was, I would've kept on assuming she was happier without me. If I'd had it all to do over, I would've made sure she knew my loving her wasn't going to change. Her underlying issue in not believing that might be different from Will's, but the part about needing to convince them seems to remain the same."

Considering Will didn't feel worthy of living a happy life because of his guilt over his brother, it stood to reason that feeling worthy of being loved by me was in that same bucket. But how could I convince him differently? And to what lengths would I go if I wasn't to lapse back into my insecurities about not feeling like I was good enough?

He went on, "He's staying in our guest apartment tonight and leaving tomorrow for LA. Then on to Australia."

"Wait, he's going to LA first?"

"Yeah, to spend time with his dad, I think he said. He didn't mention what for, but judging from your expression, that's a good thing?"

I had a flicker of hope that Will was exploring his alternative options or, at the very least, would get his father's side of the story. "It could be."

"I'll leave your name with the front desk in case you want to come by to see him tonight. I should get back, but if you need anything, you let me know, okay?"

I gave him a smile, grateful for his friendship. "I will. Thank you for coming by."

After a hug goodbye and seeing him out, I sighed heavily. He'd offered some good advice to contemplate, but I wasn't sure what to say that hadn't already been said if I did go over to see Will.

Thankfully the knock at the door made the decision for me. I opened it to see Will standing there, looking awkward with his hands in his jeans pockets.

"Hiya.

"Hi." I moved to the side, letting him in and shutting the door.

"I, uh, passed Josh in the lobby."

My lips curved into a smile. "Since falling in love with Haylee, I think he's on a mission to ensure everyone is as happy. He was here to tell me what a great guy you are. Ratted out your location for tonight and everything."

He grinned. "Guess my questions asking him how you were doing gave me away. I didn't mean—"

I stepped closer, holding up my fingers to his mouth. "I don't care if the entire world knows I love you Will, let alone Josh."

His eyes reflected surprise at my declaration. "Were you going to come by?"

I was honest in my reply. "I don't know. But I'm glad you're here."

"I didn't want yesterday or last night's drunken conversation to be the way we left things."

"Me neither."

"You have to know me leaving isn't about you."

It was just like Will to try to ensure I wouldn't beat myself up over this. "I know it isn't. Same as I know you have enough guilt to deal with without adding this to it. I have no regrets, Will. None. Well, except going to Club T that one night, which I can't help but feel put this whole thing in motion."

He shook his head sadly. "I promise that wasn't your fault. It was a ticking time bomb and bound to come up either way."

"If you say so."

"I do." He stepped closer, putting his hands on my hips. "You're the best thing that's ever happened to me, which only makes saying goodbye so much harder."

I smiled. "Yeah, well, I heard easy love is pretty bor —dull, so…"

His chuckle gave our conversation some much-needed levity. "Nice save on the word."

I put my arms around his neck. "It's our last night. Any ideas what to do with it?"

"Absolutely."

And with that, all talking was done.

I COULDN'T LIE in my bed, anticipating the moment Will would need to walk out this morning, and listen to the sound of the door closing behind him again. I didn't have it in me. So that's why, after setting an alarm to give him time to make his midday flight, I took a few minutes in writing him a note including what I needed to say goodbye and slipped out of my own condo. I grabbed coffee and went into my office. With no one else there on a Sunday, I could be alone with my thoughts.

Curled up on my office sofa, I sipped my brew, smiling while I thought about our night together, realizing there wasn't one minute I would take back.

And now, no matter how much I wished he'd include me in the game, the ball was in his court completely. Whether or not he made a decision to stay, it was clear he needed to work on his feelings of guilt from his childhood.

Simply put, I wanted a partner in every sense. And until Will could deal with his own demons, we'd only be kicking the proverbial can down the road, and it wouldn't matter where we lived—we'd eventually break apart.

Ironic that in him leaving, I'd learned a valuable lesson. Perhaps life wasn't all about the ending, but rather the journey. The expectation of a happily ever after set us up for failure from the start if anything fell short and we should instead measure relationships by what we received from them. In my case, there weren't enough words to describe what Will had done for my self-confidence. He'd also helped me believe everything happened for a reason. I wouldn't beat myself up over what I could or couldn't have done differently.

As for the future, I'd be lying to myself if I didn't admit to some hope that we'd find our way back to one another, especially if what Josh had brought up was true about Will traveling to LA to talk with his dad. But in the meantime, for the first time in my adult life, I was content to start this next chapter my life by being by myself.

Matter of fact, I was even going to embrace turning thirty-five this year. What better way to do that, not to mention give myself a much needed distraction, than to plan a party? And since it fell on Halloween, a costume party seemed in order.

Considering I'd never associated either event with much fun, it was time I changed that. Instead of panicking about turning a year older without a husband or family, it was time to embrace that I was another year wiser and be more thankful for what I did have in my life, which were a great family and amazing friends.

Energized with the idea, I sent off emails to the people I absolutely wanted to be there in a couple of weeks, worked on a venue, and compiled a guest list. I hoped that everyone could make the impromptu party without a lot of notice.

I only wished the one person I wanted there the most could be there.

CHAPTER NINETEEN

On Halloween night, I was dressed up as a cat for my costume party. Not a cute fuzzy one, but rather the Cat Woman type with the leather pants, bustier, and mask. Maybe it was a homage to channeling my inner Kat.

Plus, if in doubt, look a helluva lot better than you feel. Always. And since it had been over two weeks without a word from Will, I needed the boost.

I surveyed the hotel restaurant which I'd rented for the event and was happy with all of the spooky decorations. It had been fun to be in party-planning mode over the last few days and a welcome distraction to look forward to something. After making my rounds of the preparations, talking with the DJ and the caterers, I then focused on my guests as they arrived.

A petite woman dressed up as a pretty snow fairy came over, and I smiled in recognition. "Juliette, is that you?"

"Yes. Catherine?" She tipped her mask up so I could see her face and I did the same, both of us grinning.

"Nice to see you again. You look incredible, but, uh, weren't you blonder before?"

She appeared almost angelic in her costume with golden

brown ringlets down her back. "Ms. Clairol and I decided to return me to my roots one night. My ex loved the bleached blonde, and I got to thinking I liked it better natural, which of course meant I had to do it right then and there. Then because I did a horrible job of it, Haylee was kind enough to get me in with her hairdresser to help fix it."

Ah. Say no more. I'm sure many a box of hair color was bought and a hairdresser called to correct it with a breakup to blame. "I love it."

"I love your costume, too. You look—well, let's just say, if you had a whip in your hand, I think you could be cat woman slash dominatrix."

We both laughed.

"You know what they say, if ever you're down, wrap yourself in leather so no one's the wiser."

"Amen, but I'm sorry to hear that's the reason. Boy trouble?"

I smiled. "That obvious, huh?"

She shrugged. "Only from one woman to another."

"Well, the benefit of having been through hell is knowing you can make it through again if you have to. My new motto would be to keep taking chances. Sometimes the things that make you happy are found when you least expect it."

"You have no idea how much I needed to hear that because I might, you know, be interested in someone. And it may not be forever, but I'm sure having a lot of fun with it in the meantime."

"Maybe that needs to be an article in my next issue: romance isn't always about the destination but the journey. Enjoy it because you deserve it."

"Cheers to that," she responded, holding up her glass.

———

ALTHOUGH I'D MADE this a costume party for Halloween without any emphasis or mention of my birthday, I should've known

Haylee and Sasha, combined with my mother, wouldn't miss the chance to ensure it was, first and foremost, a birthday celebration. When they wheeled out the cake half way into the party, a rendition of a ghoulish cemetery with candles, and sang "Happy Birthday," I found myself appreciative they had. Even the thirty-five candles didn't faze me.

"Happy Birthday, Catherine," Josh said a few minutes later when he found me up at the bar ordering another drink. He kissed my cheek.

"Thank you, and love the couples costume." He was dressed as the Big Bad Wolf with Haylee as Little Red Riding Hood.

"This is the first time I've dressed up since the age of twelve."

I chuckled, thinking this new version of Josh had definitely lightened up under the influence of his lovely wife. "Well, then I feel honored you would do so for my party."

He smiled, his eyes assessing me. "It was fun. Especially to see the expression on Sasha's face when Brian came out in his costume."

I looked over to the happily engaged pair walking toward us. Sasha was Cruella De Vil and Brian had surprised her by donning a Dalmatian puppy suit. I couldn't help laughing. "It is pretty funny and typical Brian."

"Definitely. You doing all right?"

I knew he meant things with Will, but answered generically. "I am. I've embraced being mid-thirties, although that could be the wine talking. Come tomorrow, I could be in a full-on panic about being close to forty."

He smirked. "Something tells me tomorrow you won't be thinking about that at all."

I quirked a brow, about to ask him what he meant, but was interrupted when Kenzie came up on the other side.

Dressed as Harley Quinn, she insisted we all do shots together and ordered a bunch.

Brian, of course, couldn't help teasing his little sister. "Is it just me, or are your shorts getting smaller?" Then he looked toward Colby, who made a fantastic likeness to the Joker. "Seriously, Colby, you were okay with this outfit?"

Frankly, Kenzie's long legs and toned body were pretty much made for the Harley Quinn, short, sparkly shorts. However, looking at it like a big brother, well, maybe not so much.

Kenzie looked amused and then winked at me. "Wanna see three grown men instantly uncomfortable?"

"Uh, sure." It was obvious she was going to take action regardless of my answer.

And just like that, she tipped the shot, jumped up on Colby with her legs wrapping around his waist, and kissed him spectacularly. Not only her older brother, but also Josh and Mark, dressed as Superman, all groaned out loud at the action. Obviously none of them were used to the girl they'd always seen as a little sister hopping on anyone, let alone on former playboy Colby.

"By my count, that made four men uncomfortable, Kenz," Colby muttered, smirking nonetheless. He set her down gently and gave her nose a playful kiss.

She only tossed her pigtails and laughed, swinging her prop bat up on her shoulder and wiping some of the lipstick off of Colby's mouth. "Let's not forget who has the power here, boys."

Later on the dance floor, we girls were all still laughing about her stunt of using the crazy of her character as an excuse. I was delightfully tipsy and having a great time, thinking this was just what I'd needed.

But when hands settled on my hips from behind me, I froze. I turned around to tell whoever it was that I was a firm believer in *this is my dance space and this is yours.* Only I found myself staring into ice-blue eyes I'd recognize anywhere behind a mask. This time in the form of Batman.

He offered up a tentative smile. "Haylee told me once I put

on the costume she rented for me, I'd find you by looking for my match. Good thing for both of us, there's only one cat woman tonight."

"Yeah." Because when love was stuck as a lump in your throat, you said lame one-word answers like that.

"Happy Birthday, Cath. Sorry I'm late." His voice was low and husky.

"I didn't even know you were coming." Or what it meant that he was here.

"I wanted a redo of all the times I should've taken the opportunity to haul you up against me, tell you I loved you, and kissed you breathless in front of everyone."

My lips parted in surprise while I absorbed his declaration. But before I could respond, my mother's voice reverberated across the dance floor, breaking the moment as only she could.

"KISS HER."

"Your mum?" Amusement danced in his eyes although he didn't take his focus away from me for a moment.

"None other. I'd blame the wine, but I think she'd do the same completely sober."

His arm reached out, banding me flush with him while his hand moved to the side of my face. "I'd hate to disappoint her."

I could only nod as his lips met mine, and my body registered how much I'd missed him. I returned his kiss without hesitation.

The cheers were deafening, which only spurred Will on to pull me closer and dip me in dramatic fashion. He brought me back to center where my grin matched his. "Guess it's official now."

"Guess it is, but does this mean you're here to stay?" Was he home to visit? Did he have a plan now that didn't include moving to Australia?

Leaning in, he whispered, "I'm not going anywhere."

WE MADE our rounds at the party for the next hour, and I noticed that Will hardly let go of me. Obviously slipping into this new relationship role in front of our friends wasn't a problem for him. But neither did it provide me a clue what to expect from our future.

His breath came at my ear. "Would it be terribly rude if we got out of here right now?"

I shrugged. "It's my party, not to mention my birthday. So I'll be the rebel for once and say I don't care if it is."

Taking my hand, he helped me wave to the smiling couples who watched us leave. "Please tell me you have a room here tonight in the hotel?"

I nodded, thankful I'd decided it would be better to stumble upstairs later than to try heading back to my place after the party.

"Which floor?" He tugged me down the hall at a breakneck pace.

"Eleventh, but slow down. My heels can't keep up with you." I said this on a laugh and then squealed when he lifted me up over his shoulder.

He then strode into the elevator, just like he'd done in Sydney. Once he pressed the button, he slid me down his length, his lips meeting mine again. "I know we need to talk," he said in between kisses.

"Uh-huh, but I'm afraid what you might tell me is you're leaving again after tonight, so maybe it should wait."

"I told you. I'm here to stay. And here for you. That is, if you'll still have me." He kissed me like a starving man before the floor dinged and the doors opened.

This time I grabbed his hand and led him three doors down to my room. He followed me inside and flipped off his mask to reveal his handsome face before taking mine off.

"What does that mean? What happened over the last couple of weeks?"

He sat on the bed, pulling me down onto his lap. "Where to begin? I guess first by apologizing it took so long. But I had a lot of things to work out and felt like if I'd given you pieces, I'd be building false hope. I wanted to wait until I knew one hundred percent I wouldn't have to move."

I wasn't sure two weeks qualified as a long time, but I had to admit it had felt like a lifetime because I hadn't known if he would return or not. Now I stayed quiet and waited for his explanation.

"Before going to Australia, I first went out to LA to speak with my father. When I finally asked him why he'd left my mother destitute, he was totally clueless. He told me he'd been trying to give her money for years, but my mum would never take it. When I relayed some of their hardship, he broke down and said she'd always insisted she didn't need anything from him. He'd interpreted that to mean she had it covered. He's had an account set up to help pay for Thomas's care for years." He snapped his fingers. "And just like that, he prepaid the next eighteen months. He seemed almost relieved to finally be able to contribute something."

I could hear the frustration in Will's voice about learning the other side of the story after all of these years.

"After I spent a few days with him, I traveled to Australia and talked with my mum. It didn't go well when I told her my father had contributed. But once I confessed I'd been working at a risqué club, living on the floor of a bedroom, and going without medical insurance in order to keep up the payments, she broke down."

My eyes went wide. "You told her you worked at a sex club?"

"Not in those words, but I had to allude to it because she wasn't getting it. I think, in her mind, living in New York and having modelling contracts meant I'd made it and had this money to spend. Plus, if I'm being brutally honest, I think she felt like I owed Thomas, almost as if I was the proxy she could guilt instead of my dad. Her resentment over my father leaving won't change overnight, if ever, but this is about Thomas. It's not about her, the divorce, or what happened so many years ago. And you're right in saying I get a vote in whether I accept my father's contribution. Frankly, so does Thomas, who after all these years wanted to see him."

"Wow. So your dad flew out to meet with him?"

He nodded.

"How did that go?" I couldn't imagine, as a parent, facing a child who for the past seventeen years had thought I'd abandoned him.

"Rough for both of them, but I think it's an important step toward healing. My father didn't always make the best decisions, but he's willing to acknowledge that and apologize. It's up to Thomas whether or not he can forgive him. The decision doesn't belong to me and certainly not to my mother."

He paused, sighing heavily. "Hopefully, she'll eventually understand. But given how much she's sacrificed it's not easy for her. I think part of me will always feel some guilt over the fact that I'm healthy while my brother isn't, that I wasn't there to help my mum or spend holidays with them. But it wasn't as though I had a lot of choices, being a child. I need to stop punishing myself or letting my mother make me feel as though it was somehow my fault that we left."

A small part of me felt bad he'd gone to all this trouble because of me.

As if sensing my thoughts, he shifted me to the side of him so we could be face to face. Tucking my hair behind my ear, he remarked, "This was a long time coming, Cath and it's such a relief to finally deal with it. You told me things which weren't easy to hear that night I called you on the phone, but you loved me enough to say them anyhow."

He paused, taking a folded paper out of his pocket. "This here, your goodbye note, I kept it with me the entire time, counting the days until I could get back here."

I swallowed past the lump in my throat. I hadn't known how to say goodbye, nor had I known the best way to convince him that I loved him, so I'd reverted to something I did do well. I wrote a list. A list of twenty-five reasons I loved him.

"Do you know which one was my favorite?"

I shook my head.

"It's where you said I make you the very best version of yourself. That you're not perfect, but are perfectly happy when you're with me. Or maybe the one where you said you loved my body."

I laughed. "Hm, I don't remember saying anything about your body."

"Must've been an interpretation on my part." His playfulness turned thoughtful as he shifted back to the serious stuff. "I allowed my misperceptions of what happened between my parents to affect my life for too long. But until I had something or, in this case, someone to lose, I hadn't felt the need to question it. You've made me realize I deserve love and support from those close to me. I'm only sorry it took me so long to get there."

A tear slipped out that he'd spent so many years disbelieving he was worthy of love.

"Don't cry for me, love. All roads, no matter how rough, led me here to you. And I wouldn't change it for the world." He brought our joined hands to his lips, feathering a kiss over my knuckles.

Just as my road led me to him. "So you're back for good. In New York?"

"I am. After speaking with Josh, he's agreed to let me rent his extra apartment."

"Oh." My face must've given away the thought that he could've stayed with me.

"I went to him because when we move in together, I want it to be because it's an important step in our relationship, not because I need a place to stay. Okay?"

I nodded, appreciating his reasoning. "I'm impressed you asked him at all."

"Then this one will really blow your mind. I also asked Haylee to use her charity connections with the Children's Hospital in New York. I have a job interview on Monday for a patient counseling position. I'm only a semester and a thesis away from having my Master's degree, and it's what I ultimately want to be doing with my life. Working with kids and families."

I was shocked, but in a good way. For the first time, he'd demonstrated he was willing to accept help. He wasn't looking for a handout, only a chance to earn something on his own merit. "You'd be great at it."

"I'll never be the man who can take care of you financially, and I know you said you don't need that but—"

I entwined my fingers with his, holding his hand to my heart. "I'd rather have someone to take care of my spirit and, most of all, my heart. But if you break it again, I'm not sure I can take it." It warranted being said because I was all for second chances, but at the same time, I couldn't go through this again.

He blew out a shuddering breath. "Never again. I promise." He kissed me sweetly before smiling. "Sasha and your mother were also very clear about what would happen if I moved away and put you through this again."

My brows lifted in surprise. "At the party?"

He chuckled with a nod. "When you went to the restroom, they converged on me."

"What did they say?" I was both amused and apprehensive.

"Sasha, along with Kenzie, said something to the effect of stabbing me in the face with her stiletto. But to be fair, they'd both had quite a few drinks. Kenzie also muttered something about silly men taking forever to get their shit straight, which I can only assume was more a comment about Colby a couple months back, but is also applicable to me."

"Uh, okay. And my mother?"

He smirked. "She was a little more subtle, informing me that she made amazing Thanksgiving and Christmas dinners, and if I didn't fuck it up again with you, I was invited. Shirt optional, of course."

Only my mom. "Of course. By the way, Sasha's shoes are way too expensive for her to chance getting blood on them, and my mom's sweet potato casserole is legendary," I deadpanned. We both burst out laughing.

Will caressed my face, turning serious again. "God. Do you have any idea how lucky I feel?"

"Oh, I think I'm the lucky one. Lucky I requested someone else instead of Derek at Club T the second time, lucky I was horrible enough at flirting to get Kenzie to help me so you could realize I was Kat in Vegas, and even luckier that you had appendicitis."

He shook his head, smiling. "I never thought I'd consider having my appendix removed as good fortune, but clearly it was." He hesitated but then went on. "I know I still need to work on being too prideful at times, but I swear, I'll try to keep in mind the joy it gives you to be generous and not begrudge you those opportunities. I trust you, Cath."

We were both a work in progress. That he acknowledged his flaws gave me the opportunity to fully admit mine. "And I will try to be mindful to consider your feelings and input before making decisions which impact the both of us. That being said, I'm serving notice that in a few months when you earn your Masters, I'd like to take you on a tropical vacation to celebrate?"

He gave me a lopsided grin. "That sounds amazing." Pulling me off the bed, he enveloped me in an embrace. He then stepped back to meet my gaze, clearly needing to ask me something serious. "What about starting a family?"

This was the one nonnegotiable thing on my list. From his previous comments, I'd assumed he wasn't opposed to it, yet I realized we hadn't had an actual conversation about it. "You don't want kids?"

His eyes danced with laughter. "I want loads of them. Matter of fact, thinking about our future beautiful, blue-eyed, blond babies makes me want to knock you up right this very instant, but I'm wondering if you're okay with waiting a while? Just until we can do things properly and I get settled into a job."

"I don't want you to feel like I'm rushing you." The panic I'd once felt over my biological clock had calmed now that I realized the importance of having the right man versus a perceived *right time*. "And there's a chance, given my history, that we'd have to go through in vitro. Even then, it isn't a guarantee."

"First, you're not rushing. Second, we can always look into other options if the epic amount of sex we'll be having doesn't do the trick the old-fashioned way."

Swoon.

Now I knew where the expression came from. It came from moments like these where an amazing man says the perfect thing to make you realize any perceived imperfection isn't a big deal. I wasted no time in kissing him. I kissed him for the time he'd been away. I kissed him for the love I felt, and most of all, I kissed him for the promise of tomorrow.

"Uh, not to complain, but it seems over the last two weeks something changed in your pants."

He chuckled, pulling back with mischief in his eyes. "I almost forgot."

I watched him pull a handful of tootsie rolls out and started laughing. "I can't believe you remembered my favorite Halloween candy."

"Well, you did have one of the reasons you loved me was

that I remembered the little things, from how you take your coffee to your favorite salad, and that it made you feel special."

"It does."

He put the candy to the side and weaved his hands into my hair, pulling me closer while his tongue found mine, setting off a spark that had us both frantic to shed our clothes. Off came my pants first, but then Will held up his hand.

"Don't move." He stared. "Jesus, you in that leather bustier and a thong is about the hottest thing I've ever seen."

A smile of pure feminine satisfaction took over my face. "Juliette told me all I needed was a whip to display a completely different type of costume."

He grinned. "Can't say I've ever been into that kind of thing, but with you, I might be game."

We both laughed until he unceremoniously flopped onto the bed, taking me down with him on top.

"From boring to dominatrix—I don't think so—ooooh—"

His hand playfully spanked my ass, causing us both to laugh and for me to remember his *punishment* when I used the dreaded B word.

"What happens when we're in public, and I accidentally say that word?"

He nuzzled my neck, kissing down my throat. "Say it and see for yourself. After all, my alpha tendencies will not be fenced in, woman."

I giggled, considering Will was about the most thoughtful alpha I'd ever known. "Throwing me over your shoulder, smacking my ass, and calling me woman. Yeah, I think you've officially earned your stripes."

"Whew. Mission accomplished in the nick of time to balance out the other."

"What other?"

His hands framed my face, blue eyes full of such emotion that I had to remember to breathe. "The part where I say I love you, Cath, the depths of which I can't begin to put into words. And now, instead of living a life where I'm going through the motions to fulfill obligations, I'm looking forward to building a real one with you. One which is full of new adventures together."

I adored this man unequivocally. "I love you too. So much. And if we're planning new adventures, we probably need a new bucket list of sexual fantasies."

He flipped me over onto my back and dropped his lips to mine. "Mm. I can think of five things I'd like to put on it right now that we can scratch off tonight."

I smirked. "Only five? I've got twice as many, which may take us into tomorrow."

EPILOGUE

I loved the surprised look on Catherine's face when I dropped by her office on Christmas Eve morning, coffee in hand. We were due to take the train up to spend the holiday with her parents in a few hours, but she'd needed to go into work for a while first.

"To what do I owe this pleasure?" she asked in that sexy voice of hers, getting up in an equally sexy red dress, something which probably cost more than the average mortgage payment.

But over the last couple months, I'd stopped caring about things like that. Wearing high-end designer clothing was as much a part of her job as a uniform in any other. Besides, she made it easy not to dwell on such matters since not one bit of her was superficial.

"I finished up a morning appointment at the hospital and thought I'd bring you some coffee after."

She crossed the room to throw her arms around me and turned her face up for a kiss, not caring one bit that her lipstick was about to get smudged.

I gladly accommodated her.

Taking the cup, she sniffed. "Gingerbread latte, my holiday favorite. Thank you."

It really was the little things which continued to make her so very happy. If I doubted that for a moment, she reminded me with text messages whenever one of us was out of town like the one from last weekend when I'd had a modelling shoot in the Bahamas.

"I love a man who brings me breakfast in bed on a Sunday morning and miss him when he's gone."

It had been complete with a number of emoticons which she enjoyed using in her texts these days. Although we were months into our relationship and she no longer had to convince me of all the ways she loved me, it absolutely made my day whenever she did.

"You're welcome. I'll let you get back to work and meet you at your place in a couple of hours. Yeah?"

I was still staying in Josh's extra apartment but spending the weekends at her condo. We had a standing Friday night pizza-and-movies date and Saturdays were typically something with friends or a night out. Then Sunday was my favorite because we spent most of it in bed, which of course started with the breakfast I'd make and bring her.

"Actually, I was just finishing up here. I sent out an email letting everyone take off by noon and enjoy the holidays. How was your appointment this morning? Was it with the Murphy family?"

"It was, and thanks to you, they're all spending it together. Here." I handed her the paper that held a crayon-drawn picture ten-year-old Cecilia Murphy had made of the entire family together for Christmas.

She dabbed her eyes of the tears that had come and pinned the picture on her board. "You didn't tell them it was me, right?"

I shook my head. "Nope. Santa got all the credit, and I got asked to pass on that picture to him."

I'd always thought Catherine generous, but the more I got to know her, I realized that word wasn't enough. Case in point, one of the patients I'd been counseling over the last month who was battling leukemia had four brothers and sisters down in South Carolina. They wouldn't be able to afford traveling up to the hospital here in New York where their sister was receiving chemo. Catherine had not only ensured they'd all been flown up, but had also taken upon herself, with a little help from yours truly, to decorate their hotel room with a tree. Of course, this was in addition to having Santa come in to pass out toys to all of the children in the hospital over Christmas.

Three months ago, I wouldn't have believed that I could have an amazing start to a career I thoroughly enjoyed, let alone a partner I unequivocally loved even more. Or that I'd deserve it. But that was then and now—Well, now, thanks in part to working every day with people who didn't take one day for granted, I realized I'd be a fool not to appreciate the things I was fortunate enough to have in my life.

Home.

That's what Catherine represented to me. After spending equal amounts of time in Australia and the US before traveling the world over, I'd never considered any place as permanent until now. Ironically, it didn't turn out to be a location at all, but rather a feeling that no matter where I was, so long as it was with this incredible woman, I was home.

"Are you all packed?" I asked.

She smirked. "What do you think?"

The plan was that after spending a couple of days with Catherine's family, we were heading to LA to see my father and then going to Australia for New Year's to see my mother and siblings. My mum still wasn't completely over my father being once again involved in Thomas's life or paying for his care, but we were working through it slowly. However, despite it being a little awkward, I was looking forward to the trip. In part, this was because I couldn't wait to take both Thomas and my little sister, Janet, into Sydney to watch the fireworks at the harbor to ring in the New Year. It would be a treat for all of us.

"I think you probably had your list in Excel over three weeks ago, a suitcase out and ready a week ago, and everything ready to go at least two days ago." I might tease her about her tendencies to keep everything in lists or orderly, but the truth was her formidable organization fascinated me.

"I managed to wait until three days ago to take out the suitcase. And in my defense, it isn't easy to pack for winter and summer all in the same trip. Now then, have you mentally prepared yourself for another holiday with my mother?"

I chuckled, recalling Thanksgiving weekend had been—well—amusing as hell. Although in her eyes, I could see where she might not share the sentiment. The truth was I'd never had a family dynamic that I could remember over the holidays. So I'd enjoyed every moment in spite of Catherine's embarrassment.

"I packed four bottles of wine for the occasion since we can take them on the train."

A smile tugged at her lips. "Is that your polite way of saying it's me you have to manage?"

I shook my head, fighting the grin. "No, love. However, I do find the more wine you drink, the more amusing you find your mother."

She crossed back over to her desk, powered down her laptop, and began putting her things in her bag. "Indeed."

"Although I have another suggestion for a way to relax you." I lifted my chin, indicating her desk. She'd been the one to put it on our newly formed, ever-evolving sexual bucket list, but I'd been thinking about it for weeks.

Her blue eyes got big with surprise, but then her mischievous grin took over. "Forget the wine; I think you may be onto something better."

We arrived at her parents' house shortly before dinner, only taking a slight detour from the train station in order to check into a hotel a few miles away. Catherine had been adamant about staying somewhere other than her parents' house after her mother had almost 'accidentally' walked in on us one morning under the guise of bringing us coffee during the Thanksgiving weekend.

I'd found it hilarious, but I knew if it had been my mum, I would've opted for a hotel room the next time, too. Besides, having Catherine alone was preferable considering she wasn't the quietest in bed. Since it was my privileged mission to make her scream my name as much as possible while I did naughty things to her gorgeous body, the situation didn't exactly lend itself to staying with family.

I smiled as I watched her help her mother in the kitchen and give her a hug filled with affection. Despite her occasional grumbling, she adored her parents and spending time with them. It was clear the feeling was quite mutual. The only thing missing was Catherine's younger brother. He was spending the holidays abroad but was due home in time for Easter.

After a delicious meal, which included Mrs. Davenport's legendary sweet potato casserole—a legend that hadn't been exaggerated—we sat in the living room by the Christmas tree, drinking wine and visiting. Their family tradition was to open up one gift tonight, with stocking stuffers and other presents reserved for the morning.

When it was Catherine's turn to unwrap the one from me, she did so slowly, tearing the paper carefully and giving me a smirk as if to say she'd never be a rip-it-apart sort of girl. That was okay; I more than liked the fact she loved to savor things.

Pulling out the silver ball, she glanced over inquisitively until she turned it over and recognition dawned. It was a magic eight ball I'd had custom-made in silver for her office or maybe for the bedside table. I watched her hold up the card and read it, knowing what I'd put down word for word.

"For life's adventures… So long as they're with you, it doesn't matter what the ball has to say."

Her blue eyes went misty, and she threw her arms around me, whispering in my ear, "I love it and you."

"Let me see, honey. What is it?" her mom questioned.

Catherine held it up, about to explain.

But much to her horror and my amusement, her mother's gaze narrowed. "Is that a sex toy?"

"Why on earth would you think Will would give me something like that especially in front of my parents?"

"What? It's a silver ball, and they're the new thing in those smutty books I enjoy. What do they call them? Ben's balls? Or something like that. Basically, they're those things you insert—"

Cath held up a hand. "I beg of you. No more. And it's magic eight ball to which you ask questions and it gives you answers."

If she hadn't been so horrified, I'd have been laughing on the floor. As it was, I could only bite my lip and try not to make eye contact so I didn't lose it completely.

She turned toward her father. "Dad, you seriously need to monitor those books Mom has been reading lately. She's out of control."

He shrugged. "Now, honey, why would I do that when I'm the one benefitting?"

"Oh, my God. I walked right into that. I need another drink," Cath muttered, pouring more wine into her glass and trying to fight her smile despite her horror.

This time I couldn't keep it in and roared with laughter. I mean, where else could you get this sort of comedy? "I think we should all agree that first-year etiquette dictates no sex toys, but come next year, all bets are off."

Everyone cracked up, including Catherine, but then she

leaned over. "You have no idea what kind of embarrassing hell you've unleashed for next year."

Once we arrived back at the hotel, she turned and looked at me while taking off her coat and snow boots. "You know, after all this family time, we're going to need a vacation from our vacation. April can't come soon enough."

We had a week-long getaway planned for St. John with only the two of us. It was her graduation present to me for getting my Masters, and one I more than looked forward to. After my surprise graduation party, that was.

So, I may have accidentally overheard Haylee and her discussing plans, but there was no way I'd spoil it, not when Cath was putting so much effort into inviting all of our friends and making my event a big deal. Truth be told, I was grateful for the heads-up, else I might become emotional in front of everyone. I couldn't remember ever having a party thrown in my honor, not even a birthday party. I'd just have to work on my 'shocked face.'

The party wouldn't be the only surprise during that week. In a few days, I planned on getting my grandmother's opal-and-diamond wedding ring from my father with the intention of popping the question during our time in paradise.

But in the interim, there was another question I'd been anxious to ask. Between my continued modelling gigs and my counseling job at the hospital, which sometimes had odd hours, plus her job, which was equally as day-to-day, we didn't often get a chance to see one another during the week. I was hoping to change that.

I pulled her into my embrace, tugging on her earlobe with my teeth before whispering, "How long do you think it would take for you to get sick of me if we were to live together?"

She pulled back, searching my eyes. She knew the bigger deal than taking the step of living together was me being able to accept moving into her condo. Months ago, I'm not sure my pride would've allowed it. But the desire to go to bed every night and wake up each morning with the woman I loved had trumped any lingering insecurity over the fact it would be at her place.

Who cared what anyone had to say about it when I adored this smart, generous, classy woman, independent of her money, job, or material possessions?

Swallowing hard, she shook her head. "Was that a trick question? You know I'd never get tired of you."

"Would you be okay with me contributing toward the mortgage each month?" I had no idea how much it was, but I wanted to give something.

Her gorgeous face was confused, but then she smiled brightly. "I paid cash, so there's no mortgage payment."

Of course she had. I grinned at the fact I hadn't considered this.

"Um, you could pay for the groceries for all those amazing breakfasts you're going to be in charge of making daily."

"Deal." I kissed her then, running my hand up to the base of her neck and tipping her head back. "God, I love you, Cath."

"I love you too."

Not being able to resist teasing, I whispered, "Now about those books your mother has been reading…"

Her swat was well worth the jest, but then she turned the tables. "Oh, I've read them, too."

I chuckled, thinking the word 'boring' would never describe her or our future, that's for sure. "In that case, maybe it's time for you to teach me something."

Read the next book in the Something Series! Juliette and Mark's story is up next in Show Me Something.

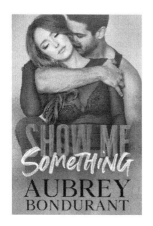

ACKNOWLEDGMENTS

Never in a million years did I think I'd be publishing a fourth book. And I'd be remiss if this time around I didn't thank my editor, Alyssa Kress first and foremost. I'm so very grateful that I lucked into finding her website from the very beginning and showed her Tell Me Something for a beta read. That first nail biting moment of knowing someone was reading something so personal that had never been shared with the world could've gone so many directions. But thanks to her guidance, support and constructive feedback, it went this one. This changed my life. And is the reason you're reading the Something Series today! Thanks for being part of the journey Alyssa!! www.alyssakressbookediting.com

To my husband and kids, thank you for allowing me to balance it all (sometimes better than others)-I love you!

And to my friends-those that have been so very supportive throughout this journey-who ask about my characters as if we're all hanging out with them-I heart you!

There is something very special about this Indie community to meet fellow authors who are always willing to help, inspire and support you. To Josephine, Owen, SJ and Rachel: Thank you!

To Kristy: Thank you for taking the time to explain vegemite to me. That scene is dedicated to you my friend!

To Sam: I can't tell you how much I appreciate you taking the time to make educate me on some Aussie-isms to ensure Will sounded at least half-Australian!

To Karen for your awesome covers and my hard copy formatting, thank you for being so quick and formatting endless pictures of shoes until I found the right ones for this series! www.coversbykaren.com

To the bloggers. Each year, I get to know more of you and can't tell you how much I appreciate your tireless efforts to support authors! You're amazing and your words lift me up and make me realize I'm doing what I was meant to do.

And last, but never least. To all the readers who choose to spend hours in this world I've created: Thank you for the privilege. For those who leave reviews, comment with my books on Facebook, join me for author takeovers: You don't have to take the time, but you do and you know what, I read and love every single review. Seriously you rock for making the effort and not only helping get the word out there, but to make my day whenever I see my books mentioned!!

ABOUT AUBREY BONDURANT

Aubrey Bondurant is a working mom who loves to write, read, and travel.

She describes her writing style as: "Adult Contemporary Erotic Romantic Comedy," which is just another way of saying she likes her characters funny, her bedroom scenes hot, and her romances with a happy ending.

When Aubrey isn't working her day job or spending time with her family, she's on her laptop typing away on her next story. She only wishes there were more hours of the day!

She's a former member of the US Marine Corps and passionate about veteran charities and giving back to the community. She loves a big drooly dog, a fantastic margarita, and football.

Sign up for Aubrey's newsletter here

Stalk her here:

Website

Facebook

Twitter

Email her at aubreybondurant@gmail.com

Made in United States
Orlando, FL
10 June 2022